MORE CHILDREN'S BOOKS FROM THE EMMA PRESS

NOVELS

The Untameables, by Clare Pollard, illus. by Reena Makwana

CHAPTER BOOKS

The Adventures of Na Willa, by Reda Gaudiamo, illustrated by Cecillia Hidayat. Translated from Indonesian by Ikhda Ayuning Maharsi Degoul and Kate Wakeling.

The Girl Who Learned All the Languages Of The World, by Ieva Flamingo, illustrated by Chein Shyan Lee. Translated from Latvian by Žanete Vēvere Pasqualini.

POETRY BOOKS

Eggenwise, by Andrea Davidson, illus. by Amy Louise Evans

Balam & Lluvia's House, by Julio Serrano Echeverría, trans. from Spanish by Lawrence Schimel, illus. by Yolanda Mosquera

The Bee Is Not Afraid of Me: A Book of Insect Poems, edited by Fran Long and Isabel Galleymore

Cloud Soup, by Kate Wakeling, illustrated by Elīna Braslina

My Sneezes Are Perfect, by Rakhshan Rizwan with Yusuf Samee, illustrated by Benjamin Phillips

PICTURE BOOKS

We Are A Circus, by Nasta, illustrated by Rosie Fencott

When It Rains, by Rassi Narika. Translated from Indonesian by Ikhda Ayuning Maharsi Degoul and Emma Dai'an Wright.

The Dog Who Found Sorrow, by Rūta Briede, illustrated by Elīna Braslina. Translated from Latvian by Elīna Braslina.

Queen of Seagulls, by Rūta Briede. Translated from Latvian by Elīna Braslina.

ANDRUS KIVIRÄHK

OSKAR
AND
THE THINGS

illustrated by
Anne Pikkov

translated by
Adam Cullen

The translation of this book was made possible by a grant from the Traducta programme of the Cultural Endowment of Estonia.

THE EMMA PRESS

First published in Estonia as *Oskar ja asjad* by Film Distribution in 2015.
First published in the UK in 2022 by The Emma Press Ltd.

Original text © Andrus Kivirähk 2015.
Cover and interior artwork © Anne Pikkov 2015.
English-language translation © Adam Cullen 2022.

English-language text edited by Kate Wakeling.

All rights reserved.

The right of Andrus Kivirähk, Anne Pikkov and Adam Cullen to be identified as the creators of this work has been asserted in accordance with the Copyright, Designs and Patents Act 1988.

ISBN 978-1-912915-78-1

A CIP catalogue record of this book
  is available from the British Library.

Printed and bound in the UK by CMP Digital Printing
  Solutions, Poole.

The Emma Press
theemmapress.com
hello@theemmapress.com
Birmingham, UK

1.

Grandma sat at one end of the table and Dad at the other. Oskar was sitting between them. They were all having meatball soup.

Oskar always enjoyed meatball soup, and not just because he liked the taste. It could be fun! *Pea* soup is nothing but green mush, so you have to try hard to make it interesting. Whenever Oskar ate pea soup, he imagined a bottomless swamp bubbling in the bowl before him. With his spoon as a shovel, he had to empty the swamp to find the treasure hidden deep beneath it. Slurping up the swamp would also reveal sunken skeletons and swamp monsters, startled by the cosy green muck suddenly disappearing around them.

There weren't really any monsters or skeletons or hidden treasure lying beneath the pea soup, of course. Oskar knew that, but eating is much more fun when you imagine things!

Meatball soup was one of Oskar's favourite meals because the stars of the show stood out so well among the vegetables. He would pretend they were chubby sea lions paddling between orange and white icebergs, which is to say between the carrots and potatoes. Orange icebergs don't really exist, but that didn't matter – they could always swim in Oskar's pretend sea! Oskar himself was like an arctic pilot wheeling around in the sky above. The sea lions did try to hide between the icebergs, of course, but they couldn't evade Oskar's sharp eyes. He scooped the icebergs up one after another until, in the end, the sea lions found themselves alone in the water with nowhere to hide.

Then Oskar would pluck them up and take them to the zoo. Well, okay – he actually just devoured them too!

Today, however, Oskar didn't have an appetite for meatball soup. The sea lions could carry on feeling relatively safe and secure among their icebergs. He had stuck his spoon into the soup but wasn't eating – more trying to push all the meatballs to one end of the bowl.

'Please eat, Oskar. Don't poke at your food,' Dad said.

'Yeah, yeah,' Oskar sighed, starting to arrange them into rows.

'How can that mother of yours just up and go to America for two whole months?' Grandma tutted. 'Dearie me – that's nearly the whole summer!'

'She's taking classes there,' Dad said evenly, 'and that's just how long they take. What else could we do? America is so far away – you can't just fly home for the weekend, you know.'

'But did she *have* to go all the way out there?' Grandma grumbled.

'Yes, she did,' Dad said, with a little note of irritation creeping into his voice. 'She's studying.'

'All people ever do these days is study, study, study,' Grandma said. 'Back in my day, kids would study while adults went to work.'

'Well, as you can see, I *do* go to work,' Dad retorted. 'And that's why I've brought Oskar here to stay with you.'

'And I'm very glad you did!' Grandma exclaimed. 'I'm happy to have him here with me. It's just a shame that you can't stay too. It's a wonderful chance to have a holiday with your son.'

'I can't right now – I don't have any days off till August,' Dad sighed. 'You know that. We've been through this several times already. Oskar's mum will be back by then too, and then we'll all take a trip together. That's right, isn't it, Oskar? And you'll have a *great* time out here in the country in the meantime!'

Oskar didn't say anything; he just kept stirring his soup. He was far from convinced that being out in the country was such a great thing, especially without his mum and dad around. He'd stayed at his grandma's house before, of course, but not very often, because she lived at the other end of the country and it was a very long drive. They travelled there once every summer and always stayed the night – but those times, his mum and dad didn't leave without him. *This* time, he had to stay with Grandma all by himself, and it felt a little scary. What was he going to do all summer?

'We left my phone behind,' Oskar said softly.

'Yes, you told me already,' Dad said. 'Why didn't you remember to bring it, then? I asked if you'd packed everything you needed.'

'I forgot,' Oskar mumbled.

'Not to worry – I've got a telephone here too!' said

Grandma reassuringly. 'You can use it to call your dad if you start to miss him.'

Again, Oskar didn't reply. Grandma wouldn't understand that his phone wasn't meant for calling people so much as it was for playing. He had masses of good games on his phone and was already missing them. Soon Dad would be driving home, leaving him all alone with his grandma – and for two whole months! If he at least had his phone, then he could curl up in a corner somewhere and tap away at the screen to pass the time. At least he'd have *some* form of entertainment. But now... Oskar felt the tip of his nose getting heavy and the muscles between his eyes starting to tighten, the way they did before tears started to come.

Dad shot him a sympathetic look.

'Come on, now,' he said, ruffling Oskar's hair. 'It won't be so bad. I lived in this house for my whole childhood, and I didn't have a mobile back then, either – nobody did. And I didn't have any brothers or sisters to play with. But I still had lots of friends, anyway! There are other houses around here and there should be some kids around too. I bet you'll make friends in no time and you'll be so busy running around with them that when Mum and I come to pick you up in August you won't want to hear a word about driving back to the city. When I was little, I couldn't even find the time to come inside and eat. We went exploring in the woods and the fields, built forts, kicked a ball around, went fishing, and came up with all sorts of other fun things to do. You're going to have a wonderful time, trust me!'

'The countryside is the perfect place for children in summer,' Grandma chimed in.

Oskar just glared at his soup. Dad hadn't cheered him up – quite the opposite. Grandma had her quirks, but at least he knew her quite well, and he'd been to her little cottage several times before so it felt at least a *bit* cosy and familiar. But complete strangers from random houses nearby, and the unfamiliar fields and forests – *those* were downright terrifying!

It was just like any time he had to go to the doctor to get a jab – there'd be this awful feeling in the pit of his stomach that morning at home. Even more terrible was knowing that there was nothing he could do about it – there was no way out and he simply had to accept his fate, get dressed, and climb into the car to go to the clinic, even though it was the very *last* thing he wanted to do.

Oskar was wrestling with a similar uneasy feeling right now – that his dad's car would have barely made it off the drive before those kids from the village would come crawling out of the woodwork to carry him off to their fort, no matter how hard he struggled. After that, they'd drag him into the woods, and then somewhere else to go fishing, and then to who-knows-what other horrible places. And Grandma wouldn't protect him at all – she'd just stand on the porch, holding a bucket and nodding in satisfaction: *Ah yes, the countryside is the* perfect *place for children in summer!*

Oskar shot his dad a miserable look. Dad tugged on Oskar's ear.

'Don't look so unhappy!' he said. 'I'll call you. And Mum will definitely be calling from America, too. It's not like she's underground or up in space, you know – you'll have plenty of chances to chat to her as well.'

'Though it *is* expensive to make calls from America,' Grandma said. 'But don't you worry – Oskar and I will have a fantastic time together!'

Oskar was sure it would be the exact opposite, but he held his tongue. The meatball soup had grown cold and cloudy from him poking at it with his spoon. Oskar stared at the bowl. He didn't like the soup *at all* anymore. He didn't like the kitchen table, or the kitchen itself. Everything felt so grim and gloomy. A fat housefly buzzed around the light-fitting and he saw a dark stain on the wall next to the stove, which he'd never noticed before but now struck him as extraordinarily ugly. *And they're leaving me here for two whole months!* he moaned in his head. Oskar felt a giant wave of sadness crash over him, nearly squishing him flat.

'Would you like some sweets for pudding?' Grandma asked. She placed a couple of pieces of hard caramel on the table – the exact kind of treat that Oskar refused to ever stick in his mouth.

'I'm not hungry,' he muttered. What else could he have expected! His whole summer was going to drag on forever, surrounded by those flavourless caramels.

2.

Dad left. Oskar and his grandmother stood on the doorstep and waved to him as he drove away. Grandma was holding a tea-towel that she swung over her head so Dad could spot them from the far end of the road. Oskar barely wiggled his fingers. What good was waving? It wasn't going to bring him back!

'Well, well, Oskar, dear,' Grandma said when Dad's car had disappeared from view. 'Now it's just the two of us. You go off and play. I've got some jobs to do in the garden and vegetable patch, but you can do whatever you please. Don't worry – I'm not going to make you work, too! When can kids be free if not in summertime? Once autumn arrives you'll be off to school, and that's when the real work begins. Make the most of this last free summer.'

With that, Grandma gave Oskar an encouraging nod and strolled off to the vegetable patch, swaying slightly as she went.

Oskar was left alone. Go and play? Easy for her to say! What was he supposed to play with when he'd left all his toys behind in the city? Even his phone! How could he have forgotten it? What an idiot he was! He'd put it on the windowsill to charge the night before, but because he was still feeling so sleepy the next morning he'd forgotten to grab it and drop it into his rucksack. By the time he realized it wasn't there, they were already halfway to Grandma's place in the countryside and it was already too late to turn around and drive home. Now that poor little phone of his was just charging away on the windowsill, all on its lonesome.

All on its lonesome, just like him.

Feeling a little unsure of himself, Oskar started exploring the garden. It was early June and the flowers were in full bloom. The whole place was perfectly nice, and Oskar actually enjoyed wandering around – that is, when he and his parents went to visit Grandma together. Sooner or later, the adults would move on to boring topics at the dinner table, eating and eating and having at least five cups of tea to wash it all down. At some point, Oskar just couldn't take it anymore and would run outside. There, from a respectful distance, he'd inspect the bees buzzing in the blossoms, search for snails in the grass, and flip over the brick that always had worms hiding underneath. If he was lucky, he might spot a lizard on the logpile, and once a big magpie had landed on a branch just a couple of yards away. At these times, Grandma's garden seemed like an extraordinary place, but it was just like any other kind of entertainment – once the fun was over, it was nice to go back home again. Nobody would want to stay at the cinema for two whole months, would they?

Oskar found his way to the brick and flipped it over. The earthworm was there as usual, as was a black beetle that scuttled off into the grass. He put the brick back the way it was.

Am I really going to come and see this worm every day now? he wondered in despair. *I'll wake up in the morning, walk outside, flip over the brick, and stare at the worm. But then what? What am I going to do with the rest of the day?*

Oskar got up, walked to the middle of the garden and stood there. All around, he could hear the chirping of birds and the soft hum of insects. He could see his grandma bent over at the far edge of the vegetable patch. White clouds were frozen motionless in the sky. A lump formed in his throat. He felt terribly alone. The whole world around him felt strange and he didn't know what to do about it.

I might as well go inside, he decided. *I'll curl up in a corner or crawl under the bed and just hide there.*

Oskar recalled their visit to Grandma's house last Christmas. Mum and Dad were sitting and talking with Grandma next to the Christmas tree, as always, while Oskar crept away to get a satsuma. Suddenly he spotted a mouse. Oskar froze, not daring even to breathe. The mouse didn't notice him, though – it pattered round the floor a little then stopped where it was. It was so tiny and the kitchen seemed gigantic around it. The mouse twitched its whiskers, its black button-eyes glittering in the light.

Then it turned tail and scampered beneath a cupboard.

Oskar felt like doing the same thing right now – hiding or crawling off into a den. Just like the mouse in the kitchen, the garden was too big and too unfamiliar for him to handle all on his own right now.

So he went inside. All three of them had been sitting together in the kitchen just a few minutes ago. Oskar could still catch the trace of his father's scent, and the seat cushion where he'd been sitting was a little wrinkled, reminding him that someone had just stood up from there. There was a bowl on the table filled with the sort of sweets that Oskar absolutely detested – ones they never bought in the city – ones which made his grandma's whole house seem far less inviting. These sweets seemed to signal the fact that he'd been dropped off somewhere far from home, in a strange land where people practised strange customs and ate strange foods. Even the plates, cups, and sugar bowl felt unfamiliar. It was odd – this hadn't bothered him when he'd visited with his parents. On the contrary, it had made him curious to inspect all Grandma's things and compare them with what they had at home. On those occasions, it'd been *exciting* to drink from a completely different cup from the one he normally used. But now, it was suddenly unpleasant. All these unfamiliar things seemed almost to be glaring at him, demanding: 'Who do you think you are? And what are you doing here?'

Oskar went into the living room. Altogether, not counting the kitchen, there were three rooms in his grandma's house: the living room, Grandma's bedroom, and Dad's old room where Oskar now slept. Whenever they'd spent the night, he usually stayed on a campbed next to his parents. There was no need for the campbed now, of course – the entire bed and the room were all his. So that's just where Oskar went now – the most familiar room in the house to him. But today it still felt somehow different and strange. The only truly familiar thing there was Oskar's rucksack, which Mum had packed with his clothes before she left for America, and into which Oskar had forgotten to pack his phone.

A mouse could wriggle into its nest and immediately feel at home there, because it was stocked with all sorts of cosy stuff. Oskar, on the other hand, was having a very hard time feeling at home in Dad's old bedroom. It was filled with all the wrong things, the wrong smells, the wrong colours. Sunlight was streaming in through the window, but the whole space somehow felt cold. The big white crocheted blanket laid over the bed glinted coldly and the pillows looked too puffy.

Oskar walked over to the bookshelf. He knew how to read but there were only grown-up books on the shelves. Dad had taken all his own old children's books back to the city for Oskar to read a long time ago. Oskar's mood grew even gloomier. There wasn't even anything to read! What on earth was he going do for two whole months? Sit and stare out the window for hours on end, just like the Ghost Lady?

The Ghost Lady lived in the house over the road from them in the city. Oskar didn't actually know her real name – Ghost Lady was just what he called her. Day after day, this woman would sit in her apartment and stare out of the window. It usually only took Oskar a single glance outside to spot Ghost Lady up on the third storey of her building. She was ancient, with snow-white skin and long grey hair. Oskar used to be afraid of her when he was little, which was how he came up with her nickname. He'd got used to her presence over time, but the name had stuck.

Before, Oskar couldn't wrap his mind around how someone could bear to stare out of a window for days and days, as if she were a potted plant on the windowsill. *He* was always busy as a bee running around town, and rarely stared out the window, if ever – only sometimes before going outside to check if it was raining or not. Or when he heard a siren wailing and wanted to see a fire engine or police car speeding by. Ghost Lady, on the other hand, would already be sitting at her window when Oskar woke up in the morning and would still be passing the time there when he went to bed at night. It had seemed bizarre to him before, but now he reckoned maybe Ghost Lady just felt lonely, too. Maybe *she* had been taken away from home, dropped off in the city with her kids, and now she didn't know what to do with herself in such a strange place, either. Just the way Oskar was feeling now.

He went to the window and stared outside. A few yards away was Grandma's shed. Next to the shed stood a lone birch tree so tall that Oskar had to crane his neck back to glimpse its crown. There was nothing else interesting in sight, so Oskar sat there gazing at the shed and the birch tree for a long time as if they were great wonders of the world. There was nothing else better to do, anyway.

The cuckoo clock in the living room chimed and the cuckoo popped out three times. An hour had passed since Dad left! Just one hour! Oskar thought about trying to figure how many hours there are in two months, but the maths was too hard for him to work out. He could already tell that the number would be frightfully large, anyway. It was better not to know.

'Still, *I* won't turn into a Ghost Lady,' he decided. 'I might as well go outside and walk ten circles around the house. Or twenty, even. Then maybe it'll be night-time and I can go to bed. And then day one will be over.'

3.

Alas, it was not as easy as that. Oskar walked his twenty circles, but it was still a long time until evening – the sun was high in the sky. Grandma emerged from the vegetable garden, flashed Oskar a look of approval, and said:

'Keep up the pace, lad! It's nice to take a walk in the countryside. It's nice being in the countryside in general – you can be out in the fresh air whenever you like. You can run and jump to your heart's content and nobody's going to stop you.'

She disappeared inside for a moment, came out carrying a gigantic pair of hedge clippers, and then went off somewhere else again.

Oskar considered running and jumping around like his grandma had suggested, but that seemed silly. Instead, he discovered a spider that had spun a web between a flowerpot and the corner of the house. He kept an eye on it for a long time, hoping a fly might get caught in the spiderweb so he could watch the way it ate – something he bet would be both horrifying and exciting at the same time. However, not one fly buzzed past. The spider sat there, motionless, and Oskar soon grew tired of watching.

He walked down to the gate and stuck his nose between the slats. Behind the gate wound a gravel road, and on the other side of that was a thicket. Oskar knew the road led to the village shop, where he'd once gone with his grandma. He wondered if going to the shop might offer any sort of entertainment. Maybe they sold decent sweets there? What if he asked Grandma to go with him?

But before Oskar could make his decision, he spotted the village kids.

There were three of them, all boys about Oskar's age. They were oddly similar: each had hair that was white as cotton, and broad button-noses. The boys were apparently brothers, the younger two probably twins. As soon as they noticed Oskar, they came to a halt. Both sides stared at each another – Oskar from the garden, the boys from behind the fence.

Oskar felt an ice-cold ball form in the pit of his stomach, just like he always did whenever he ran into anything menacing. Any second now they might invite him to come play, and then he'd *have* to go – there'd be no way out of it. There was no point in running back to his grandma, and his parents were far away – no one was there to help him. Why on earth had he shuffled over to the fence, where he was such easy prey for anyone walking past? He should have just stayed inside, staring out the window like the Ghost Lady!

'Who're you?' the oldest boy asked.

Oskar didn't answer; he just stared at his shoes. He didn't want to be rude, but how could he answer a question like that? If the boy had asked him his name, then he could've said 'Oskar'. But what when someone asks 'Who are you?' do you say you're a person? Or a boy? They could tell that already.

'Is Burnmire your grandma?' the taller cotton-haired boy asked again.

Oskar knew perfectly well that his grandma's surname was Burnmire, just like his own last name, but it seemed so weird to hear a stranger refer to her that way. It was as if he wasn't a kid, but a tiny grown-up! Still, the second question was easier to understand, so he nodded.

'You want to play football?' the boy asked.

The cold feeling in Oskar's belly shot straight up to his throat and made it ache. It was happening! They were going to drag him off somewhere past the woods and he'd never find his way back to his grandma's house again! He'd be forced to spend the whole afternoon with these total strangers, even though he didn't want to at all. Who knows – maybe they wouldn't even let him go home at night, but would make him a tantalizing offer to sleep in their fort. What boy could turn down a cracking idea like that?! And since Oskar wouldn't be able to find his own way home and the unfamiliar boys wouldn't bother to show him either, he'd have no choice but to go along with them and sleep in that fort. And the next morning, they'd take him fishing and then come up with a plan to go hiking and sailing and who-knows-where-else and he'd never make it back to his grandma's or ever see his parents again!

'You want to play football?' the village boy repeated.

Suddenly Oskar remembered there was a fence and a gate dividing them! What would happen if he shook his head? If he declared, 'No!' in a loud, clear voice? But for some reason, everyone – even his mum and dad – thought it had to be the greatest thing in the world when one boy asked another to play, and no one could refuse such an invitation. It would've been impossible to refuse the offer if any adults were around. They'd have interfered right away, saying: 'What do you mean, you don't want to? Go ahead! These kids are inviting you! It's fun to kick a ball around! Go, go on, Oskar!' But right now he was alone and no one could force him to do anything. Oskar shook his head and said:

'No, I can't... Not today.'

The cotton-haired boys eyed him curiously for a moment.

'Oo-kay,' the oldest one drawled, and they continued on their way without looking back. Oskar had gotten away with it!

Only this once, though. Oskar couldn't curse himself enough for his mistake, Why had he added 'not today' when he turned them down?! He was just being polite, of course, and just wanted to soften his tone. There was no need for that; none at all! Now the boys might think he'd be up for joining them tomorrow or some other day. It was possible they'd be back at the gate first thing next morning to make their offer again. Maybe they'd even come right up to the door and ask his grandma: 'Mrs Burnmire, can your grandson come and play football with us?' And Grandma would naturally reply: 'Of course he can! What's a kid to do in the countryside if not run around kicking a ball all day long?!' Then there'd be no way out of it.

Oskar felt downright angry at these cotton-haired yokels. What did they want from him? He would never *dream* of inviting an unfamiliar kid to play! Grown-ups don't just become friends at first sight now, do they! It'd be weird if some stranger walked up to Dad and told him, 'Let's go,' and Dad simply trotted off after him. But with kids, those things are taken as a given – as if simply being more or less the same age as someone is reason enough for friendship.

'I could tell them I'm sick,' Oskar thought, remembering how his throat had just started aching from anxiety. It was still a little sore now, so the excuse wouldn't be a *complete* lie.

He walked back to the house, sat down on the doorstep, and rested his chin on his knees. Grandma walked up and smiled:

'Tired already? I suppose fresh air does wear you out if you're not used to it. Come on in, we'll have dinner. Afterwards we can play a board game. *Life* – have you heard of it? It's your father's; he played it all the time when he was little. Come in, come in.'

Oskar obediently followed her inside. They drank tea and ate sandwiches. The tea had a strange, unfamiliar taste. Grandma explained it was wild thyme tea, which people always drank in the countryside. The sandwiches were unbelievably thick because Grandma sliced the bread herself. Back in the city, bread was always nicely pre-cut at just the right thickness and packed in a bag. Grandma added sliced sausage to the sandwiches, but since the bread was so thick already Oskar could barely taste the meat. It was as if his whole mouth was packed with plain bread, which was so doughy and chewy that it just rolled around this way and that, proving almost impossible to swallow.

Afterward, they played *Life*, which was appallingly boring. There were some exciting possible turns to the game, but neither Oskar nor Grandma were so lucky. All they could do was plod on dully to the finish. On top of that, Oskar caught his Grandma cheating: whenever she rolled a six, she would cover it with her hand and say she'd rolled a three or a four, all so that Oskar would definitely win. Oskar didn't confess that he saw straight through her trick, and just went along with her unselfish plan. Still, that made the game even *less* interesting.

'Would you look at that? You won!' Grandma cheered. 'Good boy! Wasn't that a fun game? Your father used to play it all the time.'

Oskar couldn't believe his dad could have done anything this dull as a child, but he didn't say anything. They turned on a kid's TV programme, but Grandma soon dozed off and even started snoring after a while. Oskar couldn't hear what the characters were saying anymore, but the programme wasn't very interesting anyway. He slid off his chair and walked to the window. Outside, a thick grey fog was creeping through the garden, covering all the flowers and bushes. It was pretty in a way, but at the same time it made him a little sad, too. Oskar felt like he was cut off from the whole world like a lone shipwrecked sailor on an uninhabited island. All that existed were his grandma's house and the ground close by; everything else was blanketed in an impenetrable veil. Beyond it – somewhere far, far away – was Oskar's home and his dad, and even farther away was mysterious, enticing America and his mum. Beyond that veil were all the other fantastic places he knew. Alas, he couldn't see any of them – they'd all been swallowed up by the fog.

The TV remote slipped from Grandma's hand, banged against the floor and she woke up.

'What do you know, I dozed off there for a minute,' she sighed. 'Come now, Oskar. Let's brush your teeth. It's time for bed.'

4.

By morning, the fog had disappeared and the sun was shining. Oskar was now used to the bed which had seemed so dubious just yesterday, and he no longer wanted to get up. It was nice and warm beneath the sheets. Overnight, it had become that mouse's nest he'd been looking for – a place to crawl into and curl up.

Grandma was clattering about in the kitchen. She crossed the living room with heavy footsteps and peeked into Oskar's bedroom.

'Come and eat, Oskar!' she called out. 'It's such a beautiful morning – it would be a shame to sleep through it.'

Oskar couldn't care less about the beautiful morning, but he climbed out of bed anyway. 'At least I've managed to tame *one* thing,' he thought, eyeing his rumpled bedsheets in satisfaction. He imagined himself as a caveman living in a dangerous jungle filled with all kinds of wild animals. They growled and yelped between the trees with flashing eyes and bared teeth. But then the caveman managed to win over one beast, then another... And in the end each of them came up to lick their master's hand. The frightful predators had all become pets. 'Maybe I should do something like that with Grandma's house,' Oskar thought. 'I've already tamed my bed, pillows and blankets – maybe I can get the better of the rest of the house, too!'

He went into the kitchen to eat breakfast and immediately realised that taming a jungle is no easy task. His spoon was slightly too big and the porridge slightly too thick.

How would he ever get used to that? The jam was certainly tasty, though, and Oskar could've simply spooned it straight from jar to mouth, but he doubted that would be acceptable here. At home, he'd definitely have abandoned the thick porridge and just emptied the jar of jam instead, but he was a bit hesitant to act like that at Grandma's house.

'Dig in!' Grandma encouraged him. 'This was your grandpa's favourite porridge.'

That news didn't make the meal any tastier. Grandpa had passed away a long time ago – Oskar never even got to meet him. He was like a total stranger, and if he really had loved that thick porridge then it made the meal all the more bizarre. It wasn't the first time Oskar had noticed that old people preferred weird foods, and if porridge like that had been the favourite breakfast of some long-ago grandfather then there was no way he, Oskar, could like it. Kids eat different things from old people – restaurants even have separate kids' menus!

'Grandpa would have his porridge with butter instead of jam, and he'd sprinkle a little salt on top too,' continued Grandma, with her back to Oskar as she did the ironing. 'And if there was some herring on the table, then he'd toss that into the bowl as well. That's how he ate, your grandpa.'

Oskar completely lost his appetite. The porridge now seemed downright disgusting – it gleamed weirdly like it was doused in melted butter instead of jam. Oskar could even imagine the silvery head of a dead fish sticking out of the sludge, gaping at him. Ugh! He couldn't stomach another mouthful.

'Thanks, I'm full,' he said softly. Grandma turned around and blinked in surprise at the nearly untouched bowl.

'Didn't you like it?' she asked.

'I did, but...' Oskar trailed off. 'I'd like to go outside now.'

Grandma approved at once of this idea.

'Of course, go right ahead!' she said. 'Kids *should* be outside here, in the country. You'll have more than enough time for sitting around indoors in the city next winter!'

Oskar ran out the door. It was a genuine relief to get away from that appalling breakfast! He stopped in front of the house, basking in the bright sunshine. Still, he hadn't worked out what to do next.

It wasn't bad just standing there at first – the sun was nice and warm. A woodpecker tapped on an apple tree; Oskar approached it curiously, but the bird fluttered away into the woods. He gripped his hands behind his back and began to head for the gate, but then turned on his heels and made his way back to the house. Those cotton-haired boys might be lurking just beyond the gate and lure him into joining them if they spotted him! Just in case, Oskar circled around to the back of the house.

The door to Grandma's shed was ajar, so Oskar slipped inside. Its tiny windows didn't let in much light, making the place rather dim, but he could still make out all the objects stored there.

Oskar had never seen so much junk in his life. First up, as you'd expect, came Grandma's winter firewood arranged in tall, neat stacks, but jumbled next to these were all kinds of jars, crates and unusual tools. There was a broken bicycle, an old sledge, several dusty vases, a clock with no hands, a washtub with a rusted-out bottom and much more. On the wall was a shelf holding a selection of piled-up tools: a hammer; tongs; a saw; a hand plane; and more contraptions

Oskar didn't know the names of, as well as various little boxes filled with screws and nails. Leaning in the corner was a rake, a shovel, and some kind of enormous thingammybob that resembled a fork. It looked like a weapon, just right for jabbing ogres and trolls.

Creeping through all this rubbish, Oskar felt like he was in a museum. The shed was cool and quiet; he couldn't hear birdsong or the buzz of insects outside. He didn't dare to touch anything – you don't go around patting things in a museum with your bare hands now, do you? What's more, the objects appeared to be stacked rather haphazardly, so there was a real danger that if you poked at the mountain it would collapse and you might be hit by a falling bucket or a cardboard box. It was better to keep a respectful distance.

'It's weird I've never come in here before,' Oskar thought. The idea had never crossed his mind when he'd visited with his parents, as there were many other things to do. They usually stayed for just one night, two at the very most, and never spent much time in Grandma's house or garden! They'd usually end up driving to the lake for a swim, exploring some old mansion nearby, or heading off to a waterfall a little way down the road. Oskar stuck with his parents for most of the time, and his father never showed any interest in peering into the shed. So the little building had remained unexplored.

In any case, Oskar figured he liked the shed, and decided to visit it more often. He found it fascinating to inspect all those old, broken things and wonder what they might have looked like back when they were new and undamaged.

He quite fancied poking through the lower layers of the junk mountains – it would be like digging up buried treasure.

Who knew what kinds of unusual things might be hidden there?

Oskar sat down on a stump next to the woodpile. A small axe lay on the ground next to it, covered in woodchips and splinters. He kicked them. One piece of wood stood out especially – it was rectangular and smooth like a soap box. Or a pencil box. Or a mobile phone.

He picked it up. The block wasn't anything like a normal chunk of wood that could give you splinters. It was incredibly smooth, like a pebble worn down for centuries by ocean waves. Oskar thought it felt delightful – even the corners and edges were rounded. He couldn't just leave this strange piece of wood lying in the shed, so he decided it was coming with him. Grandma wouldn't object to him keeping it, as the floor of the shed was already covered with bits of wood.

Oskar turned the newfound object over in his hands. It really *did* look like a phone. What if he were to make himself a toy one? He could colour it in, draw on buttons... He'd left his real phone behind in the city, so the least he could do was make himself a new imaginary one!

Of course, Oskar wasn't a baby anymore – he was smart and well aware of the fact that you can't make real calls on toy phones; that only actually good for playing. Toy phones are meant for babies who are still so silly that they might stick a real one between their gums and start chewing on it. Boys who are Oskar's age – boys who have a real-life Samsung waiting for them at home – have no use for a toy phone like that.

Still, he was dreadfully bored, and turning a smoothed-out woodblock into a toy phone would be *one* way to pass the time. At least for a little while.

5.

Oskar had his mum to thank for packing felt-tip pens in his rucksack, even though Dad thought Oskar wouldn't be needing them at all.

'When will he have time to draw out in the countryside?' Dad had said, shaking his head. 'There'll be so much else to do – all that running and fooling about outside.'

'But what if it rains?' Mum asked. 'Pack them, just in case.'

Of course, the weather was absolutely beautiful right now. There wasn't a speck of cloud in the sky or a hint of rain. Even so, Oskar went inside, pulled out his pack of pens, and sat down at the kitchen table.

To begin with, he coloured one side of the wood red. Oskar had always wanted a red phone, but he got a black one instead. Black wasn't bad, of course – he could still use it to make calls and play games to his heart's content – but red would've been flashier. So Oskar made himself one now.

When the back of the phone was finished, Oskar started thinking about what to draw on the front. His real phone had a touchscreen, which meant the whole front simply went black when it was off. But if he coloured one side of the wood red and the other side black, it would look a bit boring and not much like a real phone either. So Oskar decided to draw a phone with buttons on, like the one Dad had. Dad always said he couldn't be bothered to paw constantly at his phone like a dog kicking dirt over its poo. A real phone should have buttons, Dad declared! So Oskar set to work making himself an old-fashioned mobile phone.

He carefully drew ten number-buttons and two larger ones above them – one showing a tiny green phone and one a red phone, just like on his dad's. Then he drew a little four-cornered screen, and as a finishing touch he wrote 'Nokia' above it. That was what Dad's mobile had.

Finally, Oskar coloured the spaces between the buttons and the screen in red, and his phone was finished.

It was just like a real one! Except, of course, for the fact that he couldn't use it to make calls or download games.

Oskar felt a little disappointed once it was ready. Now there was nothing to do again and boredom was creeping in. That's the way it usually goes: crafts are an exciting way to pass the time, but as soon as you're done with whatever you're making, you immediately lose interest in it. Take Lego, for example. You spend hours and hours assembling a castle or a pirate ship exactly the way the instructions show, but the second the final detail clicks into place, that's it. The fun's over. It's nice to look at, your mum and dad might look at it and tell you that you did a great job, but you can't really *play* with a castle or a ship like that. All you can do is take it apart and start all over again. Right?

Oskar's new mobile was impossible to take apart. He turned his new creation over in his hands and even lifted it up to his ear for a moment. Still, it felt stupid to start talking into a chunk of coloured wood – 'Hello, hello! Who's there?' Only toddlers would do that, and Oskar had been a big boy for a very long time.

In total boredom, he looked round the kitchen. Grandma had left the iron on the ironing board. It felt out of place; too new and modern. All the rest of Grandma's things looked old, as if they'd been there since Oskar's dad was little, maybe even longer. The iron was brand new; Oskar's parents had given it to Grandma for Christmas. As a result, it felt somehow more familiar than her other things. It had come from the city too, so it looked like a little child compared to the rest of her ancient possessions. Oskar wondered if the iron felt just as lonely as him.

As a joke, he pressed the toy against his ear and said:

'Hey, iron! How's it going?'

It was a good thing none of his friends were around to see him act like such a baby!

But to his surprise, a soft click sounded in his ear and a voice replied:

'Hey, I'm doing brilliantly! Are you that boy with the arms and the legs? What's your name?'

Oskar dropped the wooden phone in shock. He stared at it wide-eyed. The chunk of wood was just the same as it had been before. Had he really heard a voice coming out of it? That was impossible! Still, there was most definitely a murmuring coming from the top end. The voice called out: 'Cuckoo! Where'd you go?' Oskar gingerly raised the phone back to his ear.

'Hello...?'

'Hello, hello!' the voice answered merrily. 'What happened, mate? I asked you what your name is!'

'Oskar.'

'That's great. And do you have arms and legs?'

'I do,' Oskar replied.

'Yippity-yay! Fantastic! How many?'

'I have two arms and two legs.'

'Well, that's just enough, isn't it!' the voice chimed. 'I bet you can use those to do all kinds of grown-up things.'

'Who are you?' Oskar asked.

'Who do you think! You're the one who called me, and now you're asking who *I* am? *You* said: "Hey, Iron! How's it going?" Did you forget or something?'

'So... you're the iron?'

'Who else would I be?! I'm a ball of gingerbread dough, right? Cut little stars and sheep out of me, would you? Baa!'

Oskar stared at the iron. There wasn't the slightest sign that it might be alive. It was an iron just like any other – standing on its end, silvery belly sparkling in the sunlight streaming into the room. Was it really talking to him?

'Hey, be a pal, would you? Since you really do have two arms, I've got a favour to ask,' the voice in the mobile continued. 'Would you mind setting me down on my belly? It feels kind of silly sitting up on my bottom like this, like I'm a dog begging for treats. Help me out, will you?'

Oskar lifted the iron and set it flat on the ironing board.

'Whew, much better!' the voice sighed. 'My bum was getting pretty stiff already. Your grandma loves to set me standing up like that and, well, she doesn't have a mobile like you do – I can't call and tell her, "Hey, Granny, cut it out!" It's just great that I can talk to *you*! I've wanted to have a friend with arms and legs for ages.'

'But how...' Oskar trailed off. 'Why... I don't get it. This is just a block of wood... How can I use it to call you?'

'How should I know? You think that since I've got a cord coming out of my bottom and some electrical gadgets inside of me that I'm some kind of electrician? Forget about it, mate! I don't know squat about those things. I'm an iron, not a scientist. You called, I picked up – end of story! What more do you need to know?'

'Does that mean I can call other... things... too?' Oskar stammered.

'If they can be bothered to answer, then sure you can!'

'But how? I don't know their numbers.'

'Calling Earth! Calling Earth! What do you need numbers for? Wake up! You're not the smartest, are you?'

'I'm smart enough!' Oskar defended himself. 'I'm just not used to... You see, when people ring each other...'

'People? You mean those things with arms and legs?'

'Yes. When people ring each other, they have to dial a number. And I thought it might be the same with things.'

'When you called me, did you dial a number?'

'No. I just said, "Hello, iron."'

'Exactly, mate! It's as simple as that! You say 'hello' and beep-beep-boop, everything works. What else do you want to call?'

'I don't know, really. I'll have to think...'

'Oi, mate – again with the thinking! Don't think so much! That's silly! You've got arms and legs – now *that's* really

something! That's something to be *proud* of! Do you get me? Fine, let's say ta-ta for now. Give me a ring again later, alright? Or I'll call you, if I feel like it.'

'Does that mean *you* can call *me*, too?'

'Well, why not? Ding-dong, ding-dong! You've really got your brain going in first gear, there. If you can call me, then I can sure as heck call you, too! It's logic, pure and simple. I'd never have thought these "people" with their arms and legs could be such ignoramuses sometimes. Don't go being offended, you hear?! See you around, kiddo! Heat things up!'

A moment later the phone started beeping, as if the call had ended. He gulped. This really made things interesting. And bizarre. And all-around awesome.

Oskar stood up, went into the living room, and looked all around. What else could he call?

6.

Oskar's gaze came to rest on a mirror. It was rectangular and hung above a little cupboard. He lifted the wooden mobile to his ear and whispered:

'Hello, mirror!'

Static immediately sounded from the receiver and an anxious voice answered:

'Yes? Who is it?!'

'I'm Oskar,' he said, flooded with a sense of thrill. The phone really worked! He could call any piece of furniture he wanted, anything at all. His coloured-in chunk of wood was truly a mighty, super-duper, mega-cool... in short, the very best toy in the world!

'Oskar...' the troubled little voice echoed, then screeched, 'Oi! Stop tickling me! Help!'

'Excuse me?' Oskar gasped.

'No, not you...' the voice groaned. 'Oh, I don't know what's to become of me! I'm afraid I'll get eaten up!'

'Why do you think that?' Oskar asked curiously. 'Nobody eats mirrors!'

'Are you sure?' the mirror said doubtfully, making a sound like its teeth were chattering. 'I'm absolutely terrified that it will bite me! Now Oskar, tell me: do you have arms and legs?'

'I sure do,' said Oskar, importantly. He'd come to realise that having arms and legs was of immeasurable worth among the things his new phone could call.

'How wonderful!' the mirror squealed in glee. 'Then you can help me! You can save me! Rescue me, my dear Oskar!

Something is climbing down my back! Something's creeping around there! Something's after me! Something big and nasty! I'm afraid of it!'

'What should I do, exactly?' Oskar asked.

'You've got to take me down off the wall,' the mirror explained, 'and then catch that awful predator! You've got arms – you can fight it! You can protect me!'

Oskar hesitated. It wasn't that he was afraid of some monster hiding behind the mirror. What could be back there, anyway? A wolf or a bear couldn't fit behind it, and Oskar didn't believe in ghosts. It must be a fly or a spider that had accidentally slid behind the mirror while climbing along the wallpaper. But how would he get it down? The mirror was hanging rather high up and Oskar was still small.

'Oh Oskar, my boy!' the mirror moaned. 'Save me! Oi-oi-oi!' it squealed. 'It's started crawling again! O-o-h, it's going to gobble me up!'

The mirror started wailing like an ambulance – so loud that Oskar had to hold the phone away from his ear. He thought for a moment. Sure, he could reach the mirror if he climbed up onto the cupboard. But what then? It might be pretty heavy – would he be strong enough to lift it? What was it hanging from, anyway? And how would he get it back *onto* the wall? What would happen if it fell and broke?

'What if I ask Grandma for help?' Oskar wondered, but then quickly abandoned the idea. The thought that that might lead to her poking into the secret of his magic phone was so unpleasant that he scrubbed it from his mind at once. No, he needed to get by on his own in this new and fascinating world that the magic mobile had opened up for him.

'Stop fussing this instant – you're making a horrible sound!' he scolded the mirror. 'Please be quiet! I'll help you in just a minute.'

'It's right in the middle of my back,' the mirror sobbed. 'That's my tenderest spot! That's where I'm the most ticklish! Boo-hoo-hoo!'

'Quiet!' Oskar snapped. He set the phone down on the table to free up his hands and climbed up onto the cupboard. Then he gripped one edge of the mirror in his right hand, the other in his left, and tried to lift. It wasn't as heavy as he'd feared and came off the wall easily. Oskar hugged it against his chest, bent down and rested the bottom edge on the cupboard.

'That's not going to fall now,' he muttered, and stood up again. A little ladybird was crawling on the wall right where the mirror had hung.

'What was it? What was it?' the mirror yelped into the phone so loud that Oskar could hear it from several feet away.

Oskar placed a finger in the ladybird's path so it would climb onto his fingertip, then jumped down from the cupboard. He picked up the phone with his free hand.

'It's just a little ladybird,' he said. 'Totally harmless. I'll go and set it free outside, then I'll hang you back on the wall.'

'Oh, thank you!' the mirror gushed. 'I was so dreadfully afraid! I'm not used to anything crawling behind me – usually people stand in *front* of me!'

'Nothing except insects can fit behind you, you know' Oskar explained while hurrying towards the kitchen door to blow the ladybird off his finger so it could fly away.

'I don't like it when things stare from *behind* me,' the mirror carried on. 'My back side is nowhere near as pretty as

my front. My back doesn't sparkle or show reflections. Don't look behind me either, Oskar! I haven't had a shower in ages!'

'I reckon you've *never* had a shower,' Oskar murmured. He returned to the living room. The hardest stage of the operation was still ahead: hanging the mirror back on the two hooks in the wall.

'You're right!' the mirror sighed, then started whining again. 'I've never had a shower! But I sure would like one! Oskar, my dear boy, take me to a shower! You've got arms and legs – pick me up and let's go! Right away!'

'No, most certainly not!' Oskar said. 'Grandma doesn't even have a shower, you know; just a bathtub. Please be quiet now, will you? I've got to hang you back up.'

This wasn't an easy task at all. Oskar fumbled around for a while, nearly dropping the mirror at one point. Sweat started trickling down his back from the fright that gave him. A strange thought crossed his mind: 'What would happen if it broke? Would it go silent? Or the very opposite – would every shard start speaking in a different voice?' He put these thoughts to one side and concentrated instead on hanging the mirror on the hooks in one piece, which he managed at last.

'Whew!' he grunted into the phone. 'You're back on the wall now and I won't be taking you down again. Next time, don't be scared of teensy little things like ladybirds – they won't do you any harm.'

The mirror started thanking him profusely, but Oskar didn't have much of a chance to listen before his grandma walked into the room. He quickly hung up and stuffed the phone into his trouser pocket.

'You're inside?!' Grandma exclaimed, washing her muddy

hands in the sink. 'But the weather's so wonderful – you should be out enjoying it. It's too bad we don't have a ball for you to kick around.'

'It's okay, I'm fine,' Oskar mumbled.

'I saw those neighbour boys walking by earlier. I'm sure they've got a ball,' she continued. 'Just try talking to them next time they go past and I bet they'll invite you to play. They're nice boys.'

Oskar froze. It was already starting! She wanted to force him to join that gang of cotton-haired kids! Now that Oskar had a magic mobile in his pocket, he hadn't the slightest desire to run about with strangers in some hayfield.

'I'm not bored,' he quickly reassured her, fibbing. 'It's just brilliant being here in the countryside!'

'Well then, that's grand,' Grandma said with a smile. 'Now, let's have some lunch. I'll make you your grandfather's favourite soup!'

Oskar was immediately reminded of his breakfast porridge, and sighed as he braced himself for the worst.

7.

Grandma was busy stirring a pot of simmering soup on the stove with a big ladle. Oskar spied on her from the living room, wondering if he could call kitchen utensils too. Maybe that ladle Grandma was holding? He lifted the mobile to his ear and whispered:

'Hello, ladle! Can you hear me?'

Oskar heard a dial tone, then a voice shouted into his ear:

'Can't talk! I'm working!'

'Are you the ladle?' Oskar asked.

'Yep, that's me! I'm busy right now, though – I've got to dive on in any moment now! Call me back later!'

The ladle's last words disappeared into the sound of bubbling, and the call ended.

Oskar chewed his lip in excitement. How great was that? He decided to call the pot as well.

'Hello, pot!' he said softly. 'Hello-o-o!'

The phone rang for a while, but no one picked up. Oskar had already accepted the notion that not even a pot might have time to chat while a gas burner was lit beneath it and soup was simmering in its belly, but then he heard a soft click and someone said in a gruff, unhurried voice:

'Pot here.'

'Hello, pot. I'm Oskar,' he introduced himself.

'Why, hello there.'

'Can you talk right now?'

'Why shouldn't I?'

'Well, Grandma's making soup inside you and I thought that maybe it would be uncomfortable. Hot, you know.'

'Hot?' the pot echoed in surprise. 'Soup in me?' He was silent for a few moments, then started to chuckle. 'Well, how about that – there *is*! I didn't even notice! How about that.'

'How could you miss something like that?!' Oskar marvelled. 'Grandma poured water in you, tossed in a handful of macaroni and she's stirring it all with the ladle now... Can't you feel anything?'

'I've got a sort of an itch... You know, I'm used to all kinds of things being stuck inside of me. Sometimes I wake up and find out that – oho! – someone's packed my belly full of mashed potatoes! Other times it's minestrone. Once there was even jam in there! It doesn't bother me, though. I fall right back asleep, and when I wake up my belly's empty again. Usually it's even been washed!'

Oskar tried to imagine what it might feel like to wake up in your bed one morning and find out your stomach had been filled with jam, but he couldn't. His belly wasn't hollow, either. In order to stuff anything in there, someone would have to cut it open first – like in the fairy tale about the seven billy goats where a big bad wolf's stomach was stuffed full of stones while he slept. In fact, the pot reminded him of that wolf just a little. Oskar wondered if the pot might want to play 'seven billy goats' with him later.

'My goodness – now I've got milk being poured into me too,' the pot remarked, bellowing with laughter.

'*Milk*?!' Oskar moaned. Grandma really was doing everything wrong!

Or at least completely different from how they did things in the city. Things had been just fine when she dumped macaroni into the pot – Oskar's mum also did this when she made macaroni soup at home. It was one of Oskar's favourite foods and he'd wait for the meal to be served without feeling the least bit afraid. But now Grandma was ruining everything by pouring in *milk*! What kind of a joke was that?! You drink milk from a glass *with* your lunch, not mixed into all the other dishes!

'Hold on a minute,' Oskar said to the pot, sticking the phone in his pocket. 'Grandma!' he called out. 'Why did you pour milk into the macaroni?'

'How else should I cook it?' Grandma replied with a grin. 'It's milk-and-macaroni soup – that's just how it's made! Your grandfather adored it – he'd even lick his spoon clean when he was finished.'

Not more about that ancient grandpa! Grandma seemed to be forgetting she was making lunch for Oskar, not a deceased grandfather!

Despair washed over him again. Why did everything have to be so weird and wrong out here in the countryside? Then he remembered he was still in the middle of a conversation with the pot, and his spirits lifted a tiny bit. At least there was *one* good thing around here – his wooden mobile.

'Pot,' he said, with a note of worry in his voice, 'it's some kind of a "milk soup". Pretty awful.'

The pot didn't answer; no doubt he was asleep again. Oskar couldn't raise his voice, as Grandma was right there and would overhear him. Instead, he pushed the red button to hang up.

'Lunch is ready!' Grandma said. 'Wash your hands and come to the table, please.'

They ate in silence. Oskar glared at the pale macaroni swimming in a white broth in his bowl. 'So *this* is where those escaped billy goats went,' he thought. 'And the wolf is sleeping on the stove with its belly sliced open.' Oskar glanced at the pot – he really did look wolf-like and just as grey. 'I bet he'll be surprised to find his belly empty again when he wakes up,' Oskar thought.

'Have a slice of bread, too,' Grandma offered. 'I'll butter it for you.'

'No, thank you,' Oskar mumbled.

'Go on! Buttered bread is the best food you can eat!' Grandma said with a smile. 'You spread a nice thick layer of yellow butter on a slice of bread and have a glass of milk to wash it down – there's nothing better than that!'

Oskar would've liked to ask Grandma why she hadn't offered him milk from a glass then, instead of pouring it all over the macaroni so now neither was fit to enjoy. But he bit his tongue. His own grandmother suddenly seemed like a total stranger. He'd never felt that way before when he'd visited with his parents. Mum and Dad had always been the ones who chatted with Grandma, while Oskar simply listened. They'd all seemed like one big happy family. But now, alone with his grandma, he discovered they really had nothing in common. The two of them sat quietly at the kitchen table while Oskar reluctantly fished white macaroni out of his bowl – macaroni that would have been much tastier *without* the milk – and impatiently waited for his chance to sneak back into the living room so he could call another thing and have a great conversation.

'Oops, I almost forgot!' Grandma exclaimed. 'Would you like some dill in your soup, too?'

'No,' Oskar replied curtly, thinking: *Dill? What next?! At least I was lucky enough to dodge that one!*

'Thanks. I'm full,' he added, sliding off his chair. 'I'm going.'

'You eat so little!' Grandma said, with a suspicious look on her face. She sighed. 'Fine, I'm not going to force you. Go ahead and run outside now! Kids should be allowed to mess about in the summer.'

Oskar actually had no desire to go outside, because all the things he could call were *inside* the house. However, that's exactly where Grandma was planning to stay as she washed the dishes. He stood on the front step and thought for a moment. Then he hurried round to the back of the house, by the shed and his bedroom window, which he'd left open just a crack. After pushing it up a little further, Oskar crawled inside. Luckily, the door to his room was already closed and Grandma couldn't see him. Go ahead and let her think he was romping around outside! Romping – what a silly word! How was he meant to "romp" all alone out there? By flopping down on his back and pawing at the sky like a kitten? No, thank you – Oskar had much better things to do.

He sat down on his bed, pulled the wooden mobile out of his pocket, lifted it to his ear, and whispered:

'Hello, wardrobe! Can you hear me?'

8.

The wardrobe turned out to be extremely talkative.

'It's great that you called!' he exclaimed. 'I have so much to tell you. You'll never guess what happened on my middle shelf this morning! It was just before dawn and still pitch-black outside. Then, all of a sudden, a scream! "Help! Help!" Two sheets had got into a fight! The white one with little cornflowers on told the yellow sheet that she looked like she'd peed her pants. The yellow sheet got really annoyed, attacked the white sheet, and started scratching at her with her claws! Just like a cat! The white sheet was the one who screamed, but the yellow one showed no mercy – she just clawed even deeper. Awful, isn't it?'

'That can't be true,' Oskar scoffed. 'Bedsheets don't have claws.'

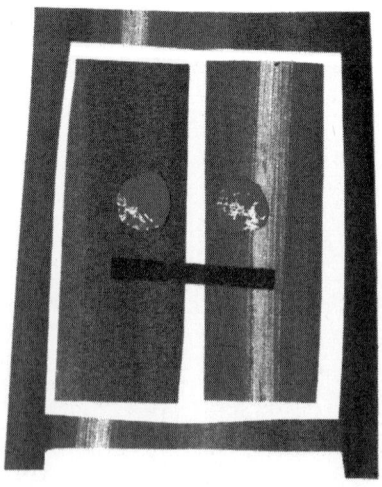

'Of course they do!' the wardrobe replied. 'At least, the ones inside of me all do. Long claws with curved tips that are so sharp you'd better watch out! And the sheets all have fangs too! The white sheet even bit off a piece of the yellow one. Crunch! There was blood everywhere!'

'I don't believe you,' Oskar said. 'Sheets don't bleed.'

'Why would I lie? It was a terrible fight with both of them clawing and snapping at each other – there were puddles of blood lying all around! Awful, just awful!' the wardrobe howled.

'Show me!' Oskar declared, swinging the wardrobe door open with one hand while holding the phone to his ear with the other. Inside was only peace and quiet: sheets, pillows and duvet covers were neatly folded and stacked on the shelves. Hanging in the other half of the space were Grandma's old dresses, along with winter clothes and other stuff that wasn't often needed. There were no pools of blood to be seen, nor the slightest sign of any dreadful struggle having just taken place.

'So where's the blood?' Oskar asked. 'You were just fibbing.'

'I was not!' the wardrobe insisted, adding in a sinister whisper: 'The winter coat drank it all up!'

'Drank what up?'

'The blood! She lapped up all the puddles till they were dry. That coat has a frightful taste for blood – she drinks it all the time. At night, she slides off her hanger and scrambles off on the prowl. Every time she returns, her buttons are all bloody and there's a chunk of raw meat in her pocket!'

Oskar looked at Grandma's brown winter coat, which was just hanging there – it appeared completely harmless.

'You made that up,' he said to the wardrobe. 'Coats can't suck blood. Why are you saying these things? It's not true!'

'What do you mean, it's not true? Of *course* she sucks blood! And she can do much worse – one time, she swallowed a poor little tablecloth whole!' the wardrobe continued in his booming voice. 'She sucked the blood dry and spat out the bare threads. She's a monster, I'm telling you!'

'You know what?' Oskar asked crossly. 'I'm going to call that coat right now and tell her all the foolish things you've said. It's not nice to badmouth others like that.'

He hung up on the wardrobe and turned to face the coat.

'Hello, coat! Hi!'

The line was quiet for a little while, then Oskar heard a strange panting noise.

'Hello!' he repeated. 'Coat! Can you hear me? Grandma's coat, am I talking to you?'

The panting grew louder. Oskar felt as if he'd called a big dog that was wheezing into the receiver with its tongue hanging out of its mouth. He hung up.

'That's weird,' he said to himself. Next, he tried calling the yellow bedsheet the wardrobe had accused of scratching.

'Hello, yellow bedsheet!'

Silence. Then something squawked and hung up.

Oskar tried again.

'Hello, yellow bedsheet! I'd like to talk to you!'

This time, no one picked up at all. Oskar called the wardrobe back.

'What's wrong? Why won't they talk to me?' he demanded. Just that morning, Oskar would never have dreamed of being able to chat to furniture or dishes, but now it seemed as ordinary as apple pie. Indeed, now it felt odd that Grand-

ma's coat and the yellow sheet *didn't* want to speak to him, but only made weird noises into the phone instead. Oskar even felt a little bit hurt. Were they making fun of him?

'They can't talk – their mouths are full of blood,' the wardrobe replied, launching straight into another fib. 'Blood and scraps of cloth. They just ate a skirt. First they pounced on it, then they gobbled it up. The little skirt cried out to be spared, but fat chance of that! They just bared their teeth and attacked!'

'Oh, all you ever do is lie!' Oskar huffed. He didn't feel like listening to the wardrobe's horror stories anymore, so he called the iron in the kitchen instead.

'Hello, iron! Oskar here!'

The iron's perky reply came through immediately: 'Hey there, mate! How's tricks?'

Oskar told the iron about his problem, but the iron merely laughed.

'You called a *coat*?! And a bedsheet?! Knock-knock, anybody home? Mate, you really didn't have to do that! A pure waste of time! Clothes can't talk, you know!'

'Why not?' Oskar asked, intrigued. 'Why can you talk but they can't?'

'Because they're clothes, that's why! What aren't you getting? Never seen clothes before, or something? All they do is growl and snort and make a whole lot of other daft noises. I iron them every day – I should know! They croak and quack and are just quite annoying. I make them nice and smooth, mind you, but give it a couple weeks and they're wrinkled up and right back under me again! I try to ask them – what's the problem? Why do you get yourselves all wrinkly all the time? Why can't you just behave? But all they do is bleat back at me. What choice do I have but to heat up my belly again and press the wrinkles out of those nitwits? It's easy for me, mate. I *like* doing it. I can't stand wrinkles. But clothes just seem to attract them. Quite the miserable lot they are – wrinkled from top to bottom and unable to speak. Don't get involved with them – it's not worth the trouble.'

'But I just wanted to check something,' Oskar said. He told the iron about the wardrobe's bloody fantasies, and the iron laughed so hard he had a coughing fit.

'Don't believe that rubbish, my boy!' he said. 'They don't have fangs or claws – just wrinkles. And I heat those out of 'em whenever I get the chance. That wardrobe is losing it a bit, if you ask me. No wonder, of course – it's filled with clothes day in day out. Stupidity is infectious. You know, mate, if I were you, I wouldn't let a single piece of clothing come anywhere near me! I noticed before that you're wearing a shirt and trousers. No point in it! Don't be chatting with fools like them.'

'I can't go walking around naked!' Oskar tried to explain. But the iron refused to understand, insisting that if *he* could get by just fine without clothes then why couldn't *Oskar*?

'What fun is there really to be had, getting involved with those nincompoops?' the iron exclaimed. 'Mate, believe me – trousers and shirts can't be your friends; they're far too stupid for that.'

Oskar promised to give the iron's words some thought and ended the call, as he'd come up with a new idea. He was curious to find out what sounds his pants and shirt made. Oskar believed the iron when he said they couldn't talk, of course, but apparently they could produce *some* kinds of noise.

First he called his shirt. It meowed pitifully for a few moments, then started hissing.

The trousers were silent for several seconds before cawing loudly.

Oskar's underpants surprised him the most, because when he called out to them several times, saying: 'Hello, underpants! Hello!' they gave him a terrible fright with a sudden and ferocious lion's roar. Could it be dangerous to be wearing underpants that roared so savagely? Oskar got rid of this thought quickly, though – underpants might make a startling noise, but they were completely harmless really.

Grandma walked past the window with a basket of fresh laundry under one arm and started hanging it on the clothesline. Oskar mused that every item must be making sounds in its own special way at that very moment: some roaring, some whimpering, some warbling like a bird; and his grandma couldn't hear any it. No one could – not a single other human. Only he, Oskar, had the power to listen.

He cracked open his bedroom door. Since Grandma wasn't inside anymore, he no longer needed to hide. The whole house was at his disposal, so he ventured out to look for new friends.

9.

In the living room there was a large dining table surrounded by six chairs. They sat there on festive occasions such as Christmas and Grandma's birthday. Otherwise, they always sat in the kitchen where it was more convenient, as you didn't have to carry the food from one room to another.

Oskar circled the table, wondering which to call: the table or the chairs? And if he did call a chair, then how would it know he was calling it specifically and not an identical one right next to it?

He decided to give it a try, anyway. Oskar crouched down next to a chair and spoke into his mobile:

'Hello, chair! I'm talking to you.'

'Hello!' a somewhat creaky voice answered. It was the kind of voice that crows had in cartoons. 'Who are you?'

'I'm Oskar and I have arms and legs.'

'I have legs, too,' the chair said. 'Four of them in total, though they're not much use as I can't use them for walking – only for standing in place. Still, that's my greatest dream! Oskar, could you help me out, perhaps?'

'What dream is that?' Oskar asked. He had no problem with helping all these speaking things around him, and was reminded of a book that his parents had read to him a couple of years earlier, back before he knew his alphabet. It was about a man called Doctor Dolittle who spoke the language of animals and could treat them better than any other vet in the world. Well, now he, Oskar, spoke the language of things, thanks to his mobile. He could listen to their woes

and come to their aid. He wasn't just Oskar anymore – he was *Doctor* Oskar!

'What seems to be the trouble?' he asked in an attentive and friendly way, just like doctors usually address their patients. 'Is some part of you broken?'

'Not at all – I'm fit as a fiddle!' the chair creaked. 'I want to go on a trip around the world!'

'A trip around the world?' Oskar echoed in surprise. 'That's impossible. I can't do that – you'd need plane tickets, and to buy plane tickets you need money, and kids aren't even *allowed* to travel alone in the first place…'

'But *I'd* be coming with you!'

'No, a chair isn't enough. Kids have to have an adult with them, but my mum is in America right now and my dad has to be at work. And plane tickets are very expensive!'

'Is a plane really necessary, though?' the chair pleaded. 'Your legs can move, even though you've only got two of them and – to be totally honest – I can't wrap my head around how it's possible to stand on only two legs. I'd topple over the very second anyone cut off two of mine! Maybe it's because your legs are made of harder wood.'

'My legs aren't made of wood at all!' Oskar snorted.

'What are they made of, then?'

Oskar thought for a moment. How was he to explain?

'Bones,' he finally said. 'They're made of bones that are covered in muscles and skin.'

'Goodness me!' the chair gasped. 'I've never even heard of materials like that. How bizarre! In any case, they help you move. Why do we need a plane? Can't we just travel with you carrying me? The world isn't all that big, you know! I was thinking of starting with the kitchen, voyaging into

Grandma's bedroom from there, and then… Are there more rooms in the house?'

'Yes, there's my room,' Oskar said. 'And then there's the hall and the loo.'

'Oh! I'd like to go there too! The loo! I've never heard of it, but it sounds grand. I definitely want to check that out!'

'So you're saying you want to travel around the house?'

'Yes, that's just what I said. I want to go on a trip around the world – the kitchen, Grandma's bedroom, your room, the hall and the loo. Oh, I had no idea the world was so big! No one's ever told me about the loo! Just think – I've been standing here in this room for forty years already and there are still so many exciting places to see.'

'I can definitely take you on a trip like that,' Oskar said with a grin. He wasn't going to start explaining that the world was much bigger than Grandma's little one-floor cottage – that as well as the house there was a garden and a road and the woods and a city beyond the woods, and then the sea, and finally there was America somewhere far, far away too. The chair wouldn't have understood and anyway, Oskar couldn't take her to the woods or the sea, much less to America. But he'd be happy to drag her around the house!

'Would you like to set off right away?' he asked.

'Oh, yes please! Could we? Of *course* I would!' the chair creaked. 'Oh, I'm so excited! I can't believe it – I'm going on a trip! I don't know what's come over me – it even makes me feel a teensy bit overwhelmed… Oskar, dearest, tell me – what's it like in the kitchen? Who lives there?'

'There are chairs there, too,' Oskar said. 'And a table. Then there's the refrigerator and the ironing board and the gas stove. On top of the stove is a little flame…'

'Oh dear! But I might burn up! I'm made of wood, you know!'

'Don't worry, the flame isn't dangerous,' Oskar reassured the chair. 'Grandma uses it to cook. There's also a tap that water flows out of...'

'My legs aren't going to get wet, are they?! I don't like the sound of that – they might start to rot.'

'Your legs won't get wet,' Oskar reassured the chair, feeling a little irritated. 'You know what? You worry too much. Once you're travelling, you'll have to put up with little discomforts. Anybody who's afraid of everything should just stay home.'

That's just what his uncle Tony had told him when Oskar had gone camping with his parents last summer and had to

sleep in a tent. Oskar complained about the mosquitos and Mum complained that it was too damp in the tent and Dad complained that the ground was too hard. Uncle Tony had said those were all trifles and a *real* camper didn't care about insignificant details like those. They hadn't camped anymore since then, but Uncle Tony's words still rang in Oskar's head.

'I'm sorry!' the chair said. 'Yes, I know it's foolish of me. But you have to understand – I've been standing around here for forty years and it's only natural that I'm feeling a touch nervy now. Fine! No more fretting! Let's go!'

'Alright. First stop, the kitchen,' Oskar declared like a pilot telling his passengers their destination. He picked up the chair and strode to the kitchen doorway. There, he set down his load for a moment and announced to the mobile, 'We're here!' Then he pushed the chair into the kitchen.

'What do you think?' he asked.

'I'd never have guessed the kitchen could be so fascinating!' the chair squealed. 'If I may, I'd like to stay here for a little while to take a closer look at this exciting room. We don't have to head to the next stop right away, do we?'

'No, of course not,' Oskar said. 'You just let me know when you've had your fill.' The iron had told the boy that things were able to call him too – it wasn't only the other way round. 'Give me a call when you're done, okay?'

'Sure thing!' the chair promised. 'I'll let you know when I'm ready to continue.'

I guess I'm like some kind of taxi driver now, Oskar thought as he positioned the chair next to the wall so it would be out of Grandma's way.

But that same evening, Grandma noticed that one of the living room chairs had been moved into the kitchen.

'How did this get here?' she asked, puzzled.

'I brought it in,' Oskar replied.

'Why would you do that, dear? This chair doesn't belong here.'

'I was playing a game,' he explained, 'and... I needed it.'

'Tut-tut – what sort of game is this?' Grandma scolded, shaking her head. 'Chairs aren't toys. You run along and play outside. I'm going to put it back in its proper place.'

'Can we let it stay here for just a little while, Grandma?' Oskar pleaded. The chair's trip around the world couldn't end so quickly! 'I'm still playing. I'll put it back tomorrow.'

'Everything has its place,' Grandma said curtly, carrying the chair back into the living room. Then she plopped herself down on the couch and switched on the telly.

'Let's see what's new in the big wide world,' she remarked.

Five minutes later, Grandma was already napping. Oskar glared at her. Cautiously, he picked up the journeying chair and carried it back to the kitchen. If he promised to help someone then he was going to do it, and Grandma shouldn't try to stop him!

After setting the chair back down, Oskar brushed his teeth and returned to the living room. Grandma was still asleep and had even started snoring. He turned off the TV, which woke her up. Drowsily, she squinted at the clock.

'Yes, quite right. Bedtime,' she said with a yawn. 'Goodnight, Oskar.'

'Goodnight,' Oskar murmured. He slipped into his room and shut the door behind him.

10.

Oskar couldn't fall asleep right away. The day had been too exciting – he had an incredible new toy and even now, in bed, he was holding it and wondering whether to call something else before falling asleep. Of course, the wardrobe was right there its door slightly ajar like a gaping mouth ready to tell new ghost stories about bloodthirsty sheets and killer coats, but Oskar didn't want to hear them just now.

What could he call? Thanks to the iron, he now knew that bedsheets couldn't talk and there was no point in bothering his pyjamas, either. But what about his pillow? That was something more substantial than an old sheet or duvet cover – perhaps it'd have something smart to say?

'Hello, pillow!' Oskar whispered into his mobile. 'Oskar here. Can you hear me?'

Crackling and rustling noises came through the receiver and Oskar started to suspect that the pillow's intelligence might be on the same level as the rest of his linens. But then something squeaked: 'I sure can!'

'Me, too!' another voice chirruped.

'But I can hear you the best!'

'I can hear you even better!'

'I called the pillow,' Oskar said, amazed. 'Why are there so many of you talking at once?'

'He-he-he – how else?!' a chorus of voices peeped. 'There's always many of us! Otherwise the pillow would be as flat as a pancake! He-he-he – we're the *feathers*!'

'Oh, the *feathers*!' Oskar took the phone away from his ear for a moment, pushed his head deep into the pillow, and listened. Funnily enough, he couldn't hear a sound – the pillow was completely silent, but when he listened over the phone, there was so much peeping and chirping inside that it sounded like the parrot house at the zoo. All the feathers were clamouring to talk at once.

'Do you know how pretty I am? I'm striped brown-and-white from tip to tip!' one twittered.

'I'm pretty, too! I'm as white as snow! Peep!'

'*I'm* black and shiny! I'm so gorgeous you'll faint! Chirp!'

'I'm brown and fluffy! Irresistible! Trill!'

'I'm the most beautiful of all – yellow with black spots! Cheep!'

'I reckon you're all very pretty,' Oskar reassured them. 'It doesn't hurt when I lay my head on the pillow, does it?'

'No, not at all! We like it! Do you like it, too? Are we soft enough?'

'Yes, very much so,' Oskar complimented them, and yawned. The feathers' twittering had made him tired. 'I'm going to sleep now. Goodnight, feathers!'

'Goodnight, dear Oskar!' they chittered. 'Downy dreams!'

They started chirping a lullaby to him in chorus, but Oskar was already sound asleep, his head nestled deep in the pillow and the phone still gripped tightly in his hand.

Oskar awoke to his grandma knocking on the door. 'Come and have some porridge!' she called out.

He yawned and stretched. The first thing that caught his eye was the wooden mobile next to him in bed, which put him in a good mood at once. It was absolutely amazing that he'd found that nifty little chunk of wood in the shed the day before. Oskar was reminded of the book *Pinocchio* and how, as soon as Geppetto cut into what seemed like an ordinary block of wood, it began crying out. Then Geppetto had carved the block into a pointy-nosed puppet named Pinocchio who could walk and talk. What if the chunk of wood he'd found in Grandma's shed was somehow related to Geppetto's? Perhaps they'd been cut from the same tree?

Of course, Oskar's mobile couldn't talk on its own like Pinocchio. But he could use it to speak to other seemingly inanimate objects, so it was definitely a little fairytale-like.

Oskar heard the clatter of dishes coming from the kitchen. He remembered the porridge waiting for him there and felt a bit miserable. No doubt it would be his grandpa's favourite breakfast again! Still, what mattered most was that he now had a fantastic phone and a ton of friends he could call and chat with every day. He'd find a way to put up with Grandma's porridge somehow.

He got dressed and looked outside – the weather was nice and the sun was shining. Then he spotted something red in the crown of the tall birch tree growing next to the shed, and he craned his neck to figure out what it was.

Dancing in the wind at the top of the tree was a red balloon.

Oskar thought it must have been blown there overnight and got caught in the branches. *I wonder where it came from!* he thought. There were balloons everywhere you went in the city – they were handed out at shopping centres, given away for all kinds of events, and even sold in certain shops. Out here in the countryside, though, the balloon seemed like a rare and unlikely guest. It was like coming across a giraffe in the middle of a bunch of pine trees.

No matter! I'll just call it and ask how it got here, Oskar decided. For a boy carrying a magic mobile around in his pocket, there was truly no problem that couldn't be fixed!

But first of all, he had to eat breakfast. Oskar walked into the kitchen, only to find Grandma dragging out the chair that was on its trip around the world.

'How strange! I thought I took this back to the living room last night,' she said. 'I suppose I was so tired that I didn't remember what I was doing. Take a seat, Oskar dear – I've spooned you out some porridge.'

Oskar trudged to the table. Luckily, Grandma had made a different kind today; one he had no problem eating. It wasn't as tasty as the porridge Mum made, of course, but there was no hope of having any like that this summer.

'I've already eaten,' Grandma said. 'I'm going to the shops. Would you like to come along? I can wait for you to finish.'

'No,' Oskar said. 'I'm not coming. Go ahead – I'll just stay and play.'

'Alright, suit yourself,' Grandma said. 'I thought you might want a change of scenery. We could go for a walk and you'd see the village and perhaps even some of the other children... But if you don't want to, I'll just go alone. Don't get scared, I'll be back soon.'

'I'm not scared of anything,' Oskar declared. What did he have to be afraid of here? What *was* frightening was a trip to the shops, because the ghostly trio of those cotton-haired kids could be lying in wait there. Now that Oskar had a magic mobile, he had no intention of ever hanging out with those three. Why should he waste his time on them when there were so many friends and acquaintances to help out right here in this very house? He'd become just as important to the things as Doctor Dolittle was to animals! No, Oskar had no time for kicking a football round with strangers – at most, he'd have a chat with a football itself, listen to its problems and help to find solutions, just like a doctor was sworn to do.

Grandma took her handbag and left. Oskar quickly finished his porridge, headed into the living room and phoned the wandering chair.

'How's it going?' Oskar asked. 'How was your night in the kitchen?'

'Oh, the kitchen was just brilliant!' the chair creaked. 'The tap dripped nonstop! I got to three hundred and seventeen drops before I lost count. Does this mean my trip is over now? I did so want to visit the other rooms! And the loo!

Will I ever get there?'

'Of course you will,' Oskar reassured the chair. 'We've just got to be clever about it so that Grandma doesn't find you during your journey and drag you back to the living room.'

'Oh, I was so startled when she grabbed me and lugged me here! I'd not even had a proper chance to fully appreciate the kitchen yet. Thank you for taking me back, Oskar!'

'All kinds of hiccups can happen while travelling,' Oskar said. 'Especially on trips around the world. A few brave explorers even get shipwrecked. Or end up dying of hunger and thirst.'

'Will I get shipwrecked too?' the chair gasped in terror. 'In the loo, perhaps? Best not to go there after all, if that's the case!'

'Don't worry – your trip isn't that dangerous!' said Oskar. 'All we have to do is watch out for Grandma. She mustn't see you. So, here's what we're going to do: I'm going to take you into her bedroom now, where you'll spend the whole day. Grandma doesn't go in there during the day – she's either out in the garden or cooking in the kitchen, so you can check out her room in peace. And later tonight, I'll bring you into my bedroom. How does that sound?'

The chair started creaking away in joy about how thrilling her travels were and how grateful she was to Oskar, but Oskar switched off his mobile mid-gush and pulled the chair into Grandma's bedroom. He closed the door so she'd have a chance to sightsee in peace, and so Grandma wouldn't accidentally spot her. Then he went outside, walked up to the tall birch tree and stared at its crown. The red balloon was still there.

11.

'Hello, balloon!' Oskar said into his mobile. 'Can you hear me?'

'Why wouldn't I?' a somewhat cheeky voice immediately answered. 'What do you want?'

'I... I thought...' Oskar was taken back. 'I was actually just... I wanted to ask how you're doing up there.'

'I'm fine, thank you,' the red balloon said crisply. 'The view from here is spectacular. It's great being up high in general. But I suppose that must be hard to imagine for someone as tiny as *you* are.'

'I'm not tiny!' Oskar protested.

'You certainly look tiny from up here,' the balloon mocked. 'It's a wonder that you can talk at all – where does a mouth even fit on someone so teensy-weensy?'

'Of *course* I have a mouth!' Oskar huffed. 'And I have arms and legs, too!' he added, playing his trump card. Just yesterday, Oskar had discovered that having these qualities made you an outright celebrity among immobile objects, but his boasting had no effect on the balloon.

'My sympathies!' she snickered. 'It must feel pretty awful having sausages hanging by your sides. They must get in the way when you're flying. Oh *right*, I nearly forgot – you *can't* fly! Poor little thing! Well, I guess it makes sense that you'd settle for a pair of arms and legs and go around showing them off all the time.'

'I'm not showing off!' Oskar yelled. 'I was just saying...'

'You were, too.'

'I was not!' Oskar was furious, especially since he had, in fact, only brought up his limbs to earn the balloon's respect. But that was a gigantic failure, because the balloon just continued making fun of him from up in the birch tree.

'Who are you again? Oskar? What a weird name! And what are your famous arms and legs called, huh? And how many of them do you have? Just two?! Ha! Why'd you even bring them up in the first place?! I hoped you'd have at least a hundred!'

'I'm not a centipede!' Oskar snorted. The balloon was getting on his nerves with all her teasing, but strangely he didn't feel like ending the conversation yet. 'Can I ask you something?'

'Me?!' the balloon gasped. 'You want to ask *me* something? What an honour! But I don't have any arms or legs! Not a single one! What could you have to ask somebody like me?'

She laughed spitefully.

'How'd you get stuck in this tree?' Oskar asked.

'How do you think? I grew here like a fungus!'

'No, you *flew* there,' Oskar corrected.

'Is that right? Well, aren't you smart!'

'Where'd you come from?'

'The Moon.'

'No, really.'

'Really – right off the surface of the Moon! Why don't you believe me?'

Oskar snorted, making the balloon snicker again.

'Fine, stop pouting,' she sighed at last. 'I didn't fly here from the Moon. I came from a house. I was blown up and tied to the porch, but I didn't feel like sticking around, so I skedaddled. Some guys chased after me, but they couldn't catch me, naturally – they had arms and legs just like you. He-he-he! They were as slow as a sack of potatoes! I bet you're all related! I didn't care. Nope – I rose higher and higher and flew over fields and forests. Once I even popped through a little cloud and left a hole in it! In the end, I came across this tree and decided to stop for a while. It's pretty nice up here. Happy now? Is that all you wanted to know?'

'Who inflated you?' Oskar asked.

'How should I know!? Why should I even care? I didn't look back,' the balloon snapped.

'I came here from the city,' Oskar said. For some strange reason, he felt like getting everything off his chest and telling it to the balloon in particular. This had never even occurred to him with the iron, the chair, or any of the others. 'My mum is in America, but my dad has to go to work, so I've got to live with my grandma for two whole months. I was unbelievably bored and felt down in the dumps at first and everything seemed so wrong, but then I made myself a toy mobile that I can use to call things like you.'

'Tch! *You're* a thing! A teensy little thing with arms and legs! I'm a balloon, if you hadn't noticed. 'Of course, *I* have no idea if you've got eyes or not.'

'I'm do have eyes,' said Oskar, trying to make peace. 'I'm sorry – it's plain to see you're a balloon. A red balloon.' He hesitated. 'And a very pretty one at that,' he added.

'You think so?' the balloon asked slyly. 'You might just be right. It's lucky I landed in your treetop, then!'

'It sure is,' Oskar agreed. 'And I'm really lucky to have a magical mobile. Otherwise I don't know what I would have done here at Grandma's. I was honestly bored to tears at first.'

'It must be constantly boring for you things down there,' said the balloon. 'You can't fly, so you spend your time on all sorts of foolish activities. Just imagine – a magic mobile! I don't even have a phone, but I can talk to whomever I please.'

'Can you talk to birds, too?' Oskar asked.

'Why shouldn't I?'

'I don't think I can...' he murmured, trailing off into thought. 'I'm not sure my mobile would let me, though I haven't tried yet... Hey, balloon! I'm going to hang up now...'

'Is that so! Tired of me already, huh? Fine!'

'No, I just want to see if I can call birds or bugs with my mobile too,' Oskar explained. 'I'll call you back later.'

'You can try, but I'm not available *all* the time, you know,' the balloon replied importantly. 'I've got better things to do than to gab on the phone all day long.'

'I can't imagine you're *too* busy up in that treetop,' Oskar said.

'You don't, huh? Well, fine! Goodbye, then!'

The balloon hung up. Oskar stared at her from the ground. Framed against the bright blue sky, she was as radiant as a red blossom.

Oskar walked over to the apple trees where thrushes and tits were hopping around. He tried to call the birds, but soon realized that even his magic mobile had its limits. No matter how much he shouted 'Hello!' into the phone, the birds wouldn't answer. They just stared with their blank button-black eyes and fluttered away whenever he stepped closer.

Next Oskar tested his mobile on bugs – first with a wasp clambering around a flower and then with some kind of caterpillar inching across a tree trunk. But neither of them picked up either. Oskar concluded that his phone could only contact things.

'Hello, balloon!' he spoke into the receiver, hoping to share his discovery with his new friend. But the balloon didn't respond. No doubt she was busy with all her important appointments. Oskar stared crossly at the balloon bobbing in the light breeze high above him.

'Well, I suppose I've got a lot of things to do, too,' he mumbled to himself at last, and went inside. Certainly there were many more things in the house that he could help somehow.

Grandma had come home from the shops and was unpacking groceries.

'I bought you some sweets too, Oskar,' she said. 'Good little boys deserve sweets every now and then, you know!'

This time, the kind she'd bought were rather tasty, so Oskar popped one into his mouth immediately. His grandma wasn't a completely lost cause – maybe living together happily would be possible if they both worked at it.

Oskar could already feel his spirits rising, just like when he saw his presents on his birthday morning or when Dad brought in the Christmas tree. It was a little like how he felt on an ordinary Saturday morning when he was allowed to lie in bed for as long as he liked and didn't have to hurry off to preschool. On days like these, it felt like there could only be fun and wonderful things ahead, like everything was going to be gorgeous and brilliant. It was a strange and excellent sensation, as if he'd accidentally swallowed the sun and it was tickling him with its warm rays.

The sweets Grandma had bought undoubtedly sweetened his mood. Still, that wasn't the main reason – his mobile was the top cause of his happiness. That, along with – for some strange reason – the uppity balloon high up in the crown of the birch tree…

12.

Grandma started making lunch, so Oskar went outside. He briefly considered crawling back in through his bedroom window again, but he decided he'd certainly find something to meet and chat with outside. The balloon was swaying back and forth in the treetop, but Oskar didn't want to call her just yet. It didn't feel right. However, leaning next to the door was a long broom – Grandma had apparently used it to sweep the front step and then left it outside. Oskar called it.

'Hello, broom!'

'Hello, hello!' the broom answered in a slightly muffled voice, as if a beard was growing inside its mouth. Or was it simply full of dust? 'Who am I speaking to?'

'I'm Oskar. I have arms and legs. Maybe you need some help? Would you like to go anywhere?' On a trip, maybe?'

'Hmm... a trip... No, thank you,' the broom said. 'I'm perfectly fine with the floor inside the house. It's so dusty all the time that I could end up sweeping myself bald.'

'What do you mean?' Oskar gasped. 'How could that happen?'

'Oh, all too easily! The bristles fall out of my head if I sweep too hard, but I *have* to sweep hard when the floor is all messy! So I sweep and I sweep, but the whole time I'm just worrying: am I going to go bald? Brooms mustn't go bald because then they can't sweep anymore. Hey, as well your arms and legs, do you have eyes too?'

"Course I do,' Oskar said, bulging his eyes so they'd be easier to see. True, he couldn't make out any eyes on the broom itself, but it probably had a pair all the same, or how else could it find dust and rubbish on the floor? The same applied to other things – the iron could see wrinkles in the bedsheets and the chair was able to appreciate the view in the kitchen. *I guess things' eyes are hidden somewhere just like birds' ears*, Oskar decided. Bird ears aren't visible at first glance; they don't stick up like a hare's or droop like a dog's. But they do still have them.

'Oh, so those round things are your eyes, huh?' grunted the broom. 'Would you be a pal and check if I'm going bald or not? Is my hairdo more or less alright?'

'It looks fine to me!' Oskar said reassuringly. 'Nice and thick and bristly.'

'That's a relief,' the broom said. 'More than anything, I'm afraid of going bald! So, I'm not off travelling anywhere. I shouldn't sweep any more than I do already.'

'You don't have to sweep when you're travelling, you know,' said Oskar.

'Do you think there won't be rubbish there too? Ha! In your dreams! There's litter everywhere you go – you've just got to be decent and clean it up.'

'No, you don't understand! Travelling isn't the same as working,' Oskar explained. 'You just wander around seeing new places and appreciating them...'

'What's there to appreciate about dust and trash? You've got to clean it up – nothing else to see there.'

Oskar gave up trying to describe the charms of travelling. He already had one globetrotter to look after! If the broom enjoyed sitting at home, then why not?

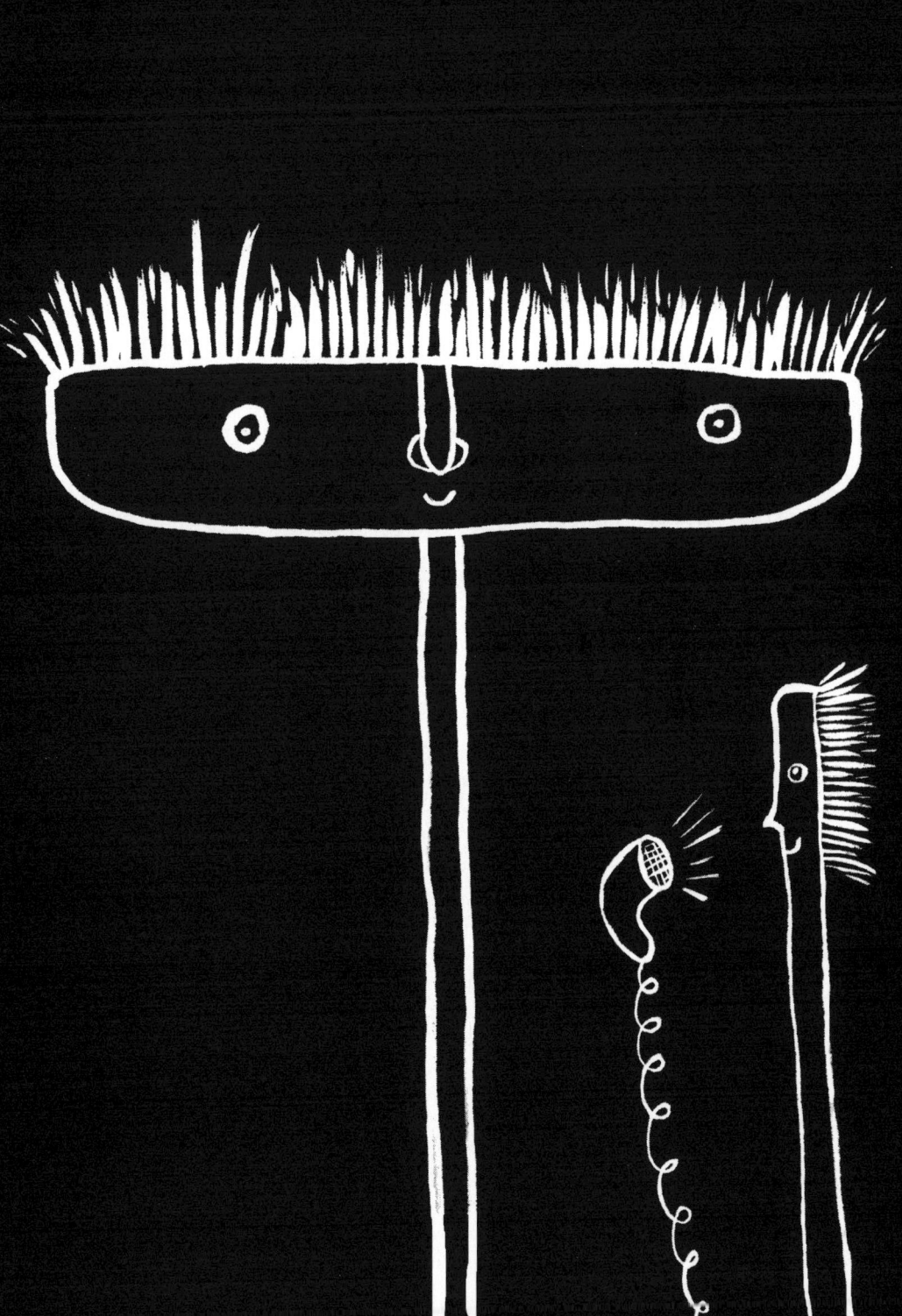

He was about to end his call with the broom and go looking for a more exciting conversation partner, but then the broom added:

'Hey, Oskar! I do have one problem. Well, not a problem exactly... I just wanted to ask... Do you know the toothbrush?'

'Of course I do!' Oskar exclaimed. 'We hang out every day. Morning and night.'

The broom was made of wood and its broomstick was green, but Oskar could have sworn that it blushed.

'I'd really like to meet him,' he whispered. 'We're related, you see, but we've never met. I've heard heaps about him – they say he's very small. It'd be fascinating to meet up. Could you introduce us, Oskar? Would that be any trouble?'

'Not at all!' Oskar replied cheerfully. 'I'll just go and bring him here.'

'Oh, you mean right now...' the broom said, taken slightly aback. 'Does my hair really look alright? There aren't any hairballs stuck in the bristles? They get caught there sometimes.'

'No, don't worry – you look very dapper! Wait here, I'll be back in five minutes.'

Oskar slipped back inside, thinking that it was actually a bit silly for him to tell the broom to 'wait here' when it wasn't able to walk, anyway.

He went into the kitchen, where his grandma was sitting next to the stove and frying pork-mince burgers amidst the loud sound of sizzling. Stealthily, he grabbed his toothbrush from the edge of the sink and crept back out. Grandma didn't look away from the pan once.

Oskar didn't run straight outside, as he thought he should prepare the toothbrush for the meeting first. He paused in the doorway, pulled the mobile out of his pocket, and said:

'Hello, toothbrush!'

'Hello, Oskar!' he replied. 'I'm glad you called. We've got a bit of a problem. You brushed your teeth too quickly this morning and a speck of porridge got caught between your canines. Oy, oy, oy!'

'That's not important right now,' Oskar said. 'Tell me – have you ever heard of the broom?'

'The broom?!' the toothbrush said in surprise. 'I sure have! He's my distant relative. I've never seen him before, but they say he's gigantic. They also say that eons ago, when dinosaurs ruled the earth, they used brooms to brush their teeth.'

'That's not true,' scoffed Oskar. 'Dinosaurs never brushed their teeth.'

'Well, then it's no wonder they went extinct,' the toothbrush mused. 'Brushing your teeth is very important; otherwise, you'll get cavities. Oskar, buddy – let's go brush your canines again right now. I just can't get that bit of porridge out of my mind!'

'No, there's no time right now. I want to introduce you to the broom. He's waiting outside,' Oskar announced.

'Waiting outside *for me*?!' the toothbrush gasped. 'Ah... Tell me – am I dry? I don't want to meet him with wet hair. And I don't have toothpaste smeared on me anywhere, do I?'

'Not at all, you look very nice. It's time for a family reunion!'

Oskar turned off his mobile and ceremoniously marched onto the porch with the toothbrush held in his outstretched palm like it was an open carriage.

'Here you are! Toothbrush, allow me to introduce – the broom! Broom, may I introduce you to – the toothbrush!' Oskar declared. He didn't hear what the two bristled things replied, because the mobile was in his pocket and he didn't think it right to bother their meeting with his phone calls. Oskar poked the toothbrush's handle into the ground right beside the broom so they could look at one another and chat as much as they pleased. He reckoned he'd call later and see how things had gone.

Oskar walked away. His gaze drifted upwards and he wondered if the balloon had watched him bring these two distant relatives together. Perhaps he should give her a call? Maybe she had finished her important errands for the day by now?

'Hello, balloon!' Oskar called into the mobile.

'So, what is it now?' the balloon replied. Oskar grinned.

'Did you see what I did?' he asked.

'No, I didn't. Why would I stare at the ground all day? I'd rather look out over the woods – that's much more interesting! You can see farther than you could ever believe from up here! Well, by "you", I do mean "me", of course. Arms and legs won't let you climb this high. You'd need to be red and pretty and full of air, just like me!'

'You must have a lot of time on your hands to be fooling around with brooms and brushes,' she continued. 'Don't you have anything better to do? Try standing on your tiptoes – then you'll be a tiny bit taller and see a teensy bit farther!'

'So you *did* see me!' Oskar said, grinning in satisfaction.

'Just out of the corner of my eye. Oh, I don't have time to chat anymore. All kinds of fascinating things are happening just beyond the woods!'

'What's going on over there?' Oskar asked.

'I told you – stand on your toes and you'll see!' the balloon said, then hung up.

13.

Grandma's porkburgers were surprising, and not in a good way. They were huge! Oskar reckoned he was as astonished as a kid who brings his rabbit some dandelions only to find discover his pet has swelled to the size of a pig.

It was the same with Grandma's burgers, which were three times bigger than the ones Mum made. Your plate could crack in half if you dropped one of those whoppers onto it!

Oskar was hit with a second miserable surprise when he sliced the burger open. Wet stringy bits of onion peeked out of the meat, like they were roots growing out of the patty. Oskar didn't like onions, even though his mum always told him ate them quite often actually; they were just chopped up so finely that he had no idea they were there. Grandma's onions, on the other hand, were downright leering at him from inside the burger!

Oskar started pulling the onion strings out one by one and imagined for a moment that he was digging for glittering flecks of gold in a heap of dark soil. Onions certainly weren't gold, though! They were more like pale-faced zombies climbing out of their graves. He could spot a few slimy heads, but who knew how many more lay in wait for him! Oskar quickly lost his appetite.

He scowled at his grandma, who seemed untroubled as she ate, sticking one forkful after another into her mouth. *Can she even taste the food at all?* he wondered. She certainly didn't seem to care, and was eating with the same blank expression she wore when washing dishes or tidying up.

'Grandma, are there any foods that you don't like?' Oskar asked.

'I can't say any come to mind,' she replied. 'As long as it fills my tummy and doesn't scream when I chomp down on it.'

Oskar eyed her warily. He doubted that even a scream would stop his grandma – she'd still pop the struggling morsel into her mouth, swallow, and sigh: 'That sure hit the spot!' Then she'd get up to wash the dishes.

'Why are you poking at your burger?' Grandma asked. 'Is something wrong?'

'There are lots of onions,' Oskar muttered.

'Onions are one of the main ingredients,' she replied. 'They're good for you. Your late grandfather would pick up a raw onion and bite into it like an apple.'

Always more about that grandpa and his bewildering antics! Oskar wanted to snap back at Grandma that just because sword-swallowers swallow swords it doesn't mean you should sprinkle nails into your burgers. But he held his tongue. The phone rang in the living room and Grandma left to answer it.

Oskar seized the chance to hide his last half-eaten burger under the others on the tray – for there were even more! A whole ton of them! Each was as big as a hot cross bun, only packed with onion instead of fruit. Grandma apparently planned to stick to a strict diet of burgers alone from now to the end of summer.

'Your father wants to talk to you!' Grandma called from the other room.

Oskar ran to the phone. Dad asked how he was doing and if he was dying of boredom.

'Not anymore,' Oskar replied.

'You've found some friends, then?' Dad asked.

'I have,' he replied. The friends weren't the kind Dad would have liked, but that didn't matter. What mattered was that they existed at all.

'Have you played football yet?' Dad asked. As if it were impossible for a boy to have a proper summer without football!

'Not yet,' Oskar replied. 'There's been so much else to do.'

'That's good. I'll let you go and enjoy your holiday, then!'

Oskar hung up and turned to go outside. But Grandma was standing in the doorway holding his toothbrush.

'What's this all about?' she demanded. 'A toothbrush stuck out in the ground? Did you put it there?'

'I was just playing...' Oskar tried to explain, but Grandma shook her head vigorously.

'This is not a game. This is really silly. Dear me! Your toothbrush will get filthy, stuck in the ground like that. A fly might land on it, or... and then afterwards, you'll brush your teeth and get ill. We're going to have to boil it in hot water.'

'Why?!' Oskar gasped. Boiling a toothbrush sounded dreadful – like actual torture! Weren't there some old, awful fairy tales where an evil king wanted to throw a brave hero into a cauldron and boil him alive? Sometimes even in tar?! Luckily, the cruel plan always failed, and it was the evil king himself who fell into the cauldron and was never seen again. Boiling water was for soup and potatoes – not putting a toothbrush in bubbling water! He could not let that happen!

'I don't want you to boil my toothbrush,' Oskar said, with a quiver in his voice.

'We must!' Grandma insisted. 'That will kill all the germs.'

Oskar was afraid the toothbrush might die along with

them. True, *things* were tough; much tougher than humans. The pot could chat to Oskar while boiling-hot milk soup simmered inside him. Perhaps being boiled would have no effect on the toothbrush. Even so, Oskar couldn't bear to think of the object he'd just been talking to being tossed into a bubbling pot. He grabbed the toothbrush out of Grandma's hand.

'I'll wash it myself,' Oskar insisted.

Grandma tried to argue that washing alone wouldn't help, because the garden was dirty. In her opinion, boiling was the surest way to deal with germs.

'Back in the day, we'd boil all kinds of things,' she said. 'Bedsheets...'

'Did you eat them later, too?' Oskar growled poisonously. No doubt they did – he bet she added a huge helping of onions and then his late grandpa devoured them with a ladle! That was how they lived in the olden days.

Oskar felt angry. Everything Grandma did was wrong, and she did it at the wrong time and in the wrong place. The toothbrush just wanted a chat with the broom, but Grandma had brought him inside. The chair had to hide like a fugitive because otherwise Grandma would put a swift end to her journey, saying 'a chair's place is in the living room!' Just like she said, 'You mustn't take your toothbrush outside!' What did she know?! The toothbrush himself wanted out! Why was she poking her nose into everything?!

Oskar started rinsing his toothbrush at the sink. The whole time, his grandma stood behind him shaking her head.

'You'll get a tapeworm at this rate, behaving like this,' she warned. A few seconds of silence followed. Then she sighed: 'I suppose you *are* rather bored all alone here, and that's why you get into this mischief. You should really make friends with those neighbourhood boys. You can all play Tag and Crocker and Last Pair Out and Olly Olly Oxen Free. They're polite children; they always say hello to me nice and clearly when we pass on the street.'

Oskar could just imagine the cotton-haired creatures greeting his grandma in unison in the village: 'Hi, there, Mrs. Burnmire!' It would be such a pain if Grandma decided to force them into a friendship now! Oskar cast a pleading glance over his shoulder.

'I have a brilliant time on my own too. I'm used to playing by myself in the city.'

'What kind of fun is that, though?! You take your toothbrush outside and stick it into the ground like a beanpole?' Grandma clapped her hands together in exasperation. 'I've never heard of that kind of a game before. Did you think it would start to grow?'

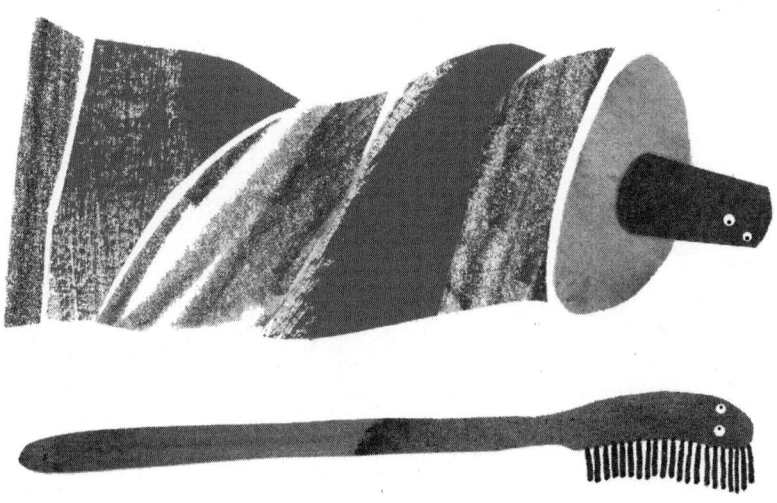

What Oskar was thinking was that he'd never heard of any games like "Crocker" or "Olly Olly Oxen Free" before, but he wasn't going to admit that out loud. He was amazed that Grandma really didn't understand *anything*, so there was no point in trying to explain. He could talk to things about anything, on the other hand. Things like the balloon... and others too, of course. Chatting with them was much more enjoyable.

Oskar seized his squeaky-clean toothbrush and took it to his room. Grandma stayed bustling about the kitchen, packing her gigantic burgers into the fridge.

He called the toothbrush.

'How'd it go?' he asked. 'Were you two interrupted? It wasn't my fault – Grandma found you. I can take you back to him later.'

'No need!' the toothbrush replied. 'We actually made plans for the broom to come and visit me next time. If you'd be so kind as to help, naturally...'

'No problem!' Oskar promised. 'What else are my arms and legs for?'

14.

The toothbrush was still on cloud nine after his meeting with the broom and rattled on incessantly about all the stories he'd heard. Once, the broom had swept a broken bottle into the dustpan without being at all afraid of the nasty shards threatening him with their needle-sharp claws. He'd even swept up a dead mouse.

'Can you imagine? A dead mouse!' the toothbrush repeated queasily. 'I'd faint on the spot if I ever found a dead mouse stuck between your teeth. But the broom wasn't afraid at all!'

Naturally, the broom's main focus was his constant war on dust balls and other rubbish. The broom compared himself to a policeman who, time and again, went on patrol to catch the clumps of lint and hair that had crawled out of their dens by brushing them into the dustpan. These were epic battles – the dust and litter certainly resisted with all their might and tried their best to escape, but never could. The broom always managed to sweep the floor clean and not one villain got away.

'I told him that my job is quite similar,' said the toothbrush. 'Only I'm more like a detective. All kinds of crumbs and nasty bits of food hide between your teeth, and it's my job to track them down and drag them out into the open. They can be very sly sometimes, slumping their heads down between their shoulders and crouching low without moving, but I've got a trained eye and they can't fool me. My darling toothpaste helps me a great deal, of course. You know, Oskar – we were thinking that the next time we meet, we could both bring our wives along. I'd come with the toothpaste and the broom would bring the dustpan. That wouldn't be any trouble, would it?'

'Not at all,' said Oskar. 'I had no idea that you and the toothpaste were married.'

'Oh, yes!' the toothbrush exclaimed. 'For two whole weeks already!'

'That's not very long at all,' Oskar said, frowning. 'My mum and dad have been married for ten years.'

'There's not a tube of toothpaste in the world that would last that long,' the toothbrush replied somewhat glumly. 'They run empty after a month at most, and then I have to take a new wife.'

'How many times have you been married?' Oskar asked.

'This sweetie pie is my thirty-sixth wife,' the toothbrush said.

Oskar thought this was a bit strange, but no doubt it was normal in toothbrush world. The two briefly discussed details for the next get-together and decided it could take place in two days' time. Oskar suggested that they meet under his bed this time. Grandma was hardly going to find them there! The toothbrush was very pleased with this plan, and told Oskar that he'd never been under a bed before. The broom, on the other hand, regaled him with stories about the tight space beneath beds, where especially large dust balls lurked.

Oskar took the toothbrush back to the kitchen. Grandma had done the dishes and disappeared; the kitchen was all his. He rubbed the mobile between his hands and wondered what to call next.

His eyes landed on the dustbin. How about that? It might have something interesting to say. What would a dustbin chat about? What kind of a voice would it have? For some reason, Oskar felt sure the bin would talk in a raspy voice, just like the old man who lived in their block of flats in the city and enjoyed sitting in the park, feeding pigeons, and drinking beer in the summer. The old man's voice sounded like someone tooting a rusty trumpet. Whenever he heard it, Oskar was reminded of the Tin Man in the book *The Wizard of Oz*. Well, this dustbin *was* made of metal! He reckoned he might as well call and find out what sound it made.

'Hello, dustbin!' Oskar said into the receiver.

'Hello, my boy!' the bin replied. But his voice wasn't raspy at all – instead it was velvety and mellow, just like on an advert for chocolates. 'It's so nice of you to call. And what impeccable timing! I was just getting full!'

'Would you like me to empty you out?' Oskar suggested helpfully.

'Oh, no, my generous chum!' the dustbin said. 'I'm on fine form, as it were. Whenever I'm empty, I can't seem to create a thing – I feel just helpless and miserable. Luckily that tragedy never lasts for long, and soon I start to fill up with all kinds of valuable things. I swell and burst into bloom like a rose bush!'

'You bloom like a rose bush!?' Oskar couldn't believe his ears. 'I'd sure like to see that. When do you start?'

'That was just poetic metaphor!' the dustbin explained. 'That's how poets speak, and *I* am a poet. Here, listen to my latest: 'I hope to never bid farewell / to you, my fair cream-white eggshell!' I came up with it just this afternoon.'

Oskar peered into the bin. It was heaped almost to the

brim with rubbish of all kinds, and lying right on top was indeed the empty eggshell that Grandma had tossed in while making the burgers.

'Do you write poems about everything that falls into you?' Oskar asked.

'But of course!' the dustbin replied. 'The more that piles up, the greater gusto I have for crafting verse. Today has been very fruitful, indeed – my poetic steed truly soared! What do you think of this poem: "I gain resolve to forge ahead / from this green heel of mouldy bread!"? Or this one: "A star has fallen into this bin / in the form of an ochre sausage skin." Isn't that nice?'

'It really is,' Oskar agreed. A thought crossed his mind: if he tossed something else into the dustbin just now, would it write a new poem about it that very instant? His eyes scanned the kitchen. The floor was clean – the broom had evidently been at work earlier and swept up all the rubbish from underfoot – but there was a dead fly lying on the windowsill. That would do just fine!

Oskar picked up the fly between his fingertips and tossed it into the dustbin, still holding the mobile up to his ear.

Immediately the bin declared:

'Oh, I've just had another idea!'

'What's that?' Oskar asked.

'I thought I'd write a poem about a dead fly. What a genius idea! Sometimes I amaze *myself* with my talent. Alas, what am I to do. That's just what I am – a bin full of great ideas! Now, quiet! Quiet! Silence, world! Everyone, hold your breath! The poet is at work!'

Indistinct murmuring came from the mobile for a few long minutes. Oskar waited with bated breath. Finally, the bin announced proudly:

'The poem is ready. I could declare that I've never written anything as fine as this before, but that would be a lie, because all my poems are equally wonderful. And so it is with this one. What's more, it is very sorrowful. I'll read it to you, but be warned – I might burst into tears at any moment!'

With that, the dustbin began reciting his poem in a trembling voice:

'Oh, dearest fly! You left so young. Why must you from the mortal world be flung?'

The bin began bawling as soon as he uttered the word 'flung'. Oskar tried to peek and see if the inside of the bin turned wet when it cried, but he couldn't make out any streaming tears because it was too full of rubbish.

Oskar tried to soothe the dustbin by praising his poem, but all it did was blubber. Oskar wasn't sure what to do. As a last resort, he tore a piece of paper towel off the roll on the counter, blew his nose into it, and threw it away.

Suddenly the dustbin fell silent.

'I've got a new idea!' he declared triumphantly. 'I can't believe how fast-paced my imagination is today! I'll have a new poem ready in two shakes of a lamb's tail!'

Oskar quietly ended the call as the dustbin began muttering to himself again. He'd heard enough poetry for one day.

15.

Day began to turn to night, and Oskar remembered it was time to move the globetrotting chair from his grandma's bedroom to his own before it was too late.

He gave her a call: 'How's it all going? Are you ready to carry on your journey?'

'Oh, I've seen so many wonderful things!' the chair chattered. 'And I feel so rested! What incredible silence there is here! But I'm ready to keep going – I *do* want to see the whole world.'

Oskar dragged the chair into his own bedroom. His gaze drifted to the window and up to the top of the birch tree. The red balloon was dancing in the breeze.

He felt very tempted to call her again, but got a grip on himself before he pulled out his mobile. The house *was* filled with all sorts of different things that he hadn't yet spoken a single word to; things that were still total strangers – he couldn't just go chatting on and on with a single balloon! There could be objects in trouble right here all around him. Oskar went into the living room and scanned the space.

What if he struck up a conversation with the clock? It was a grand, old-fashioned cuckoo clock with a pendulum that swung from side to side and two pinecone-shaped weights dangling from chains. A tiny carved bird peeked out of its hatch on the hour and cried out: 'Cuckoo!'

Oskar lifted the phone to his ear and said: 'Hello, clock! I'm Oskar. Pleased to meet you.'

'Hello, Oskar!' the clock immediately replied. 'It's very nice of you to call. I've been hanging here on this wall for fifty-one years, three months, fifteen days, seven hours, and twenty-one minutes, but I haven't spoken to a single human being that whole time. You're the very first.'

'I reckon it's because no one's ever had a phone like mine,' Oskar said. 'I can use it to call things and talk to them.'

'Is there a cuckoo in your phone, too?' the clock asked.

'Of course not!' Oskar laughed. 'Cuckoos don't live in phones.'

'Some other bird or beast, then?' the clock pressed.

'Nope, nobody,' Oskar replied.

'How sad!' the clock said, sounding like it was frowning. 'I wouldn't know how to manage without a pet. I'm so accustomed to my little cuckoo. She keeps me company, especially at night. I have insomnia, you know – I have to keep working and ticking away without sleep. The cuckoo is a great help during those long hours.'

The clock sighed.

'When I was just a kid, I dreamt of having lots of animals one day!' he said mournfully.

'When were you a kid?' Oskar asked. 'How can a clock ever be a kid? Clocks don't grow!'

'I mean the time just after I was built,' the clock explained. 'Before I was assembled, when all my gears were strewn about the clockmaker's table. Back then, I wanted to become a zoo director as soon as I was finished. And I was absolutely thrilled when the clockmaker gave me the cuckoo! Alas, I've never received any more birds or beasts.'

The clock fell silent and Oskar didn't know what to say either. They were both thinking the same thing. The clock was the first to speak again.

'Oskar – perhaps *you* could give me an animal?'

Oskar had already been considering that, only... what animal could it be? Where would it live? Probably inside the clock, right next to the cuckoo behind her little hatch. He could put a bug inside – an ant, for starters – but there was no way it would enjoy living inside a clock where it was dark and cramped, there was nothing to eat, and you were in constant danger of being mashed up between the gears. No, and he couldn't put a live beetle in there either.

Still, the cuckoo that popped out on the hour wasn't real – she was just a bird-shaped toy.

If Oskar were at home in the city, he could have moulded animals out of Play-Doh, but his grandma definitely didn't have any of that lying about. What's more, Play-Doh might be bad news for the clock's mechanism – the gears might stop working if any got stuck between them. Then he'd be in big trouble.

But what if he *drew* the animals? He could make them on little scraps of paper, roll them up, then poke them through the cuckoo's hatch. Tiny little bits of paper shouldn't cause any harm to the gears!

And Oskar had a set of felt-tip pens handy – the same ones he'd used to colour his magic phone.

'I think I know what to do,' Oskar said. 'What animals would you like?'

'A dog, of course,' the clock replied. 'I've always wanted one of those. And a hippo. I'd also like a monkey. And a parrot. A lion, a polar bear, and a hamster.'

Oskar had quite a job ahead of him. The animals would be especially hard to draw because they had to be very, very small. He had no trouble drawing the polar bear and the

hippo, or the dog. The lion wouldn't turn out right at first, but then Oskar realized he simply needed to draw a cat and scribble a fluffy mane around its neck. The monkey took a lot of work too. The parrot kept looking too much like a crow, and for some reason the hamster turned out to be the hardest of all. Oskar kept at it, biting his tongue between his teeth, but the best hamster he could manage to draw looked suspiciously like a sausage with legs.

'Well, I guess that'll just have to do,' Oskar decided at last. 'It's a rare breed of sausage hamster.' He rolled up the tiny pictures, pulled a chair under the clock, climbed onto it, carefully pried open the cuckoo's hatch, and dropped the new animals into the opening one by one.

'There you go, zoo delivery!' he announced into his phone.

'How amazing they are!' the clock gushed. 'Thank you so much, Oskar! Finally I'm the zoo director I've always dreamed of becoming.'

Oskar would have liked to chat with the clock for longer, but he heard his grandma's footsteps climbing the porch. He barely had time to hop off the chair before she stepped into the kitchen, glanced into the living room and spotted him.

'What are you doing in there, Oskar?' she asked. Then she saw the chair pushed up beneath the clock. 'Don't you be playing with that clock!' she warned him sternly. 'Clocks aren't for playing with – they're very delicate machines. Your grandpa and I were given that for our wedding.'

'I wasn't playing with it,' Oskar protested.

'Why did you push a chair up under it, then?' Grandma asked. She marched into the room and carried the chair back to the table. 'Did you touch the clock?' Grandma's expression was unsmiling. 'You shouldn't touch it.'

'I only looked at it a little,' Oskar said. 'I wanted to... see the cuckoo.'

'The cuckoo's place is inside the clock – it only comes out to sing,' Grandma lectured him. 'You could break the clock if you try and yank it open.'

'I won't do it again,' Oskar promised. Oh, how frustrating this all was! The poor clock had hung on the wall for fifty-one years and longer, yearning to become a zoo director all that time, and now that Oskar finally made his wish come true, Grandma had showed up and started scolding him not to yank at it! The word itself was bad enough. Oskar was no fool – he never yanked at anything! He was just doing good deeds for things.

Grandma walked up to the clock and inspected it fretfully, as if afraid she'd discover a hole or a scratch. Then she turned one ear towards it and listened carefully to see if it was still ticking.

'I didn't do anything, I swear!' Oskar repeated. 'I was just looking.'

'We look only with our eyes!' Grandma instructed, then stroked the side of the clock and went back into the kitchen.

That tiny gesture helped Oskar to understand her just a little. The clock was no doubt dear to her in a very special way, but she simply couldn't speak its language or realize what its own problems and wishes were.

Luckily, she had Oskar and his phone with her for the summer. He thought of the hippo, the monkey and the other animals lying side-by-side at the bottom of the clock, and imagined Grandma would be in for a big surprise if the lion were to one day pop out of the hatch instead of the cuckoo and roar a couple of times.

16.

That evening, Oskar and his grandma played *Life* again. Oskar didn't really want to play, of course, but Grandma insisted. It was just as boring as last time, and she still cheated to make sure he won. Whenever Grandma rolled the dice, she'd cover it with her hand (sneakily, so she thought) to hide the number from him. Even so, Oskar caught a glimpse of it almost every time – whenever she rolled a six, she'd tell him it was a one. If Grandma had done the opposite, lying that the one she really rolled was a six, then Oskar would certainly have made a fuss and demanded she play fairly, but now it seemed somehow rude to expose her. So he simply kept his mouth shut and waited impatiently for the game to end.

Unfortunately, Oskar had unlucky rolls over and over again. His counter kept landing on squares that sent him tumbling back to the start of the board. Grandma suggested they pretend it hadn't happened and just keep on playing, but Oskar refused to accept. Being sent back to square one wouldn't have been all that bad if Grandma herself played fairly, sped on to the finish and won the game. But she started to drag it out even longer, making sure her piece always landed on the squares that sent it tumbling back as well, in the hope that Oskar would soon catch up and get ahead of her. He started to feel like this game of *Life* would never end.

'Grandma, you rolled a four – why did you only move three squares?' Oskar finally demanded after losing his patience.

'You don't have to be sent back. Keep going!'

'Oh, you're right. I'm not wearing my glasses,' Grandma apologised. However, she cheated again on her very next turn. Oskar was already so fed up with the stupid board game that he didn't let a single one of her wrong moves go unnoticed.

'You didn't roll a one – it was a five! I saw it!' he complained. 'You've got to land here. Right, now it's my turn to roll. Two. Now, it's your turn. Show me!'

'The die fell a little funny. I'll just roll again,' Grandma lied.

'Nothing fell a little funny; you rolled a four. So – one, two, three, four. You've won. Game over!'

Oskar felt downright giddy. *I bet this is how people who recover from some terrible disease or make it out of a war alive feel*, he thought.

Grandma, on the other hand, looked stunned.

'How could it be that I, an old lady, won against you?' she sighed, spreading her arms. 'Would you like to play again?'

'No!' Oskar almost shouted. 'No more!' At the same time, he was thinking, *I never want to play this stupid game ever again.* 'I think I'll just go to bed. Goodnight.'

'Don't you want to watch telly?' Grandma asked. 'There's a nice film on tonight about a poor girl who meets a millionaire and marries him.'

'No thanks, not interested.'

'Maybe you're right,' she agreed. 'I suppose it's not a kid's film, really. You go ahead and go to bed; I'm going to stay up and watch a little.'

Grandma made herself comfortable in front of the telly, but was snoring softly even before the poor girl had a chance to meet the millionaire in the first place.

Oskar snuggled in under the covers. The globetrotting chair stood in the corner sightseeing and the wardrobe seemed once again to be wearing a sickly sweet expression that pleaded: *Call me and I'll tell you something bloody and horrid!* The pillow was soft beneath Oskar's head and his thoughts drifted to the colourful giggling feathers inside. Staring out the window from his bed, he could see the birch and the red balloon, which was incredibly vivid in the bright June night. Oskar decided to call her.

'Hey, balloon! I'm already in bed,' he said.

'Is that so?! You can't even be bothered to come out to the tree anymore – you just call me while lounging around! Pitiful!' the balloon said. 'You shouldn't be so lazy. Get a move on!'

'It's night-time. I've got to go to sleep,' Oskar explained.

'Sleep?! Already?!' The balloon snorted. 'It's just getting interesting outside and all sorts are starting to happen. Oh boy, what amazing stuff I can see from up here!'

'Like what?'

'Guess you'll have to come and see for yourself.'

'No, I'm not going out anymore today,' Oskar replied, yawning. 'It's so cosy here in bed. Do you ever sleep?'

'Never!'

'Liar.'

'How can you say that?! Me? Lie? Shame on you! I always tell the truth. I'm not a sleepy little teddy bear like you, who pulls up his blanket and sucks his thumb on a beautiful summer night like this. There's a fog rising, night's scents are spreading, and weird noises are coming from all around... I want to see it all; I've got no time for lying around. Sleep is boring. Boo-riing!'

'Okay,' Oskar said just to appease her. 'Maybe you do see funny things from way up there in the treetop. But I can see you when I'm lying here in bed, and that's a nice way to fall asleep. Goodnight, balloon!'

'Goodnight, Oskar!' the balloon replied. 'Go ahead and get some shut-eye, I guess. Teensy-tiny boys *need* their sleep if they want to grow a little bit taller. Who knows – maybe you'll be taller than a dandelion by morning!'

'I've been taller than a dandelion for ages already,' Oskar said matter-of-factly. 'Actually, I'm even taller than you!'

'Oh yeah? What a riot! That's a fib if I've ever heard one! Come up here and we'll measure!' the balloon giggled.

'You come down here and we'll measure us on the ground!' Oskar proposed.

'Never! Down there? Pff, as if! A balloon's place is up in the sky!'

And as if to prove her words, the balloon, buoyed by a sudden gust of wind, rose a little above the tree-top and wheeled round in circles against the deepening summer twilight.

'That's very pretty,' Oskar said.

'Sleep tight, giant!' the balloon replied warmly.

Oskar hung up and tucked the phone under his pillow. He was in a particularly bright mood and felt like hugging someone.

In the living room, the remote control clattered against the floor as it slipped from Grandma's grip.

'Would you look at that – must have dozed off,' Grandma murmured to herself sleepily. 'How is it that as soon as I sit down in front of the telly, I just can't keep my eyelids open... Oskar, dear, are you asleep already?'

Shuffling footsteps approached and Oskar's bedroom door

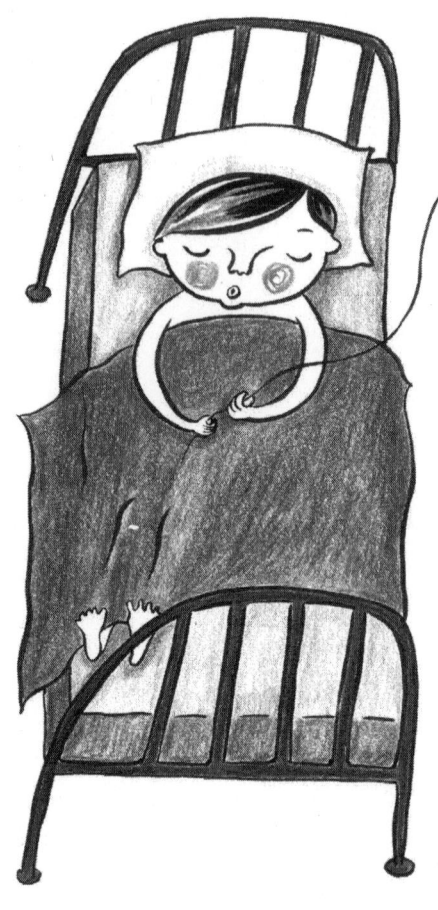

creaked open. He stayed motionless under the blanket and crossed his fingers, hoping Grandma wouldn't notice the chair on its trip around the world. Did she really have to check on him?! Why couldn't she just go to bed for the night? Why did she have to come into his room first?

'Fast asleep...' she murmured, crossing the doorstep and tucking him in. 'Good lad.' With that, she yawned loudly and left the room.

Oskar breathed a sigh of relief, then rolled over onto his back and stared out the widow until he drifted off to sleep.

17.

The next morning, Oskar was woken by his phone making strange sounds under his pillow. It wasn't an ordinary ringtone – a jingle or a song – but a peculiar rasping noise. It sounded as if someone were grinding away at the wooden telephone with a big saw. There wasn't really a saw under his pillow, of course – the phone was lying there in perfect solitude. But when Oskar grabbed it, he felt as if it was vibrating a little and even warm to the touch.

Is somebody calling me? Oskar wondered in amazement. Nothing like this had ever happened before – he was always the one to call things. Oskar lifted the mobile to his ear.

'Hi!'

'Hello, is this Oskar?' a gruff old man's voice spoke.

'I am indeed. Who's speaking?'

'I'm the table. The living room table. I have a little problem... One of my chairs is missing.'

'She's not missing at all,' Oskar replied, glancing at the corner of his room where the globetrotting chair was currently camped out. 'She's travelling.'

'Travelling! You don't say...' the table echoed in surprise. 'Well, I'll be... And when is she coming home?'

'I can't say for sure,' Oskar replied. 'She still needs to visit the hallway and the loo. It'll definitely be a couple more days.'

'A couple more *days*... That's an awfully long time! I'm not used to my chairs being away from home,' the table moaned. 'Especially at night. It makes it impossible to fall asleep.

All I do is worry about what might happen to her. What if she breaks a leg? What if her bottom falls out? I start fretting about that silly little chair.'

'There's no need to worry or be afraid,' Oskar reassured him. 'The chair is in perfect shape. She just wants to see the world. You've got five more chairs around you – what difference does it make if one is off exploring?'

The table sighed mournfully.

'I do have five other chairs, yes. But I'm used to the whole family being together. None of them have ever been away from home for so long. It'd be nice if she just came back to us soon. The other chairs are heartbroken too – all they do is ask: Where's Rickety? Where's Rickety?'

'Why do you call her "Rickety"?' Oskar asked, narrowing his eyes.

'That's just her nickname,' the table explained. 'Now, be a good boy and tell her to come home, will you? Everyone misses her.'

So Oskar called the chair and passed on what the table had told him. But the chair only grew angry hearing about it.

'Of course he did, of *course* he did!' she squealed in a flustered, high-pitched voice. 'Come home, eh? Right this instant? Oh, he'd love that! Now, this very moment, when I'm having such a good time travelling through other rooms and experiencing so many incredible things. Nope, I've got no intention of giving up my trip. All I've done my entire life is stand around in one place with the table and the other chairs as if I was nailed to the ground. I want to have a little fun for once!'

'Is your nickname "Rickety"?' Oskar asked.

'It is *not*!' the chair screeched. 'That's a terrible nickname!

Only that stupid table calls me that! No, there's no way I'm going back to him. I want to be free, not "Rickety"! I want to keep on going!'

'Then it's settled,' Oskar agreed. 'I'll take you into the hallway next, but not right now – once Grandma leaves the house. Wait here till then.'

Oskar got dressed and went to eat breakfast. Grandma started tidying up the kitchen after he finished, so he went outside. He would have to be patient, because the chair's journey couldn't continue until the coast was clear. The hallway was a cramped little space and there was nowhere for the chair to hide, so it would easy for Grandma to stumble upon the traveller and take her back to the living room. The table would be quite pleased to have all his little lambs back together again, but Oskar sided with the adventurous chair.

It's like a spying game, Oskar thought as he stood in front of the house, trying to look as if he hadn't a care in the world while actually keeping an eye on Grandma through the kitchen window. She had just finished washing the dishes and was now drying plates. When she'd finished that, she left the house. Was this the right moment? Oskar peered at her out the corner of his eye. Was she off to the vegetable patch? Unfortunately not – she'd just gone to hang the tea towel out to dry before going back inside. As far as Oskar could tell, she had started mopping the floor.

That meant it would take even *longer*! He had to stay patient, just like spies and thieves in films – ones who waited long, long hours before they got their chance to set off an explosion or steal a pearl necklace from a jewellery shop. Oskar had nothing criminal in mind, of course – he merely wanted to carry a chair into the hallway – but thanks to

Grandma it had become a dangerous task that required him to stay on his toes. He crouched behind a peony bush, concealing him from Grandma while giving him a clear view of the front door. It was a great spot for spying.

Above the roof of the house, Oskar could also see the birch tree next to the shed and the red balloon gleaming at its tip. He thought it was just the right moment to say good morning to his friend, so that's what he did.

'What do you mean, "morning"?' the balloon snorted. 'The sun's been high in the sky for ages and *now* you come and wish me good morning?! I bet all you'd do is sleep if you could. And why've you crawled under a bush? Are you eating leaves down there?'

'How can you see me?' Oskar asked in surprise. He'd thought he was perfectly hidden from sight, and the balloon *was* some distance away.

'How can I see you – ha, what a great question!' the balloon jeered. 'With my *eyes*, silly! Did you think you'd be invisible by wiggling into a shrubbery? Or that you'd pass for a flower? In your dreams! You're nothing like a flower at all. By the way, there's a bee crawling up your trouser leg.'

Oskar leapt up in horror, but there was no bee to be seen. 'You lied!'

The balloon giggled.

'Oh, you think so? You'll have to get used to bees if you've decided to start pretending to be a flower, you know – they're only gathering nectar.'

'I'm not pretending to be a flower,' Oskar insisted, and tried to explain what he was up to. But the balloon started deliberately yawning before he could finish.

'Boo-riing!' she announced. 'As if I give a hoot that you're dragging some chair from room to room and afraid of your grandma finding her. Boo-riing! Stop your yapping before I turn grey.'

'*You're* the one who's not doing anything except bobbing about in some tree,' Oskar snapped, feeling a little offended.

'Is that right! Only someone who spends his days down amongst the worms and the moles could think that way!' the balloon said primly. 'You simply can't imagine all the things I see and do up here! Every now and then, a new breeze comes to visit. We chat, he tells me how pretty I am, spins me around, asks me to dance... And then we twirl! He doesn't hide from his grandma in some bush! He-hee!'

'A breeze is just air,' Oskar scoffed. 'You can't talk to air.'

'*I* can! I'm filled with air too, you know! I get along just fine with breezes!' the balloon declared. 'Here comes one just now! And he's a southern breeze – all gentle and warm! I reckon I'll be off to the ball with him just now, so I can't talk anymore!'

'Well, bye then,' Oskar grumbled.

'What's wrong? Are you pouting? You can go dancing too, you know! You and your chair! Or your grandma! Pick whichever you like most! Toodle-oo.'

The balloon hung up, giggling hysterically. Oskar slid the phone into his pocket. He glared at the balloon bouncing about on the treetop and tried to imagine what that gentle, warm southern breeze she was dancing with now might look like. Pretty ugly, no doubt!

Then he spotted Grandma coming outside and heading towards the vegetable patch. That meant it was time to act. He darted out from behind the bush, ran straight to his room, grabbed the chair and hauled her into the hallway. Then he pulled out his phone.

'I don't know how long you can stay here,' he explained. 'But I'll keep an eye on Grandma, and I'll rush to the rescue if you end up in any danger.'

'Thank you, Oskar!' the chair squealed. 'How can I ever repay you? Would you like to sit down and rest for a spell?'

'No thanks,' said Oskar. 'I'd better go outside and be on the lookout.'

With that, he walked out into the garden and stood with his hands on his hips, eyeing Grandma as she busied herself in the vegetable patch, bravely resisting the urge to glance up at the crown of the birch tree.

18.

The air outside was scorching, so Oskar crouched down by the side of the house. There he was shaded from the sun and could lean back against the pleasant cool of the brick wall. Grandma was weeding in the blazing heat of the vegetable patch. Oskar hoped there was lots to pull up so she'd have her hands full till suppertime.

But before long, he got bored just crouching there. What if he called something for a chat? On the ground nearby was a small milk churn that was missing its cap. Oskar decided to give it a ring.

'Hello, milk churn!' Oskar said, lifting the phone to his ear. 'I'm Oskar. It sure is hot today.'

'Hello!' the milk churn replied. 'Hello! Who's there? Hello!'

'It's me, Oskar!' Oskar said a little louder. 'Nice weather today, isn't it?'

'Hello!' the milk churn repeated. 'I can't hear you very well. I've lost my ears.'

'What do you mean, you've lost your ears?' Oskar now yelled into the receiver. 'How can your ears get lost?'

'Yes, good, much better! Now I can hear you. You've got to talk loudly to me; I've been deaf for a whole year. What a tragedy, eh! And nobody can help, either. How could they? You'd need arms and legs for the task.'

'*I've* got arms and legs!' Oskar yelled. 'I can help! What do you need?'

'My boy, is that really true?' the milk churn gasped. 'Well then, I've certainly got a favour to ask! You see, last autumn, Grandma used me to collect berries, and she lost my lid in the process! I have no idea where it went – all I know is that Grandma brought me inside and rinsed me out, but my lid was nowhere to be seen. Missing. And I have all kinds of important things on that lid, like my ears. She can't have gone far; she must still be lying here in the garden. Be a good boy and have a look around, would you? Maybe you'll spot her. She's white and looks just like me – I'm sure you'll know her when you see her!'

'I can try,' Oskar promised. He liked the milk churn's mission. Now he could pretend to be a detective searching for lost treasures. Or trying to catch a dangerous criminal who lurked somewhere in the garden, hatching evil plans!

Oskar tried to decide which one was more exciting, but couldn't choose. All he knew was that he was no longer just Doctor Dolittle, but also Sherlock Holmes facing a dangerous and important task.

'It's no good standing around with my top open either, because anyone can peek inside,' the milk churn continued. 'You can see straight down to the bottom! How embarrassing! You wouldn't want anybody peeking inside you, would you? Everyone's got their own little secrets that they don't want to show others. I, for instance, have two little rust spots down there. I don't want any old person gawping at me! But how can I stop them when I don't have my lid? They don't just *look* inside, either – they *climb* inside me sometimes. A snail lived there for three days on the trot. You wouldn't believe how uncomfortable that was! Be a good lad and start looking for my lid at once. I've been without her almost a whole year, can you imagine!'

'I'll look for her right away!' Oskar declared, though the earless milk churn didn't hear him. Oskar left him to babble to himself and walked into the garden.

How would he find the lost lid? The milk churn said Grandma used him last autumn for gathering berries, which meant she'd probably forgotten the lid somewhere in the berry bushes. But there were countless bushes in Grandma's garden – who could possibly look under all of them?

Oskar did, however, have his amazing phone. Would the lid answer if he tried ringing her?

Oskar put the mobile to his ear.

'Hello, milk churn lid! Oskar here! Hello, milk churn lid! Pick up! Someone's looking for you!'

Nothing happened at first, but then, he heard heavy static

and a frightened voice yelling: 'Yes, yes! I'm here! Help! Rescue me! I've been in such grave danger for a whole year now without my milk churn! Help! Help! Help!'

'Calm down!' Oskar soothed. 'Help is on the way. I can hear you, but I can't see you. Where are you right now?'

'Under a bush! Under a bush! Help! Help! There's a big frog here! It's going to eat me up!'

'There's no need to panic! Frogs don't eat milk churns, or their lids,' Oskar reassured her. 'I can't believe you've been living out in the wild for a whole year and still don't know these things. I'll rescue you as soon as I can find you, but there are lots of bushes in Grandma's garden. You'll have to be more precise. What kind of a bush is it?'

'A gooseberry bush! Help! I want to go home! I want my milk churn!' screeched the lid, starting to wail like an ambulance rushing to someone's aid.

'Hush!' Oskar snapped. 'All this whining is going to get you nowhere. Can you describe the gooseberry bush in a little more detail? What's growing around it?'

'Rhubarb! Big rhubarb plants!' the lid squealed. 'Oh, how awful they are! Don't leave me here! Help!'

Oskar couldn't understand what was so awful about rhubarb, but at least he now had an idea of what bush to look for. There was only one gooseberry bush growing by Grandma's rhubarb patch and that's just where he headed. At first the lid was nowhere to be seen and Oskar started to wonder if homesickness had made her go bonkers. But when he took a closer look (which wasn't at all easy, because gooseberry bushes are notoriously prickly!), he noticed something white nestled in the low but dense nettles beneath the branches. It was the lost lid!

'Found you!' Oskar announced. 'Hold on a little longer and I'll try to scoop you out.'

He found a stick under the apple trees and used it to poke through the nettles until he got one end hooked under the lid. It was impossible to tell that she'd been outside for a whole year, including a long winter. The lid was certainly a little smudged and dirty, but she looked as good as new after Oskar had wiped her on the grass.

'Thank goodness!' the lid cheered. 'I can't believe it! I'm saved! I can see my dear milk churn again! I don't have to live with the snails, ants and that frog anymore! I don't have to sleep in the snow or under rotting leaves! I can go home! Hooray! Three cheers for my brave rescuer!'

Oskar felt his chest swell with pride. It was nice to receive that kind of praise.

'Now let the last stage of the rescue operation begin –' he declared, 'the journey home!'

Oskar lifted the lid high above his head so her white surface glinted in the sunshine and marched slowly towards the house, where the milk churn stood waiting for his lid and long-lost ears. Oskar called him. It turned out the milk churn hadn't even noticed Oskar leave, and was still going on and on about his tough life.

'So, laddie, would you please just do us a tiny favour and go find my poor little liddie? There's just no way I can carry on without her!'

'I already found her!' Oskar announced.

'Huh? I can't hear you, sonny – my ears are on my lid, you know. What did you say?'

Instead of answering, Oskar grandly set the lid on top of the milk churn, as if crowning a king. Shouts of joy sounded from the phone at first, followed by slurpy kisses. Oskar slid the mobile into his pocket.

Just a few seconds later, the block of wood started buzzing and vibrating again. Oskar guessed it was the milk churn wanting to thank him, and answered.

'*I* could have told you where that flimsy old lid was hiding, you know,' said the red balloon, brightly. 'I could see her down in the nettles all along. It took you forever to find her! I thought you'd be looking till Christmas.'

'What are you talking about – it only took me a moment!' Oskar protested, though he was thoroughly pleased that the balloon had been keeping an eye on him from up in the birch tree. And he was especially chuffed that this time, *she* had called *him*! 'I thought you were dancing with your stupid southern breeze,' he added poisonously, so as to not betray how glad he really felt. 'I bet he stank like monkeys and hippos.'

'What?!' the balloon sputtered. 'Monkeys and hippos? Come off it! He smelled like an orange or an orchid! What a spectacular time we had! Way better than crawling around in the bushes, looking for the lid to a potty.'

'She wasn't a potty lid!'

'Of course she was – I saw her! And you carried her over your head, he-he-he! Yeah, *that* sort of a hat would really suit you.'

'You're a twit!' Oskar said, grinning.

'No, you are!' the balloon replied. 'And by the way, your grandma's coming. She's going to find your chair, and guess what'll happen then!'

Oskar glanced towards the vegetable patch. She was right – Grandma was walking his way!

19.

Grandma's front door swung inward, which meant that, if you hid directly behind it, you were invisible to anyone walking in. Unless, of course, they glanced back. Oskar could only cross his fingers and hope his grandma would just head straight to the kitchen. So he wedged the chair behind the door and squeezed in next to it.

Grandma came in, breathing heavily. Now only the door separated her from Oskar and the chair. If she decided to close it behind her, their hiding place would be revealed instantly. Luckily, it was hot outside and Grandma left it wide open. She went into the kitchen without glancing back, poured herself a glass of water and drank it. She must have got hot while gardening out in the blistering sun.

The chair was safe for now. Oskar heard the clattering of dishes, which meant she was probably starting to make lunch. He peeked into the kitchen: Grandma was standing at the stove with her back to him, so he seized the opportunity to move the chair to the other corner of the hallway, where it would be hidden from sight from the kitchen. Of course, this wouldn't help the intrepid explorer if Grandma decided to leave at any point. She would spot the globetrotting chair immediately and send it packing, right back to the table. Oskar's job was to make sure this didn't happen!

He went into the kitchen to keep an eye on Grandma.

'What's for lunch today?' he asked, hoping to strike up a conversation and keep her in one place.

'Yesterday's leftover burgers,' she replied. 'We've got to finish them, or they'll keep taking up room in the fridge.'

Oskar sighed. So that's what it had come to – they were eating not because they liked the taste of the food, but to make space in the fridge! If there was a brick in there, no doubt Grandma would set it on the table, chop it up and chew on it as if that was was perfectly normal.

'I don't want any more burgers today,' Oskar said. 'I ate my fill yesterday.'

'What will I make you, then?' she asked worriedly. 'I can cook some macaroni, but you won't get full just from that.'

'Of *course* I will!' Oskar exclaimed delightedly. 'I have macaroni all the time at home.'

'Plain macaroni...?' Grandma frowned.

'With ketchup!' Oskar explained.

'That's not a proper meal...' Grandma said, shaking her head. It wasn't the first time Oskar had noticed how greatly Grandma underestimated macaroni. It almost didn't even deserve to be called a food, in her opinion, and on the very rare occasions she did make it, she always apologised. Oskar's mum had explained to her that there were whole restaurants in the city that served nothing but macaroni – though they called it 'pasta', of course. Yet Grandma just couldn't bring herself to believe it. The way she saw it, people should only eat macaroni if they were starving.

Oskar, on the other hand, loved macaroni and ketchup, and the news that today's lunch wouldn't offer any nasty surprises made him feel like a weight had lifted from his shoulders. Grandma could go ahead and dig into her heap of onion-stuffed burgers – *he* was going to dine on macaroni! It was already boiling in a pot on the stove, which meant it'd

be ready soon. They'd sit down at the table, leaving the chair to look around the hallway in peace.

But then Grandma bent down to pick up the dustbin.

'Grandma, what are you doing?' Oskar asked in shock.

'The bin's almost overflowing; I have to take it out and empty it,' Grandma replied. That meant she was planning to leave the kitchen and go outside! She was sure to see the chair! Oskar quickly blocked the doorway.

'No, don't! Let me empty it!'

'You?' she asked in astonishment.

'Yes. I want to help,' Oskar said. 'I know where the big bin is behind the fence. You stay and cook; I'll just be a minute.'

'What a good boy you are! But won't it be too heavy for you? You might pull a muscle.'

'I won't,' Oskar reassured her, grabbing the bin by the handle. It turned out the bin actually *was* very heavy! The bin must have been coming up with a lot of poetry lately, and those poems were very heavy. Still, Oskar had no choice – he couldn't let Grandma go into the hallway. Biting his bottom lip, he heaved the bin into the air and walked out.

The first few yards weren't too bad, but before long he felt like his arm was going to drop off. Oskar would have gladly set the bin down to change hands because the handle was digging painfully into his palm, but he was afraid Grandma might be watching from the window and would storm outside to help.

So instead he grunted and groaned his way to the gate before he let himself have a little break – he did, in fact, need to put it down for a second to open it. Oskar looked at his right palm – it was bright red and tingling. With his last remaining strength, he lifted the bin with his left hand and shuffled in short, quick steps to the big bin. Emptying it was easy after that walk!

Now the bin was empty, it was light enough for Oskar to swing it back and forth as he walked. Oskar would've liked to call him and ask how he felt without any poems rattling around inside, but there wasn't time – if he didn't get back to the house, Grandma might come looking for him and come across the chair. Oskar sped up and was back in the kitchen just moments later. The chair was where he'd left it, so in that sense everything was fine.

'You're a wonderful helper,' Grandma praised him. 'Here, lunch is served! I was worried about you having to eat plain macaroni, you poor thing, so I poured it into a pan and cracked a couple of eggs over it.'

Oskar didn't know whether to cry or scream in rage. Everything had been right as rain – moments ago, he couldn't wait to come inside for lunch, but now Grandma had managed to go and ruin a decent meal in mere seconds.

He could stomach the macaroni-and-egg mix, but he wouldn't enjoy it. Ketchup and scrambled eggs didn't go together at all. If he hadn't had to take the bin out himself, he'd have been able to put a stop to Grandma's foolish plan. Alas, Oskar had been left with no choice, and those few seconds were enough for Grandma to mess everything up.

He poked at the eggy macaroni and only ate half, as he'd lost his appetite.

'I told you macaroni isn't a proper meal for anyone,' Grandma sighed. 'I feel terrible to see you going hungry.'

Oskar didn't reply.

'Would you like half my burger?' she offered.

He slid off his chair, mumbled a thank you and ducked outside.

20.

Oskar sat outside on the front step and sulked. Thanks to his magic phone, he'd stumbled across the mysterious world of things – a world where everything was fun and exciting and always went without a hitch. But there was also the real world inhabited by Grandma and her burgers, macaroni with scrambled eggs, and *The Game of Life*. That world was miserable and exhausting. It was impossible for Oskar to enjoy – he just had to grit his teeth and bear it.

On top of that, the real world was foolish and intrusive, constantly interfering with the secret world of things and trying to arrange everything however it liked – oblivious to the joys and woes experienced by those things. It was only now that Oskar realized how selfish an act like emptying the bin really was. You might think you're filled to the brim with poems, but all Grandma can see is plain old rubbish that should be thrown away. And he, Oskar, had helped her do it! He promised himself that, the very first chance he got, he'd throw away lots of bits of rubbish so the bin could start composing fresh poetry.

First, however, he needed to take care of the chair. It was still in the middle of the hallway, defenceless and in plain sight. As soon as Grandma had finished tidying up the kitchen, she'd head outside, notice the chair, and end its trip around the world in an instant, just as she'd cracked eggs over Oskar's macaroni. Grandma lived according to her own stupid rules and had no idea how much trouble they caused others. She was like an old bear who loped around the woods, failing to see how each of her steps crushed a tiny bug or snapped a stalk plump with red berries.

Oskar crept into the hallway. Grandma was doing the washing up and the water was splashing noisily, so he could move the chair without getting caught. He carried it outside and hid it behind a lilac bush.

Then he rang her.

'There's been a slight change to your around-the-world itinerary,' he announced. 'Since conditions got too dangerous in the hallway, we've taken a slight detour into the garden.'

'What was so bad back there?' asked the chair.

'Wicked bandits are roving around. They might have nabbed you and sent you back home. I think it's best if you stay here till tonight. Once it's dark, I'll carry you back inside and put you in the loo.'

'Oh! I've been waiting so long for that!' the chair chittered happily. 'I'm already bursting with new impressions from everything I've seen, but if I can visit the loo to boot, then I'll have tales to tell the table and all the other chairs till the end of my days. What room is this, again? It's very strange. The floor hasn't been swept or mopped and there's no roof at all. Is it being renovated?'

'This isn't a room,' Oskar explained. 'You're outside. There is no floor or ceiling here, just the ground and the sky.'

'There *is* a floor!' the chair argued. 'I can see it. But someone's spilled dirt all over it. And what's this green stuff? Is it a rug? Eew, it looks like bugs are crawling around in it! What a filthy place! Someone should take a damp rag and mop up a little.'

'This isn't a rug, it's grass,' Oskar explained. 'The bugs live in the grass, so it's only natural for them to be crawling around. This isn't the house anymore, alright? It's the garden! The garden never gets cleaned – it's supposed to be dirty.'

'I don't like it here,' whined the chair. 'Everything's too strange and different. I'm used to living on a clean wooden floor and I like having a white ceiling overhead, not some shimmering blue thing. And why is the ceiling lamp turned on in the middle of the day?'

'That's not a lamp, it's the sun!'

'The sun...' echoed the chair doubtfully. 'All the silly things people come up with. Why do you need a sun when you can buy nice a light from the shop?! I'm not sure about this... I'd like to go to the loo now, please!'

'You can't just yet; Grandma would find you just like *that*,' Oskar said, snapping his fingers.

'At least put me next to the wall, then, away from this vase.'

'There's no vase here.'

'What about these branches next to me then, huh? Haven't they been put in water? They'll wilt if not.'

'This is a lilac bush!' Oskar laughed, realising what the chair meant. 'Lilacs just grow here in the soil. You don't keep outdoor plants in vases. And there's no wall for me to put you by – there *are* no walls outside.'

'How can that be?!' the chair gasped, getting choked up. 'How can there not be any walls? I can't even begin to imagine! A room without walls! That's impossible! I'm getting scared, Oskar!'

'Don't you understand? This isn't a room; this is the garden!' Oskar said, starting to get irritated. 'Don't be such a fusspot. There have to be some unbelievable adventures during a trip round the world. Columbus didn't know that

America existed, either, but he went and found it and wasn't afraid at all.'

Oskar left the chair to get used to the New World and went back inside. He slipped past Grandma, who was just finishing in the kitchen, and went to his room. It was too hot to be outside any longer, but pleasantly cool inside. Oskar closed the door and flopped down on his bed. He'd taken care of the chair and had earned a little rest.

Lying down for a little while was quite nice. The balloon was bobbing at the top of the birch tree outside. He didn't reach for his phone to call her, but just watched her and wondered whether there really were breezes living up in the treetops; ones who were invisible to the human eye and took the balloon dancing? Could it be possible? Why not! Not too long ago, he wouldn't have even believed that you could call things and talk to them. Maybe the balloon was dancing with a breeze right this moment?

The thought made Oskar's stomach churn. He rolled over onto his belly. Through the half-open doors of the wardrobe, he could glimpse the ruby red belt on Grandma's coat. It looked like a big dog with its tongue hanging out while it panted and stared anxiously, pleading: 'Pet me! Play with me!' Oskar could almost physically feel the wardrobe wishing with all its might to regale him with new horror stories. He picked up his phone.

'Hello, wardrobe,' he said. 'How's everything going inside of you? Is blood gushing like rivers?'

'Oh, and how!' the wardrobe started blabbering without a second's hesitation. 'Hi, Oskar! We've got blood spurting here in streams and lying in big puddles everywhere. An awful thing just happened; it's terrible to think of it even now. On my uppermost shelf lived a flower-patterned blouse. She was very kind-hearted, even sunny, and would chirp like a cricket every evening. She'd never hurt a fly and mostly kept to herself. It had been ages since anyone had worn her – I suppose she was pretty old and worn out, but she didn't let that get her down; she just stayed mellow and kind. Then one day Grandma started rummaging through my shelves, found that blouse, and do you know what she did then? She tore her to pieces! Rrrip, rrrip, rrrip! Grandma shredded her into little squares. It was terrible to watch, just terrible! Then, Grandma gathered up the bits and took them away. And the poor blouse was never seen again. Until yesterday.'

The wardrobe held a dramatic pause, then repeated threateningly: 'Until yesterday!' before falling silent again.

'So, what happened yesterday?' Oskar asked.

'It was late at night and all the clothes were asleep,' the wardrobe spoke in a raspy whisper. 'Suddenly the door flew open, and there she stood: the little scrap of flower-patterned blouse. But she was no longer the same kind, well-mannered blouse who chirped like a cricket to entertain the other clothes every night! The blouse had changed! You could still make out the little flowers clearly, but she'd been turned into a duster! Dust was caked on her – she'd never been shaken out, and she no longer chirped now, but hissed! She stood in the doorway for a moment, hissing angrily like a cobra, and then she lunged!'

'How could she lunge? Dusters don't have legs,' Oskar interrupted.

'Why not? She'd made herself legs out of the dust itself – a dozen legs!' the wardrobe continued without missing a

beat. 'The dust had made her sly and evil! She attacked the other clothes – you wouldn't believe how she bit and gnawed! She shredded the bigger bedsheets with her long fangs and gulped the tablecloths and handcloths down whole. Blood sprayed in every direction. It was terrible, just terrible!'

The wardrobe finished his story, feeling quite satisfied with himself. Oskar yawned.

'Yeah, that was pretty good,' he said. 'What happened to the duster next? Where is she now?'

'No-one knows!' the wardrobe replied in a conspiratorial whisper. 'Once she'd torn everyone to shreds, she hissed once more, so loud that the floor shook, and then vanished into the darkness. But you know, she just might be standing right behind you now!'

Oskar applauded.

'What a great ending!' he said. 'Bravo!'

'I can tell you another tale about a wool sock who became a strangler,' the wardrobe offered, but Oskar reckoned he'd heard enough horror stories for one day. He hung up and rolled over onto his back. The balloon was swaying softly in the breeze. Oskar had never liked taking daytime naps, which had seemed like the most unpleasant thing in the world when he was still in nursery school, but right now drowsiness was forcing his eyelids shut. His bed felt so cool and comfortable. Oskar curled into a ball and fell asleep.

21.

Oskar didn't nap for long. Soon the telephone started buzzing in his pocket again. He woke up and answered.

'Hello,' he said with a yawn. 'Who's there?'

'Are you that brave boy who saved the milk churn's lid?' squeaked an unfamiliar voice.

'That's me. Who are you?'

'I'm a lid, too,' the voice peeped. 'Or a cap... Yeah, actually I'm a cap. A helpless little bottle cap. I've gotten lost in the garden too. I want to go home! Come and rescue me!'

'Sure thing!' Oskar said, getting out of bed. 'When were you lost?'

'Oh, it was a very long time ago!' the cap moaned. 'Last year. Or even the year before that! It's so awful here, so cold! Please come quick!'

Oskar went outside. The air seemed to have cooled down a bit. He could see Grandma crouching in the vegetable patch, and peered behind the lilac bush to check – the chair was still there.

'Are you coming?' asked the tinny, miserable-sounding voice. For some reason it reminded Oskar of a little lamb. 'I miss home so badly!'

'Where are you?' asked Oskar. 'Where should I go?'

'I'm in the tall grass past the apple trees. I don't know if you'll ever be able to find me; I'm so very tiny,' whined the cap. 'What have you got on your feet?'

'Sandals. Why?'

'Best if you take them off and go barefoot,' the tinny voice said. 'You'll be able to feel around for me with your toes.'

This advice seemed a bit strange to Oskar.

'I'm sure I'll find you either way,' he said. 'I can crouch down and sweep my hands through the grass. Are there any flowers growing near you, maybe? That would make it easier for me to spot you.'

'No, there's not a single flower here!' said the voice, now almost choked with tears. 'Oh, you'll never, ever find me! You just won't notice me! I'm too small!'

'I suppose I could take my sandals off if you think it'd help,' Oskar said. He didn't particularly like the idea of walking around outside barefoot, because he might step on a pinecone or some pine needles and hurt his foot. Bees could sting him. An ant might crawl over his toes. All kinds of things could go wrong, but if it was a question of that or rescuing somebody teensy-tiny from the tall grass, then feeling around with his toes might be just the right solution.

Oskar passed beneath the apple trees and came to the patch of grass. Or rather, it *would* have been a patch of grass had anyone ever mowed it. But Grandma had never had the time, so it had grown wild and was now as high as Oskar's waist. It wasn't just grass anymore – it was a meadow!

He slipped off his sandals.

'Where are you?' he asked. 'Make some noise!'

'Here I am, here!' she squeaked, though that wasn't much help to Oskar because the voice was coming from the phone, giving no clue to exactly where the little cap might be lying.

'Come quick!' the high-pitched voice said. 'Just walk forward and feel around with your toes. You're sure to find me.'

Oskar stepped into the tall grass and tried to peer among

the blades. He couldn't see much because the grass was so thick, but he put out a foot and prodded the earth with his toes.

Suddenly the phone started making a strange noise. It whined and rattled like when Dad drilled holes in a wall at home. It seemed like he had another call waiting – someone else was trying to get in touch.

Oskar lifted the phone to his ear.

'Hello!' he said.

'Listen up, bat brains.'

He recognized the balloon's mocking tone at once.

'Where do you think you're going? Why have you gone climbing through that tall grass? And why have you taken your shoes off?'

'I'm rescuing a bottle cap,' Oskar explained. 'I'm barefoot so I'll be able to feel when I step on her.'

'I don't doubt it,' the balloon said. 'But I'd stand still right now if I were you – there's no bottle cap in that grass! Just a rusty nail with its pointy end sticking up. You're pretty close to it already – squat down and you'll see.'

Oskar squatted down and flattened the surrounding grass with his arm. Poking out of the dirt just a couple steps away was indeed a long, rusty brown nail with its pointy end sticking up skyward.

Oskar would have stepped right on it if he'd kept walking!

Oskar got an awful feeling in the pit of his stomach. He sat down in the grass and glared at the nail.

'But... the call came from a cap,' he said to the balloon. 'She had a really nice, high-pitched voice...'

'A nice high-pitched voice!' jeered the balloon. 'Well, how about that! And you went and fell head-over-heels in love with her, didn't you? And you leapt to the rescue! Even took your shoes off! Fine, I'm not going to warn you next time. Have a nice happy life with your lovely nails! Maybe you *like* it when they jab you in the foot! Maybe you think that's pretty great. They're your dearest darling angels...'

'Oh, come on...' Oskar interrupted. 'I'm glad you called and warned me. Thank you! How were you able to see her? The grass here is so thick and you're so far away.'

'Pff, of *course* you don't believe a silly little balloon could have sharp eyesight,' she snapped. 'You think all I'm good for is bouncing around in a treetop. Well, fine! I'm not going to bother you anymore. You keep getting calls from nails with nice high-pitched voices – who am I to rain on your parade.'

'I didn't know it was a nail!' Oskar protested. 'I really did think it was a bottle cap and I just wanted to help. In fact... you're the one I like.'

'Nyah!' the balloon scoffed.

'Honestly,' Oskar reaffirmed.

'Nyah, nyah, nyah! I don't have time to talk anymore. There are all kinds of interesting breezes here... And they're all asking me to dance... *Everyone* likes balloons, you know! We're just so pretty and irresistible! Bye, teeny boy! Have a nice night with your nice-sounding nail! Sing together, why don't you!'

The balloon hung up. Oskar scratched his nose with the phone and thought. Imagine that – the balloon had called to warn him! She'd been keeping an eye on him from up in the birch tree and rang the moment she saw him walking unsuspectingly towards the rusty nail.

Oskar supposed he and the balloon really had become friends.

It made him feel great.

Oskar looked down at the nail. It was thick and as long as his index finger. They'd have had to call for an ambulance if he'd stepped on a whopper like that.

He picked up his phone.

'Hello, nail!' he said.

For a while no one answered, but eventually a grumpy voice grunted:

'So, what do you want?'

There was no trace of the nice, high-pitched voice. Oskar was reminded of the fairytale about the wolf and the seven little goats, where the Big Bad Wolf changed his voice to sound like their mum so he could get inside and eat them. That was just how the nail had tried to fool him.

'Why did you do that?' Oskar asked. He wasn't even angry, just stunned. Up till then, he had thought all the things he could talk to on his phone were kind and well-meaning by nature. But now it turned out there were also mean, spiteful things who wanted to cause harm. He might as well start believing the wardrobe's tales about bloodthirsty dusters!

'I was bored,' the nail growled. 'I thought I'd play a trick on someone and make a hole in their foot. I saw you dig that silly milk churn lid out of the bushes and realised I might be able to lure you over here too. I'm so nice and sharp, it'd be a blast to jab somebody!'

'Hurting others is no "blast"! It would have been really painful for me.'

'So what?' snapped the mean nail. 'I can't feel pain – I'm made of metal.'

'How long have you been hiding in the grass?' Oskar asked. 'How did you end up here in the first place?'

'It was way back, years and years ago. Some men were building a fence and dropped me. And I'm glad they did! I wouldn't have wanted to be stuck inside some fence post, pounded into the wood up to my ears. It's better to be a free bandit!'

'Well, I'm not going to leave you here to lurk in the grass,' Oskar said sternly. 'We don't need a bandit living in the garden. Nail, you are under arrest!'

Oskar felt like a real police detective. He would have liked to add: 'Hands behind your back!', but the nail had no hands. So Oskar simply clenched the caught criminal in his hand and went looking for a suitable prison.

22.

Had Oskar found the nail in the grass the previous summer, back before he had a magic mobile, he would have just buried the rusty thing – it wouldn't have been able to cause anyone harm deep underground, where the moles and worms would keep a safe distance from her. But now that he'd talked to the nail, he thought of her as a living creature. And how could he bury something alive underground! It was an awful thought. Even if she was mean-spirited and had wanted to poke a hole in Oskar, she didn't deserve such a cruel punishment.

But Oskar couldn't just toss her into the woods or a ditch either, because she might start plotting new evil deeds there. She'd stick her sharp point skyward once again and hunt for innocent feet. He had to find a place where she couldn't harm anyone but wouldn't feel too alone either.

Who could keep an eye on the nail? The shed suddenly came to mind – right where he'd found that smooth block of wood shaped like a phone in the first place. The shed had a lot of nails and Grandpa's old tools in it, including his hammer. Yes, the hammer would be the ideal guard for the nail! Who else would a nail respect and fear if not a hammer, who could give her a knock on the head if needed?

Oskar went to the shed and tried the door. It was locked this time, but he knew where Grandma kept the key – it was always hanging from the window in the kitchen. He slipped inside, grabbed the key, and unlocked the door.

Inside, it was dark and smelled like old junk. Oskar searched for the tool shelf. There he found a nice hefty hammer perfect for keeping watch over the outlaw nail.

Oskar phoned it.

'Hello, hammer! I brought you a rusty nail. She's a dangerous criminal who lived outside for years, stalking people from a patch of tall grass. Today she tried to jab me. I arrested this bandit and would like you to take care of her now.'

'Sure thing,' the hammer replied gruffly. 'It's a shame to see a nail like her go down the wrong path. Nails are usually honest and friendly. I think the loneliness is to blame. Nails are used to living in a big flock, lying side-by-side like bees or ants. Being abandoned has a bad effect on them – they can get sick and even go crazy.'

'Do you think she still has a chance of getting better if she's kept with other nails?' Oskar asked.

'I don't see why not. Put her in that box with the others. With any luck, being around her own kind will have a positive effect and help drive away any bad thoughts.'

Oskar placed the outlaw in the big box filled nearly to the brim with nails of every shape and size. Then he rang her.

'I'm going to leave you here with your relatives,' he said. 'You can talk to them and spend some quality time together. I hope you'll become a good nail one day.'

She ground her teeth angrily.

'I've got nothing to say to these nincompoops!' the nail growled. 'They're just simple-minded lumps of metal, all the same colour grey and just yearning for somebody to bang them into a wall. *I've* led a daredevil life! *I've* lived under the snow and in a puddle! *I'm* an infamous bandit and a bloody cutthroat!'

'You've never *actually* cut a single throat. And no one has ever stepped on you, so you've never been bloody, either. All you've ever done is to lie in the grass, not doing much at all. So you're not that special, you know. But you did disguise your voice very well. You could be an actor!'

'A what?' sputtered the nail.

'An actor,' Oskar repeated. 'You could do your sheep impression for the other nails. Give it a try! Actors can be famous too, not just bandits. And you won't be out in the garden making trouble anymore, so you'll have to get famous here in the shed.'

The nail was quiet and seemed to be considering Oskar's suggestion. He re-locked the shed door and hung the key back in the kitchen. The sun was sinking lower in the sky. Oskar knew he would have to wait for Grandma to fall asleep before he could creep back out to the lilac bush to fetch the chair and hide it in the loo, quiet as a mouse. He couldn't wait for the moment to arrive. Grandma was already finishing her work in the garden. She came inside and set the table for dinner. They ate. Then, just like every evening, she suggested that they play *The Game of Life*, but Oskar refused.

'You lost yesterday and now you don't want to play anymore,' she sighed. 'Don't you worry – I bet you'll win today!'

Grandma wore an especially sly look on her face as she said this, and Oskar could imagine just how hard she would try to cheat in his favour.

'No thanks, I don't feel like playing,' he said. 'I'm tired of that game.'

'That's a shame and I don't have any others,' Grandma fretted. 'What are we to do then...'

She looked at him worriedly.

'How about some riddles? What's orange and sounds like a parrot?'

'A carrot,' Oskar groaned. 'I'm going to my room.'

Having made his escape, he lay in bed waiting for Grandma to finally decide to go to sleep. First she would turn on the TV. Then she would doze off and start snoring. Soon after that, the remote would slip from her hands and hit the floor, Grandma would wake up, potter around a little, go to the toilet one last time, and finally go to her room. Then, at last, it would be Oskar's chance to bring the chair inside and place it in the loo.

What was he to do till then? The red balloon was swaying in time with the birch tree's branches. Oskar could tell her about what he did with the nasty nail. But for some reason he felt shy about phoning her so often. He rang the pillow instead and listened for a while to the feathers showing off and complimenting one another on how pretty and fluffy they were. Time crept by at a snail's pace. Grandma had turned on the TV but wasn't snoring yet. Oskar looked up and decided to give the ceiling light a call.

'Hi!' he said. 'We haven't met yet. I'm Oskar.'

'Hello, Oskar!' the light boomed in a deep voice. 'Would you like me to predict your future?'

'You know how to do that?' Oskar asked in amazement.

'Of course I do! It's my job,' the ceiling light said. 'I do fortune telling for the flies every day.'

'So *that's* why they buzz around you all the time! Got it!' Oskar grinned.

'It is indeed. They come up and ask me to tell them what's going to happen so that's just what I do. I say, for instance, that you'll find some jam on the table tomorrow. Or that someone will forget to put the lid back on the sugar bowl in two days' time and you'll feast to your heart's content. But not all the fortunes I tell are optimistic – I might tell them they'll be hit with a flyswatter that very evening. Or they'll be swallowed by a swooping swallow tomorrow! Or they'll get caught in a spider's web.'

'And do your predictions always come true?' Oskar asked.

'Ah, that's not what matters,' the light scoffed. 'Flies have no long-term memory. They forget everything you tell them within five minutes flat and come back asking again. I tell some flies their fortunes fifty times a day!'

'What would you predict for me?'

'I predict you're going to fall asleep very soon,' said the light.

'I could have predicted that for myself,' Oskar said disappointedly. 'I go to sleep every night.'

'So I'll be right!' the light chuckled. 'But I've got to go – a client just arrived.'

Oskar noticed a big fat housefly buzz up to the lampshade, where it then fell silent. No doubt it was listening attentively to the light as he told its fortune, only to forget it five minutes later.

Just then, Oskar heard the TV remote go *thunk* as it hit the living room floor. He pulled the sheets up over his head without changing into his pyjamas. Soon afterwards, Grandma put her head round the door.

'Already sound asleep...' she murmured. 'Good night, little Oskar.'

He waited a few minutes more before sneaking out of his bedroom. It was dark and quiet in the living room, and soft snoring drifted from Grandma's bedroom. She was asleep! He could finally get to work.

Oskar went outside and carried the chair back into the hallway – she was already damp with dew. Wedging her into the loo posed quite a challenge, because the space was cramped and the door swung inwards, meaning that once the chair was inside, the door wasn't easily closed again. But after trying it various different ways, Oskar finally got the chair inside. Her dream had come true – she was in the loo!

Oskar went to sleep with a contented smile on his lips.

23.

Oskar woke to a rattling sound from the hallway. It was still dark, both in his room and outside. He was groggy and couldn't work out at first what was happening or why Grandma was grumbling and banging on the toilet door.

Then he realised what was happening and leapt out of bed in a flash. Grandma had woken up to go to the loo in the middle of the night, but the chair was still inside! He had managed to get the door shut before going to sleep, but now the chair was blocking it from being opened.

Oskar ran into the hallway. Grandma was pushing at the door of the loo, barefoot and wearing a long nightdress, but it would only open a tiny crack that wasn't big enough for her to fit through. She jiggled the handle angrily.

'What the devil is going on? The door's jammed! It won't open! It's like something's blocking it!'

She glanced at Oskar.

'Oh, and now I woke you up as well!' she said, guiltily. 'Do you also need a pee? Go outside behind the bush. It's like something's caught behind the door, but I've no idea what it could be. It's never been this tricky before.'

'I'm fine,' Oskar replied. 'I just... came to see what was happening. I couldn't sleep.'

'Well, of course you couldn't with your grandmother knocking about and making a racket in the middle of the night! Who could? Hold on, I'll get the broom and we'll try to pry the door open with the handle. There's something behind there, I'm sure of it! Must be the devil at work!'

Grandma went to the kitchen to fetch the broom, but couldn't find it, and then remembered she'd left it leaning against the side of the house. She pulled a coat on over her nightdress and went outside.

Oskar had to hurry. He was small enough to fit through the crack just fine. Once inside, he picked up the chair and was able to nudge the door open with his shoulder. Then he quickly carried the chair into the hallway and managed to hide it behind a long coat hanging from a peg, just moments before Grandma came back with the broom. Oskar stayed in front of the chair to hide it with his body while pointing at the open door to the loo.

'I fixed it.'

'How on earth did you do that?! What was wrong with it?'

'I dunno. I just jiggled it a little and all of a sudden it opened,' Oskar explained.

'What a clever boy you are! It's a whole different world having a man around the house. I just kept pushing and pulling away here to no end. Thank you, Oskar! I'll have to oil the hinges in the morning; they get stuck sometimes. Now go back to bed. It's only four a.m.'

'I will,' Oskar promised. He waited for Grandma to disappear into the loo and then carried the chair to his room. What a close call! Her trip around the world was adventurous, indeed! All thanks to Grandma, of course. Who could have guessed that Grandma would need to use the loo at night?! Oskar never needed to. Grandma certainly had some strange habits.

Oskar snuggled into bed and fell back asleep.

First thing next morning, he rang the chair.

'How are things?' he asked. 'Did you like the loo?'

'Very much so!' the chair exclaimed. 'It was so exciting in there! You can't imagine what an unusual chair-fellow I met. He was hollow inside! I've never seen anything like it in my life.'

'That wasn't a chair, that was the toilet. They are a bit rare, you're right about that, and they only live in bathrooms. You won't find one in a regular room. They're kind of like the koalas and kangaroos you only find in Australia.'

'What an incredible world!' the chair gushed. 'Do you think any other chair has ever been to the loo before?'

'I doubt it,' Oskar said. 'I reckon you're the first to have ever set four legs on the surface of the loo floor.'

'Oh, that's magnificent!' the chair cheered. 'I sure do enjoy the rambler's life! Where to next?'

'I'm not sure. You've finished the tour of the house – you've been to all the rooms. Wouldn't you like to go home now? The table has been waiting a long time.'

'No!' the chair almost screamed. 'I want to keep travelling! I don't want to go home yet!'

'But where can I put you?' Oskar wondered out loud. 'You didn't seem to like it outside very much.'

'No, it's nasty out there! There's no floor, no ceiling, no walls. I want to travel indoors. Tell me, Oskar: does the world have more rooms?'

'The world has lots of rooms, but unfortunately they're a long way away from here,' Oskar replied, then paused for a few seconds to think. 'Okay, I'll put you in the shed for a day,' he decided. 'But after that, you'll have to go back to the living room because I don't have any more rooms to offer.'

Oskar got dressed and went to have breakfast. Grandma immediately brought up what happened last night.

'It was as if the door was under some kind of a spell,' she murmured, opening it and swinging it back and forth cautiously a few times. 'I almost feel like it was a dream. It's opening just fine now, so what could have been wrong last night? This door has never played tricks like that before. Was something jammed behind it, Oskar? Did you see anything?'

'No, it was too dark,' Oskar fibbed.

'Well, that's true enough. And in the absolute middle of the night! How about that! Like some spirit was holding it shut from inside. Almost makes you believe in ghosts!'

Grandma shook her head and finished her coffee.

'Would you like to come to the shops with me?' she asked. 'I need to pick up some bread.'

'No thanks,' Oskar said. 'I'm going to go out and play.'

'That's a good idea,' Grandma agreed. 'What's there for a kid to do at the grocer's, anyway? Go out and have a good time. You were a very good helper last night, fixing that door. Quite the talented young man you are!'

Grandma picked up her shopping bag and left. Oskar waited until she'd gone out of the gate before carrying the chair to the shed.

He also used the opportunity to take a peek at the rusty nail. She was still lying with the others, just as he'd left her. Oskar called the hammer.

'How's our little bandit doing?' he asked. 'Is she behaving well?'

'Oh, yes indeed!' said the hammer. 'It turns out she's quite the cool cat. All she did was mope around and mutter to herself at first, but after a while she became rather talkative. She's very good at mimicking funny voices. First she pretended to be a kitten, then she croaked like a frog, and finally she sang the *Pinocchio* song at an amazingly high pitch. It was like being at the theatre! She promised to perform *Little Red Riding Hood* for us today – and I might add, by the way, that she'll be playing the parts of Little Red Riding Hood, the Wolf, Grandma and the Hunter all by herself! The other nails just can't get enough of her – a natural-born talent!'

'That's brilliant!' Oskar exclaimed, then called the rusty nail himself. Her voice was totally unlike before – there was a kindness to it, and she sounded a bit embarrassed by her dark past.

'I actually wanted to thank you for taking me out of the garden and bringing me back to the other nails,' she said sheepishly. 'And please forgive me for wanting to jab you. I don't know what came over me. In fact, I had really always wanted to be an actor. I was just practising the voice of Grandma for the show tonight. Tell me, how does it sound?' In the shrill voice of an old woman, the nail cried out: 'Come in, Little Red Riding Hood! I'm in bed.' Then, back in her normal voice, she asked: 'Was that alright?'

'I think it was great,' Oskar said. 'You've got it just right. Do the Wolf's voice for me, too!'

'Where does your grandma live, Little Red Riding Hood?' the nail snarled into the phone. 'Go and pick me some flowers!'

'Wow! That was fantastic!' Oskar praised her. 'You sound just like a real wolf. It's so nice that you're putting on a show for the other nails. What else are you planning to perform?'

'I was thinking of doing *Puss in Boots* soon,' said the nail. 'And then *The Gingerbread Man* and *The Ugly Duckling*.'

Oskar was very happy that the nail had found such a great way to apply herself.

It's nice to take care of things, he thought as he went inside to sort out the reunion of the broom and the toothbrush under his bed.

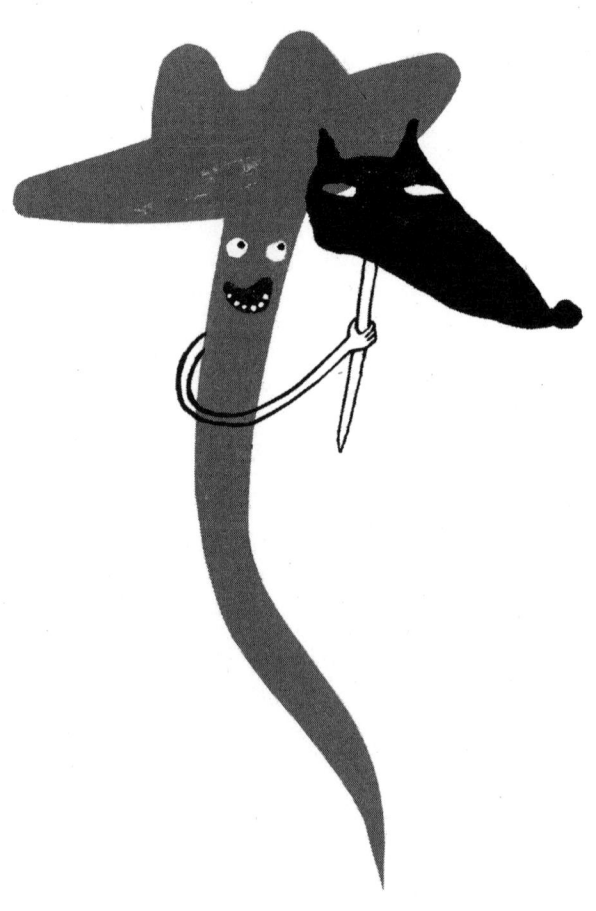

24.

Grandma was still at the shops, giving Oskar free rein to move things around as he pleased. He fetched his toothbrush and toothpaste from their place next to the sink and put them next to each other under the bed. Then he brought the broom and dustpan inside and slipped them under there too, trying to position the broom so its long pole wouldn't stick out. He didn't need Grandma to stumble across the brush family gathering again.

Once that was done, Oskar went outside. He immediately spotted something very unpleasant. The white-as-cotton-haired neighbour boys were standing on the other side of the fence and staring into the garden like three ghosts. At first Oskar thought they were looking at him. But then he noticed the boys' eyes were directed upward towards the crown of the birch tree. They were eyeing the red balloon.

Oskar didn't know what to do. His gut feeling was to duck back inside straightaway before the boys noticed him – then they wouldn't be able to invite him to go anywhere, because they were unlikely to follow. But why were they looking at his balloon? What were they up to? Oskar couldn't just leave the balloon alone. He had to stand guard and make sure those pale creatures didn't cause his friend any trouble.

The boys noticed him.

'Our balloon's up in your tree,' one of the smaller ones said.

'How is it "your" balloon?' Oskar asked, having to remind himself not to call her a 'she'. He stood his ground in the centre of the garden, with no intention of getting any closer to the trio.

'I got it for my birthday,' the oldest boy said. 'Actually, I got lots of balloons. My dad blew them up and tied them to the flagpole. But this one got away and flew off. Stuck up in your tree, now. Way up at the top.'

The boy fell silent and all of them stared at the treetop, including Oskar. He hated knowing that the red balloon had anything to do with these white-haired idiots. It made her background and her past feel somehow repulsive. Oskar would have liked to believe the balloon had appeared out of nowhere or had come from a mystical land of invisible winds and transparent clouds, born out of the radiant red sky during a sunrise, before making her way straight to him. But instead it turned out his balloon had been inflated by the father of these ghouls. And who knew what *that* man looked like! No doubt he also had pale hair, a potbelly and a bluish nose. It was a good thing the balloon had escaped from those villains, but it was unfortunate she'd had anything to do with them in the first place.

'How we goin' to get her down?' asked the smallest boy, making Oskar's hands go clammy in shock. They wanted to take his balloon away! There was no way he could let that happen!

Luckily the biggest of the three shot down that idea on the spot. 'We can't; too high up.' Oskar sighed in relief. But the littlest one wouldn't give up and carried on nagging:

'There's got to be some way. Like if we climb up there and poke it with a stick.'

'No, the higher branches aren't thick enough. They won't hold a person,' the oldest boy explained to Oskar's relief.

But then, narrowing his eyes, the tallest boy squinted at the balloon and said:

'I guess we could try to shoot it down if we had a rifle.'

Oskar's legs, back, and heart now went clammy, as well as his sweaty palms. Shoot the balloon?! How could they even imagine such a thing?! That was dreadful! What for?! Why oh why had these three murderers happened to walk past his fence and glimpse the poor balloon? It was too bad that she was stuck so high, or the house would have hidden her from the road.

On the other hand, if she'd been just a few branches lower, those agile, crafty little country boys would've had no trouble shimmying up the tree like wildcats and carrying off the balloon. From that perspective, it *was* a good thing she was bobbing high up by the slender branches.

But a rifle...

Oskar felt dizzy as one of the smaller boys sighed and said:

'We don't have a rifle.'

'Yeah, too bad,' the bigger one said. 'Otherwise it'd be great for target practice. I bet I could hit it.'

'Me too!' the smaller ones cried in unison.

'No you couldn't,' the bigger one scoffed. His younger brothers didn't dare to argue back.

They all went silent again, staring up at the red balloon. Oskar was both hot and cold at the same time and could feel sweat trickling down his spine. If only those boys would go about their own business and leave his balloon alone!

'Anyway, it's mine,' the big boy finally grunted, shooting Oskar a glare. 'You remember that.'

'It's up a tree,' Oskar snapped back with a note of defiance.

'You've got more balloons at home; go play with them.'

'They all popped a long time ago,' the boy replied. 'We stuck needles in them. Made some pretty good bangs.'

He motioned to his brothers.

'Let's go,' he said, and the trio started shuffling away, their white hair sticking up like the seeds on a dandelion.

Oskar sat down outside the house. He felt like the wind had been knocked out of him by all the danger he'd just overcome. Worse though, all kinds of frightening and unpleasant thoughts started popping into his head. True, there was no way the village kids could get the red balloon down from the treetop. They didn't have a rifle either, and with any luck they wouldn't be able to get their hands on one. Who in their right mind would hand a weapon over to babies like them? They might be able to make themselves a bow and arrow. Oskar had heard somewhere that country kids were good at those sorts of dangerous arts, but they probably wouldn't dare to step foot in a stranger's garden to start letting arrows loose, and, all in all, the arrows weren't likely to fly high enough, either. So, he actually didn't have

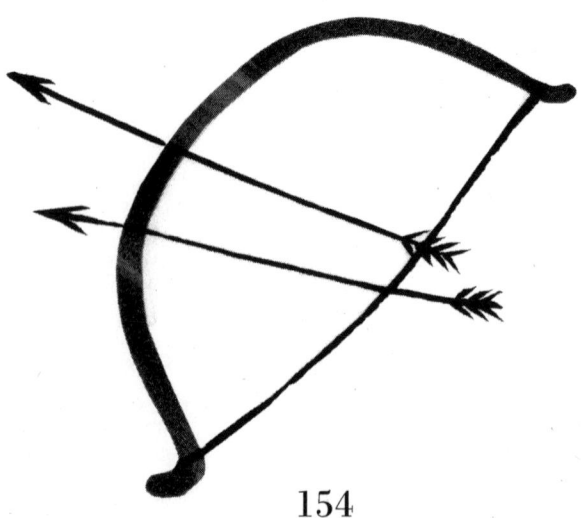

to worry too much about those white-haired boys – they posed no danger to the balloon.

And yet...

For the very first time, Oskar realized how incredibly fragile and delicate his know-it-all friend really was. A balloon wasn't a chair or a table that could practically last forever. It wasn't a clock that Grandma had received as a wedding present which still ticked on to this day. The balloon could come loose from the branch and fly away at any moment; or, even worse, it could pop with a deafening bang! That is what had happened to the cotton-haired boys' other balloons – the ones their father had tied to a flagpole, where they were powerless to escape the mean boys' needles. There weren't any needles at the top of the birch tree, but there were certainly branches, birds, rain and hail. Breezes swung the balloon around as they danced with her and could tug her away at any moment, or even push her against the sharp end of a bare twig.

Oskar realised it was all too easy for him to lose the balloon, even this very second. Or just a few moments from now. Someday, for certain. And likely very soon.

This knowledge felt so cruel and unfair that Oskar couldn't bring himself to glance up in her direction. All he could do was sit on the step and stare at his toes poking out of his sandals. Grandma came through the gate, carrying her bulging shopping bag, and asked:

'Did I just see the boys from the village walk past?'

'Yeah,' Oskar replied hollowly.

'Didn't they ask you to play with them?'

'No.'

'What's wrong with them? You four would get on very

nicely. They're about your age. I suppose I'll have to speak to them myself.'

'Don't, Grandma!' Oskar shouted. 'I don't want to! I like being alone! Just let me be!'

He jumped up and stomped off behind the house.

'Well, I'm not going to force you,' Grandma said, startled. 'I suppose you're right – city boys and country boys do play different games. I just can't stop being worrying that you'll get bored. You've got no-one to talk to; no friends.'

Oskar could hear his grandma talking but didn't answer. He stood at the base of the birch tree and stared up at the balloon with fear in his eyes. She wasn't about to drift away, was she? Or even worse... Oskar didn't even want to consider it.

25.

'Hi balloon!' Oskar said.

'Ugh, you again?' her cheerful, teasing voice replied. 'What have you come up with this time? Are you combing the grass for more nails? No surprise, I guess – when someone's as tiny as you, all he cares about is tiny things like him. Nails, bottle caps, specks of dust, pine needles, pebbles. He likes talking to *them* much more than me.'

The balloon giggled.

'Never even crosses his mind that he could look just a little higher than the tip of his nose and appreciate things of true beauty. Things up in the sky. Things like the sun, the clouds, and balloons,' she continued. 'Those white-haired boys down on the road were definitely looking at me, and for a long time, too. They're tiny and are stuck way down there, too, but at least *they* have taste! *They* know what real beauty is and don't go chasing after rusty nails.'

Oskar snorted.

'Those cotton-haired boys just wanted to work out how to get you down from that tree. They said you belong to them.'

'I don't belong to *anybody*,' the balloon squealed. 'I fly wherever I please. A balloon isn't a comb or a wallet that you can stick in your pocket. Balloons don't fit into anyone's pocket – we're too nice and round.'

'I know that,' Oskar said, 'and I don't want to put you into my pocket either; I like you just the way you are.' He hesitated for a moment. 'Are you sure you're tied tightly to those branches?' he asked, shyly.

'What do you mean?' the balloon snapped. 'Tied tightly? Do you mean "am I stuck here"? Trapped? I'm not trapped. Don't even think about it!'

'I'm not, I'm not,' Oskar tried to defend himself, but the balloon cut him off.

'I can fly away any time I want! I'm just resting a little. It's cosy up here. You can see wonderfully far, and all kinds of incredible breezes come to dance with me. They beg me to go along with them all the time! And maybe I will soon. I'll find a nice handsome breeze and fly off with him.'

'Please don't,' pleaded Oskar. 'I'd feel so sad if you weren't up there anymore.'

'Ha! Do you really think I'm going to stay here forever? Balloons aren't like moss that just grows on a tree. Balloons are made to float and soar. The world is so big, the sky is so endless, the breezes are so enticing... It feels absolutely out of this world to rise higher and higher and ride a brisk breeze to who-knows-where! *You* couldn't fathom it, of course – you're too heavy and would plummet like a stone. It's strange... you're so little and yet so heavy!'

'I wouldn't want to fly to who-knows-where,' Oskar said defensively. 'That's dangerous.'

'Of course it is, at least according to you and your mates! You *are* friends with nails that are hammered into walls and spend their whole lives stuck there,' the balloon jeered. 'Maybe *you'd* like to wiggle into a wall, too! What do you say? Though I guess you kind of do already – each and every night, you go into that house like a nail into a wall and stay there till morning. I think that's boring! I want life to be fun! I like to fly!'

'But you might pop,' Oskar protested softly.

'You're a ninny!' The balloon was quiet for a few moments. 'I don't want to talk to you anymore,' she said at last, crossly.

'No, please!' Oskar begged her. 'I didn't mean to... You won't pop, don't worry. You're wound nice and tight around those branches and nothing bad will happen.'

'You nincompoop! I *told* you: I'm not stuck anywhere! I'm just resting, alright?! Any time I want, I could... Oh, what's the point of it. Good*bye*!'

She hung up. Oskar glared at his silent mobile, then arched his neck and studied the balloon. There was no doubt her string was wound tightly around the branches, even though she herself stubbornly denied it. Watching her, it seemed like she had suddenly started making fruitless attempts to tear herself loose.

'Don't do that...' Oskar murmured. He called the balloon again, but she didn't answer.

Oskar walked round to the other side of the house. The cotton-haired boys' visit had drained him of all his peace of mind and suddenly he wasn't so chuffed about his magic phone anymore. True, he could use it to call all kinds of things, but what good was that if anything should happen to the balloon? There were countless things in the world. They'd still be there, and Oskar could keep talking to them, but it wouldn't make up for the loss of the balloon. It was so outrageously unfair that *she* was the one in danger, not some random table or cupboard that Oskar wouldn't even miss.

Of course, the balloon *was* still there right now. Maybe it was too soon to worry. The branches could keep hold of her for a very long time. Maybe nothing bad would happen.

Maybe they'd miraculously made a one-of-a-kind balloon that would never ever pop! Oskar's block of wood had turned into a phone, which meant miracles *could* happen.

Oskar stared at the balloon bobbing over the roof of the house and tightly crossed his fingers with both hands, as people often do when wishing for something with their heart and soul.

Grandma came outside.

'Oskar dear, I bought hot dogs from the shop today,' she said. 'You do eat those, don't you? Come in, lunch is ready.'

Oskar had in fact lost his appetite, but he had no choice but to go inside. He did like hot dogs, of course, though he had a sneaking suspicion that Grandma would manage to mess them up somehow, like when she turned macaroni into scrambled eggs. Maybe she'd spread something over the hot dogs? Or she just *thought* they were hot dogs, but in reality they were bratwursts. That had happened to Oskar once before when he and his parents were visiting some distant relatives. There'd been talk of hot dogs at first, too, but then bratwursts were served, and when Oskar brought it up the adults said: 'What's the difference? A bratwurst is just a plump hot dog.' There *was* a big difference, actually – Oskar despised bratwursts because they had gross thick skins and tasted much, much worse.

This time, however, Grandma really had bought hot dogs. True, she'd boiled them instead of grilling them in the oven. Oskar was a little disappointed, because oven-baked hot dogs are nice and brown, split at the ends, and crunch between your teeth. Ones fished out of a pot of boiling water, on the other hand, are pale pink and all waterlogged and squishy. Oskar imagined they were swimmers who'd been saved from drowning and were now lying limp on the corner of his plate.

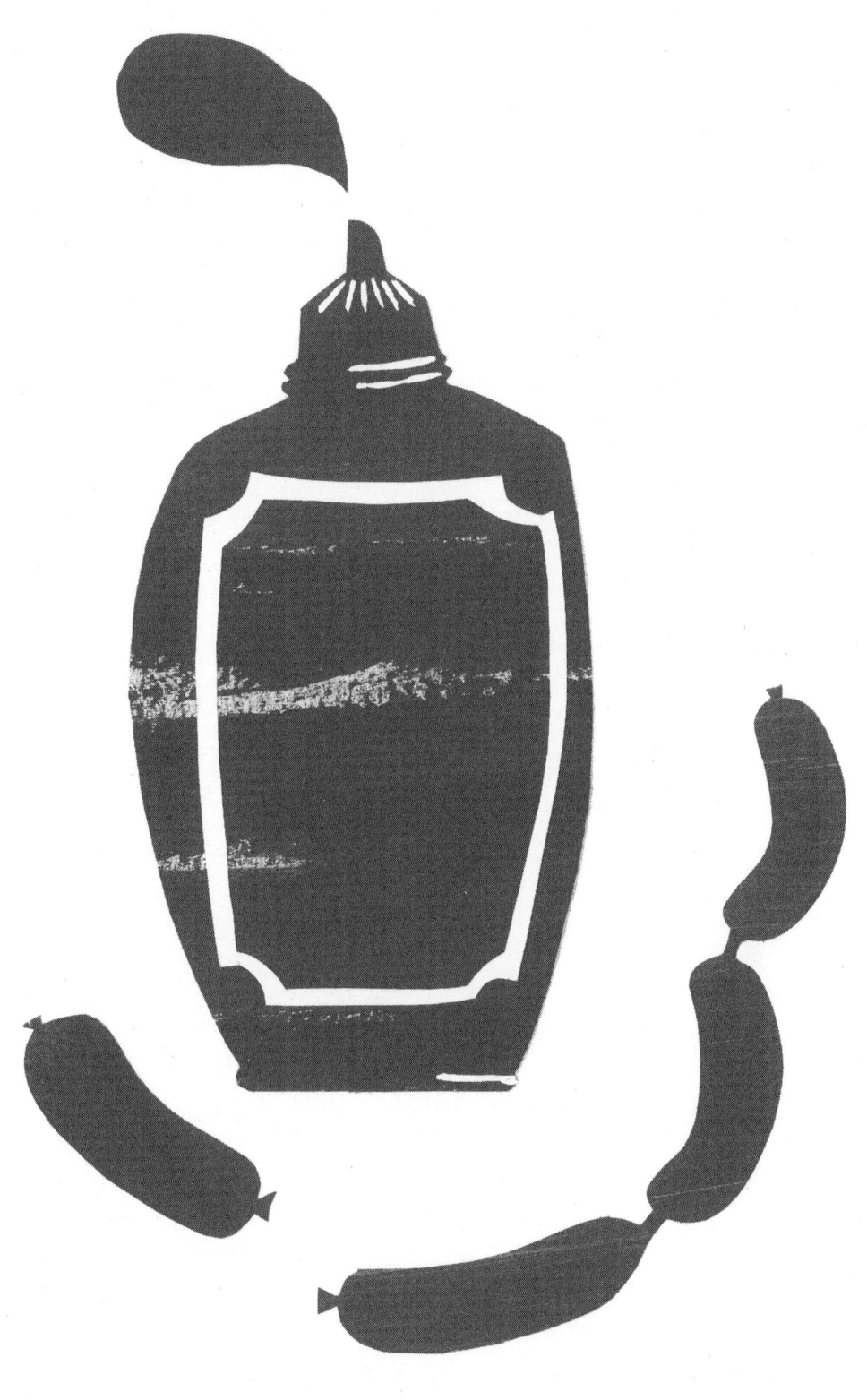

He squirted ketchup in their faces to revive them.

'Finally, the lad's eating something,' Grandma murmured in relief. 'Not just pecking at his food like a sparrow. You're a city boy, alright. I ran into a neighbour at the shop and she said her sons just shovel down their food. They eat like grown men – extra helpings of porridge in the morning and always asking for meat at lunch. You can't fill a belly with just soup, as they say. All they want is meat. You've met them – they're the ones who walked by this morning. All white-haired like little lambs.'

It came as no surprise to Oskar that the cotton-haired boys had werewolf properties. It seemed quite logical – first they pop helpless balloons with pins, then they storm the kitchen and start devouring all the meat they can find. For some reason, Oskar imagined the meat rare and still a little bloody. The cotton-haired kids would cram their mouths with it, blood dribbling down their chins.

Grandma finished her lunch. She stood up and patted Oskar awkwardly on the head.

'Oh, don't mind me; just talking to myself,' she said. 'Children don't have to gobble up everything they see. Your father didn't have much of an appetite when he was your age, either. All that matters is that you're a good boy. It's wonderful that you came to stay with me this summer – it's so much nicer having someone to talk to.'

Grandma continued chattering on about something and patting Oskar on the back, but his mind was somewhere else.

26.

After lunch, Grandma went off to do her chores while Oskar stayed inside. He paced restlessly through the rooms, peered beneath the bed to see how the brushes were doing all nestled together, then cast an uneasy glance through the window. Still there.

Oskar had already taken the phone from his pocket and was rubbing it thoughtfully in his hand when it started making that buzzing noise. Something was calling him.

'Hello!' he answered quickly, hoping it was the balloon. To his slight disappointment, he heard the gruff voice of the sitting-room table instead.

'My chair still hasn't come home yet! What the devil is going on? Where can she be gallivanting about, the poor thing?'

'Don't you worry about her,' Oskar reassured the table. 'Your chair will be just fine. Her trip around the world is about to end and she'll be back in the living room before you know it.'

'I don't believe you!' snapped the table. 'I believe she's in grave danger! Someone must be holding her captive somewhere. There's not a chair in the world that would stay away from home for so long. I want to go looking for her.'

'And how do you plan on doing that? You can't even walk!'

'Then you'll have to help me. You're the one to blame for her running away from home in the first place. Take me to her this instant.'

'That's impossible,' Oskar groaned. 'There's absolutely no way I can carry you on my own. You're too big and heavy.'

'But you must!' the table insisted. 'I want to find my Rickety. Who knows what awful place she's ended up in…'

'She's in the shed right now,' Oskar replied. 'And, by the way, she hates it when you call her 'Rickety'.'

'In the *shed*?!' the table roared. 'That's the most dreadful place of all! That's where old, broken things are carried away to! I must go and rescue her at once. Pick me up and let's dash, on the double!'

'Don't be silly! Do you have any idea how big you are?' Oskar asked, a little irritated. 'Have a good look in the mirror one of these days. I'd have to be a giant to pick you up, not to mention *run* with you. Just be patient and don't panic. The chair is alive and well. She'll be home tonight, I promise.'

Oskar hung up. On the one hand, it was understandable that the table missed his chair: they'd been standing side by side for years and years. But on the other hand, what harm could come to a sturdy wooden chair? It would be completely different if she were fragile and inflatable…

He glanced out of the window again. Everything was still alright. For now.

Just then, his phone rang.

Can it really be the table again? he thought frustratedly. But this time there was an unfamiliar voice on the line. It was mellow and extremely polite.

'Please do excuse me – am I speaking to Oskar?' it asked.

'You certainly are,' Oskar replied. 'Who's this?'

'Oh, I do apologise! I forgot to introduce myself. I am the cream jug, calling from the living room cabinet. Do you have a moment to chat?'

'Yes, of course,' Oskar said. 'Do go ahead.' The cream jug's politeness was infectious, and even made him slightly uncomfortable: Oskar was still just a little boy and wasn't used to anyone talking to him in such an adult way. 'How may I help you?' he asked.

'Forgive me for inquiring, but is it true that you have arms and legs that move?'

'It certainly is,' Oskar replied.

'Oh, how delightful that is to hear! Then perhaps I might be so bold as to ask a little favour. Unless you are busy today? I imagine that if one has arms and legs which move then one must have so much to do! I can call you back tomorrow; it can wait.'

'No, please, go ahead and tell me!' Oskar reassured him. 'I'm in no hurry.'

'Well, I don't know where to begin...' the cream jug sighed. 'But alright, I will lay my heart before you. Perhaps you can be of assistance. You see, I am but one piece of a grander coffee set. In addition to me, there are six cups, six saucers, a coffee pot, and... a sugar bowl. We are kept in the cabinet and taken out only on the most festive of occasions; which is to say, very rarely. This is of no consequence, of course, except... Grandma uses the sugar bowl every day and keeps her in the kitchen – not in the cabinet with the rest of the set. We are kept apart and I almost never get to see her. Yet, I am dearly fond of her. You could even say I love her. I do apologise, but would it be possible for you to open the cabinet door for a moment so I may peer into the kitchen to see if I can spot her? I wish for no more than to simply gaze upon her from afar. If it isn't too much of a bother, of course – I don't wish to cause you the slightest inconvenience!'

'It's no problem,' Oskar said, opening the cabinet door. The cream jug was set upon a stack of saucers surrounded by cups and he looked very handsome with his curved white belly covered in little pink butterflies.

'Thank you! Thank you!' the cream jug rejoiced down the phone. 'I can already see into the kitchen! And there's the table! But... I can't see the sugar bowl anywhere. What bad luck... Grandma must have put her somewhere else. How unfortunate...'

'I'll go and look for her and put her in the middle of the kitchen table, right where you can see her,' Oskar promised.

'Would you really do that for me? I'd be ever so grateful!' said the cream jug. 'You'll certainly have no difficulty recognising her. She has just the same pattern as me, but is naturally a thousand times prettier.'

'I'm sure I'll recognise her,' Oskar said. He knew Grandma's sugar bowl well, as he scooped great spoonfuls of sugar out of her into his tea every evening. Grandma usually put her on a shelf while she cleaned the table, and that's just where Oskar found the sugar bowl now. He took out his mobile.

'Hello, sugar bowl,' he said. 'My name is Oskar. I'm going to place you on the table and, if you look into the living room, you might see one of your friends there in the cabinet.'

'Who could that be?' the sugar bowl asked, in a high-pitched voice.

'The cream jug.'

The sugar bowl squealed.

'The *cream* jug...' she echoed in delight. 'We haven't met in so long... How do I look? Is there too much sugar in me?'

Oskar couldn't imagine how a sugar bowl could be too full of sugar, but he reassured her anyway that there were only a couple of spoonfuls inside. That put her mind at ease.

'All right, we may go,' she said. 'But wait! One more thing. Could you tilt my lid to one side, just a little? It makes me look a bit cuter.'

'Sure,' Oskar said, putting her lid on a little crookedly. 'Are you ready for the two of you to meet?'

'Yes!' the sugar bowl squeaked. 'Now I'm ready.'

Oskar made sure the table was clear and that there were no random dishes lying about which might intrude on the romantic moment. Then he placed the sugar bowl carefully in the centre of the table.

'Can you see him?' he asked.

'Yes, I can!' the sugar bowl whispered. 'Just as round as always. What a prince!'

Oskar went into the living room and called the cream jug.

'Is everything all right?' he asked.

'Above and beyond, my boy – everything is marvellous!' the cream jug confirmed. 'I can see her! Oh, how lovely her little tilted lid is... My princess!'

Oskar didn't want to bother the two of them any longer, so he left them to gaze at each other in awe and went outside.

27.

The sky was overcast now. Oskar spied his grandmother crouched at the far end of the garden, as usual. *What does she do there non-stop?* he wondered. *What could she be up to?* Still, the thought wasn't intriguing enough to make him want to go and find out.

He sat down on the front step. Let her potter about on her own there – the more she was away from the house, the better. So many important things were happening at the moment: the brush reunion under the bed and the cream jug and sugar bowl's long-awaited meeting through a doorway. On top of that, the chair was still finishing her trip around the world in the shed. The cuckoo clock was directing a zoo and the bedroom ceiling light was predicting flies' futures. Grandma had no idea any of it was going on, and nor should she.

Oskar's thoughts turned to the balloon again. Life at Grandma's would have been pretty superb if not for that single (but very troubling) worry, which had crashed down on him so unexpectedly that morning. What's more, there was no one who could do anything to help. It was quite an unusual feeling, having a problem that no one could come and help with. Nothing like that had ever happened to Oskar before – Mum or Dad always found a way out of any tough situation. But right now, not even they could have made anything better. That was life, and he just had to deal with it.

Oskar sighed and pulled out his mobile. He wanted to chat to something to brighten his gloomy mood a little, and next to the front step was Grandma's big watering can.

'Hello, watering can!' he said into the phone. 'I'm Oskar. What are you up to?'

'Hello, Oskar! I'm watching the sky.'

'Why?' Oskar asked.

'I'm waiting for my parents to come.'

'Your parents? So your parents live up in the sky?'

'They certainly do!' the watering can replied merrily. 'They're gigantic and can hold lots of water. Tons and tons of it. Way, way more than I can. They drift across the sky and water the ground. That's my mum and dad – big grey watering cans.'

'You mean clouds?' Oskar asked. 'Rainclouds?'

'What do you mean, "clouds"?' The watering can sounded confused. 'I'm a watering can, which must mean my mum and dad are watering cans as well. Children look like their parents, right?'

Oskar was about to explain that actually those were clouds bringing rain and that the watering can had no connection to them at all – that he'd been made by people and purchased in a shop – but then, Oskar started to think. The watering can's story was much more pleasant. Indeed, what was wrong with referring to rainclouds as 'big watering cans'? There wasn't much difference between them – both sprinkled the ground with water. If the watering can wanted to believe that his mum and dad were clouds, then why not? There was no reason for Oskar to interfere.

'How did you end up here on the ground when your parents live in the sky?' he asked instead.

'I'm not quite sure. I don't remember. But I reckon they must have laid me as an egg. The egg fell down and I hatched from it.'

'Does that mean you've never actually met your parents?' Oskar asked.

'Of course I have – they come and see me quite regularly,' the watering can said. 'They love me! Every once in a while, they fly over and gently drizzle water on me. Oh, they're extremely good at watering! The way they do it, the whole ground gets wet, water drips from the trees and there are puddles everywhere. I've got a lot to learn before I can be just as talented and fly away with them.'

'Can you fly?' Oskar asked. The watering can's story seemed to be getting more and more outrageous.

'No, not yet. I'm not a grown-up watering can; I'm just a chick. That's why Mum and Dad don't take me with them – I wouldn't be able to stay up. I have to just wait and grow.'

'For how long?'

'I'm not sure,' the watering can said, with a slight note of regret. 'But it's probably going to take a good while longer, because I'm still so small compared to Mum and Dad. They're so big that they can cover the whole sky! When that day will come for me... Well, I'm afraid it'll take years.'

Dinosaurs came to mind, for some reason. They had been enormous too, just like clouds. Dinosaurs also laid eggs and the tiny dinosaurs that hatched might have been more or less watering can-sized. No doubt they also waited in the tall grass back in prehistoric times, watching, wide-eyed, their parents' huge bellies swaying above them as they plodded through the jungle.

'Are those clouds above us now your parents?' Oskar asked, craning his neck to stare at the hazily overcast sky.

'Oh, no – those aren't watering cans. They don't hold any water. They're lazy and cotton-white; all they do is fly past

and be no help to anybody. But I can sense that my mum and dad aren't far off. I reckon they'll get here pretty soon, and I'll be able to see them again. They'll probably be proud of me, because I've watered a lot of ground lately! Mum and Dad don't always have the time to get round everywhere. A plant here or a bush there might start to dry up, and that's when I help.'

Listening to the watering can, Oskar suddenly started to miss his own parents. They were far away as well – even further than the watering can's mum and dad. Clouds at least drifted over people's roofs, but his mum was in America and his dad was in the city. And then there was the whole matter with the balloon... Oskar felt his spirits sink again.

'Come sit next to me,' he said, lifting the watering can onto the step. 'Is there anything I could do for you? I've got arms and legs, you see. I could carry you somewhere, or vice-versa – can I bring you anything? Just tell me.'

'There's nothing I need,' said the watering can. 'I've just got to wait here patiently and keep growing until I'm big enough to soar through the sky with my parents and water the whole earth.'

The watering can thought for a minute.

'Actually, perhaps there is one thing you do,' he said. 'You could fill me with water. I don't like to be empty, especially when Mum and Dad are coming to visit. An empty watering can looks sloppy and lazy. Mum and Dad are never empty – they're always chock-full of water.'

'No problem!' Oskar said. He knew just where the tap and hose were that Grandma used to fill the watering can every evening. He called the watering can back once he'd filled him up to the brim.

'Is that better?' Oskar asked.

'It certainly is,' the watering can replied in a slightly bubbly voice, as if water kept getting into his mouth. 'Now I'm ready. They'll be pleased to see me like this.'

Staring at the watering can, an image flashed through Oskar's mind – one of a little boy who had put on a white shirt and bow tie, and was now waiting impatiently for his parents to get to the school Christmas party so he could perform the songs and poems he'd memorized. The boy kept glancing at the door and nervously chewing his fingernails.

'I'm sure they'll come soon and pour rain all over you,' he said.

28.

Grandma was still busy in the garden, but Oskar knew it would soon be time for supper and he'd need to put everything back before then, so nothing unusual caught her eye.

First he went to fetch the chair from the shed.

'I think your journey is over for now,' he said. 'The table misses you terribly and even wanted to come looking for you himself. You have to go home.'

'Alright then,' said the chair. She sounded a little tired and no longer upbeat like before. 'I actually miss the sitting room a little, too. It's been ages since I slept under a blanket!'

'Where do you have a blanket in the sitting room?' Oskar asked, wrinkling his eyebrows.

'I mean the tablecloth.'

'Oh. But that's on top of the table.'

'True, but we're pushed partway under the table every night so it's like he holds us while we sleep,' said the chair. 'That way the tablecloth covers us, too. That's where I longed to be that one time I stood outside under the sky.'

'Did you enjoy the shed?' Oskar asked.

'I did...' The chair sounded a little hesitant. 'There are so many old friends here... Chairs I haven't seen in a long time. Ones who were taken away when one of their legs broke. It was wonderful and so emotional to talk to them again.'

The chair was silent for a few moments.

'It was actually right here in the shed where I realised that the sitting room is the loveliest room in the whole wide world,' she declared proudly. 'And I'm unbelievably lucky to be able to live there. Imagine if one of my legs snapped or my back broke off! I'd be taken to the shed for good! No, no – that's the last thing I want! Let's go home now. Moley's waiting.'

'Who's "Moley"?' Oskar asked.

'That's what I call the table sometimes,' the chair confessed, sheepishly. 'Whenever he calls me "Rickety".'

'I thought you didn't like that nickname,' Oskar said.

'Actually, I do,' whispered the chair. 'It's quite sweet!'

Oskar shrugged. The relationships between chairs and tables were beyond him! He wedged the chair back under his arm, crossed the garden and carried her into the house, watching to make sure Grandma didn't notice. She was hanging out the washing and didn't even turn her head.

Oskar put the chair back in the sitting room just the way she wanted. It wasn't night-time yet, but cuddling your loved ones is the best thing to do when returning from a long trip. The long white tablecloth draped over the edge, covering everything except the chair back.

Let's hope Rickety and Moley are happy now, Oskar thought as he went to deal with the sugar bowl and the cream jug.

'Well, have you had enough of each other yet?' he asked. As soon as the words slipped off his tongue, he remembered in dismay how polite and formal the cream jug had been when addressing him earlier. 'I mean, what I meant to ask was – have you and your princess admired each other for long enough?'

'Oh, no!' the jug sighed. 'It is still far too little! I could gaze in wonder upon her crooked little lid and rounded sides for all eternity. But I understand; our time is up.

It cannot be helped! Yet I do have one more request! Please do not think poorly of me because of it! Tell me, are there also fingers on your hands?'

'Yes, of course. Five on each.'

'Oh, you favourite of fortune! Could you do me a tiny deed, then? I promise not to ask anything more of you!'

'I'm glad to help. What can I do?'

'Would you be so kind as to rest one finger upon my nose? And then to place that very same finger upon the sugar bowl's dainty little neck? I'd like to send her a kiss, you see. Please deliver it for me!'

It was undoubtedly the strangest thing Oskar had ever been asked to do, but he agreed all the same. *I'm like a postman*, he thought as he walked from the sitting room into the kitchen, his index finger holding the invisible kiss held stiff in the air. *Or like Little Red Riding Hood. The wolf comes up to me and asks: 'Little Red Riding Hood, what are you bringing your grandmother?' 'Cake and milk.' 'But what is that on your fingertip?' 'A kiss. If you don't go away this instant, it will open op and swallow you.'*

Murmuring this to himself, Oskar approached the kitchen table and called the sugar bowl.

'The cream jug sent you a kiss; it's here on my fingertip. Where should I place it?' he asked.

'Oh... A kiss!' squeaked the sugar bowl happily. 'On my neck, perhaps?'

'That's what he thought, too,' Oskar said. 'The thing is... I'm sorry, but you're the first sugar bowl I've got to know this well, so I'm not sure where exactly sugar bowls' necks are.'

'Just beneath my lid!' she replied. Oskar pondered that if a lid was essentially the same thing as a hat, then the *head* should be under it, but he decided not to say anything. He gently placed his finger against the neck of the sugar bowl, who sighed blissfully.

'Could I send a kiss just like that back with you?' she asked.

'Of course,' Oskar said. 'But after that, I need to put you back on the shelf and the cream jug will have to be behind the closed cabinet table door, because Grandma doesn't like it left standing open.'

'What a shame. But perhaps you could help us again someday? I just can't live without seeing my precious cream jug anymore.'

'No problem at all!' Oskar said, then picked up her kiss on his fingertip (a kiss that was invisible to the naked eye, of course) and carried it back to the cream jug. Having listened to the jug's gushing words of thanks, and promising to arrange another meeting soon, Oskar closed the cabinet table door, went into the kitchen, set the sugar bowl back where he had found her and then remembered that the brushes were still waiting their turn under his bed.

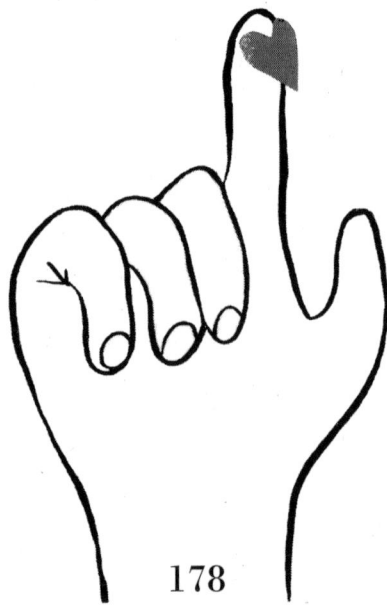

'Hello!' he said into the phone, dropping down onto his knees. 'Hi, broom! How are you all doing down there? It's time to wrap things up.'

'Oh yes, I suppose it is!' the broom said in his bristly voice. 'There's work to be done – no doubt balls of dust and all sorts of other rubbish have crept inside since I've been away. They do it the second I'm caught off my guard. It was very nice to meet my young relative, though. He's a smart lad, well-educated! All the things he told me about teeth – by George! What terrible germs live among them! I can't even remember their names. Life's not so bad chasing dust and scraps of paper round – imagine catching those little baddies from behind a set of teeth. He's a fine young man and is doing our family proud!'

'Do you really think he finds *that* many germs in there?' Oskar asked doubtfully, as they were almost certainly talking about his own teeth. He couldn't believe there were great herds of germs living inside his mouth!

'The toothbrush said they're in the thousands,' the broom confirmed. 'And another thing – have you ever heard of an incredible creature called a tongue? It lives in your mouth, too – long, pink and plump like a giant slug. I asked the toothbrush why you don't just spit it out, but he explained that's not possible – tongues are tied to mouths by their tails. How about that! This world certainly has its wonders. Tell me, honestly: have you ever heard of such a peculiar creature before?'

Oskar carefully shifted the 'peculiar creature' in his mouth and told the broom he had heard of it, and had even seen it.

'Where?!' the broom gasped.

'In the mirror.'

'Is that right? I've never looked in one before,' the broom admitted. 'So there's a tongue living in the mirror, too! Interesting, interesting...'

At that moment, Oskar heard footsteps coming from the hallway. Grandma had come in. He ended the call, hid the toothbrush and toothpaste in his pocket and hurried out of his room holding the broom and dustpan. Grandma spotted him instantly.

'What are you doing with those?' she asked. 'They're not for playing with, you know – they're dirty.'

'I wasn't playing. I... was sweeping up a little. There was a ball of dust in the corner, just there.'

'Oh my!' she gasped. 'And I just mopped all the floors yesterday. How about that – dirt really does spread quickly. You're a good boy, Oskar. Now go empty the dustpan into the bin, please.'

Oskar pretended to shake something off the dustpan into the bin and thought: *If I had a real ball of dust here, it would be turning into a poem right now.*

29.

After dinner, Grandma tried to get Oskar to play tic-tac-toe.

'Have you heard of that game before?' she asked, searching for a pencil and piece of scrap paper from the drawer. 'You make Xs and I make Os and whoever gets three in a row wins.'

'I know,' Oskar said. 'But I don't feel like playing. It's a pretty boring game.'

'How about a game of *Life*, then?' she suggested, but Oskar didn't want to open up that can of worms either. Instead, he said he was going back outside.

'Absolutely, you go right ahead,' Grandma said. 'Summer nights are so long and bright. The only downside is that the mosquitoes are around again and in quite the temper. Put on a long-sleeved shirt so they don't get you too badly.'

Oskar did, then skipped outside. Heavy clouds covered the sky and the air was very still – there seemed to be no wind at all.

He went behind the house and looked up at the red dot above the crown of the birch tree. Oskar had thought a lot about the balloon during the day – he'd felt worried about her. Still, everything was alright for the time being. He realised it had actually been silly to put himself into such a state so soon. It was like being afraid you might one day ride your new bike into a ditch and bash your knee before you'd even bought the thing. If you're going to fall, then you're going to fall – there will be time then for tears and limping home, feeling disappointed. Right now, the balloon was still bound nice and tight to the tree in Grandma's garden, and he, Oskar, had a magic phone in his pocket that he could use to call his friend. It would be silly not to take advantage of the opportunity.

Oskar put the phone to his ear.

'Hello, balloon!' he said. She'd been annoyed with him that morning, and he wasn't even sure she would answer.

But she did.

'Hello, Oskar!' This time she wasn't her usual cheeky self, but sounded a little gentler and more friendly. 'How has your day been?'

Oskar told her. He talked about the broom and the toothbrush, the watering can, the chair who had gone home after a long trip, and the sugar bowl and cream jug's date. The balloon giggled.

'You do have a lot of patience for messing around with things that need help! Day in, day out, all you do is drag them around from one place to another. I saw you crossing the garden with the chair. And I also spotted you nestled up to the watering can like a couple of puppies. You even look the same. He-he! So he really believes that his parents are rainclouds? And he's made of *aluminium*! What can I say – your friends are real characters!'

'What did you do today?' Oskar asked. 'There's no wind, so I guess you weren't able to dance.'

'Oh, there are a lot of other exciting things for me to do instead,' said the balloon. 'Like reading leaves.'

'What leaves?' Oskar asked, puzzled. 'You mean tree leaves?'

'What do you think I mean? Of course tree leaves! You go ahead and read some cabbage leaves the next time Grandma makes you cabbage soup. Just scoop them out of the bowl and enjoy!'

'I don't like cabbage soup,' Oskar retorted. 'And I don't want to read cabbage leaves, either. What's written on those tree leaves, then? I can't see anything.'

He pulled a tiny leaf off a low-hanging branch and inspected it closely. There were some lines on it, but none of them looked even close to letters of the alphabet.

'Buy yourself a pair of specs!' the balloon said. 'Though they won't be much good if you don't know how to read.'

'I know how to read just fine,' Oskar said. 'Kids' books and comics. But there's nothing at all written on this leaf!'

'Of course there is! You've just got to be able to speak the tree's language. For instance, there's a very funny story here about a teeny-tiny boy who becomes best friends with a watering can. They water the flowers together every day – the little boy pees on them while the watering can sprinkles them with water. He-he! And in the end, they both grow up, turn into rainclouds and get married. What a great story!'

'That's a fib,' Oskar said. 'I bet none of these leaves have stories like that on them.'

'You think so?' giggled the balloon. 'Well, *I* read it, in any case. And there's another nice little tale here, too – it's about a gorgeous red balloon whom everybody's crazy about. Mosquitoes fly around and around her, buzzing in admiration. By the end of the story, the balloon becomes Queen of the Mosquitoes!'

As soon as she mentioned mosquitoes, Oskar realised the air around him was thick with the droning insects. There were thousands of them relentlessly barrelling in to attack him. Oskar started swatting at them.

'That's rubbish,' he said. 'Mosquitoes don't care about you because you don't have blood. They're buzzing around *me*.'

'Right, because they've chosen you to be their dinner,' the balloon said mockingly. 'Of course I don't have any nasty blood inside of me – I'm not a blood sausage like you! Mosquitoes are attracted to my red colour; they think I look like a giant drop of blood. I'm perfect to be their queen!'

'Keep dreaming!' Oskar scoffed, and started skipping around the tree to escape the clouds of mosquitoes.

'You dance pretty well, you know!' complimented the balloon. 'You're not as graceful as the mosquitoes twirling in the air, but you're better than the ants. They crawl around the branches up here, but they don't dance – all they do is wiggle their bottoms. Poor little things! They don't have wings. Can you imagine how far they've travelled, just to come and visit me?'

Oskar could see the ants scurrying up and down the trunk of the birch tree, and suddenly he had a funny idea. That afternoon, he'd carried kisses on his fingertip from the sitting room to the kitchen and back. What if he were to send something like that to the balloon? And what better way to deliver it than one of the ants bustling on the tree trunk?

Of course, it was impossible to talk to an ant to explain the important task with which it was entrusted. It was entirely possible that the ant would turn around halfway and crawl right back down the tree trunk. But if he were to send off several ants, *lots* of ants, then some of them might just make it all the way to the balloon!

'Hey, I'm going to send you something,' Oskar said.

'What?'

'It's... a kiss.'

Oskar blushed. Before then, he'd only ever kissed his mum and – on rare occasions like birthdays – his dad. There was no way he'd have ever wanted to kiss a girl. Impossible! And if anyone ever asked him to, he'd have climbed into a wardrobe to hide! But the balloon was different. She was like a girl, in a sense – she spoke in a girl's voice and was just as cheeky as any other kid at school. But at the same time, she was still a balloon, not a real person. That made it feel alright to send her a kiss. It wasn't scary, but the exact opposite – it felt nice, somehow.

'A kiss?' the balloon asked slowly, sounding very surprised. 'You're sending me a kiss? I can't believe my ears!'

'That's right. On an ant.'

The balloon laughed.

'You're sending me a kiss on an ant!' she repeated. 'You really are dotty. Which ant? There are so many!'

'I'm sending it on a few,' Oskar explained. 'I don't know which ones will climb all the way to the top, but if you do see some ants up there, then just know a few of them have a kiss on their shoulders.'

'You're daft,' the balloon said fondly. 'A real nincompoop. Sure, send a kiss if you want, I guess. I'll keep an eye open for your ants, and will try and find the right one.'

Oskar placed his finger on his lips and then started passing the kiss onto various ants. He picked ones that were scurrying up the trunk already, and tapped them lightly with his fingertip. The ants froze for a moment, before scuttling even faster on their way, carrying Oskar's kisses on their backs like invisible rucksacks.

He put kisses on about twenty ants, reckoning that was probably enough. Some of them were sure to find their way to the balloon! The mosquitoes were starting to get bad again and Oskar had had enough of their attacks.

'I'm going inside now,' he told her. 'Or the mosquitoes will eat me alive. The ants are on their way!'

'I suppose I'll just wait for them, then,' she replied sweetly. 'Goodnight, Oskar!'

Later, after Oskar had brushed his teeth and was lying in bed, the phone started making the sawing sound from its place under his pillow. He lifted it to his ear.

'Hello!'

'Got it!' said the balloon. 'Thanks!'

That was all she said. Oskar slid the phone back under his pillow, fell asleep and dreamt very wonderful dreams that night.

30.

Oskar's room was still dark when he opened his eyes in the morning. *Is it really still night?* he wondered sleepily, then heard loud pattering against the window. It was raining. The watering can's mum and dad had finally arrived.

Oskar's second thought was of the balloon. *She's going to get all wet!* He climbed out of bed and went to the window to check on his friend.

The scene outside was terrible! Rain poured down as if from a giant tap and, on top of that, a powerful wind was whipping the trees back and forth and snapping branches and leaves off the bushes. A storm was in full swing, and thrashing about in the middle of the gale was the red balloon, looking like she was being yanked every which way by giant invisible hands.

Oskar stared out the window, open-mouthed in horror. At any moment, the balloon could be ripped from the tree and vanish from sight, stolen by the howling winds! There was no way she could survive being pulled about so violently. Oskar felt like he was witnessing some dreadful crime – a murder, even – and had no way to step in and help the victim. All he could do was watch in dread as his friend fought an unstoppable foe.

Wait, but I can at least call her! Oskar remembered. He rushed to pull out his phone from under his pillow.

'Hello, balloon!' he said. 'Hello!'

He suddenly heard the roar of the storm and the balloon's cheeky voice:

'I can't talk right now! Can't you see?! I don't have time! I'm dancing! Oh, how I'm dancing!'

She hung up. Oskar glared at the balloon bouncing in the treetop. He had wanted to give his friend courage; to tell her how much he liked her and how frightened he was that the wind might sweep her away. He'd wanted – if the unspeakable horror were actually to happen – to spend those final fateful moments together with his friend, but it turned out she didn't even need him. The balloon thought it was all just a delightful dance and marvellous fun. The possibility of leaving the treetop behind apparently didn't seem all that tragic to her – on the contrary, it'd be a gleeful escape with some dance-loving breeze.

Those breezes and winds! Oskar couldn't see a single one of them, of course, but there was no doubt the balloon was surrounded by a fair share at the moment. All her attention was turned to jumping and jiving, to doing headstands and somersaults with their help. So *that* was what mattered most to her! Had any of those winds ever sent her a kiss on an ant like Oskar did just yesterday?

Fine, fly away then! Oskar thought, feeling hurt. *I don't need her. She can go ahead and have fun with all her wind-friends until they carry her to the top of some pine tree and she pops with a bang when she crashes into one of the needles, for all I care.*

He stepped back from the window and even drew the curtain to hide what was going on outside. But he could still hear the rain lashing down and the howling of the wind, and couldn't shake from his head the image of the balloon spinning in cartwheels with her string pulled taut to its breaking point.

Oskar heard dishes clattering in the kitchen. He got dressed and went to have breakfast. Grandma was also looking out the window, nodding in satisfaction.

'At last, some rain,' she said. 'And it's coming down nicely, too – the plants will get a decent drink. That's good. The ground was terribly dry before; nothing'll grow in that.'

She glanced at Oskar

'Though I suppose this kind of weather is awfully boring for you,' she sighed sympathetically. 'You can't go outside or do anything. These rainy days are the worst for kids – I know it all too well. When I was a little girl, my brothers and sisters and I couldn't stand staying indoors when it was raining cats and dogs outside. And as soon as Mum and Dad weren't looking, we ran straight out of the house. We jumped barefoot in puddles and splashed mud on one another. It made us so happy! A child's happiest dream! Oh, we were so silly back then.'

Oskar couldn't agree with her more. Nothing could have made him jump in puddles or splash around in the mud. Just the thought of it made him feel all slimy and gross. Grandma and her siblings were definitely weirdos if they'd liked those kinds of games. But apparently prancing about in the rain hadn't lost its charm for her, because she gave him a sly look and asked:

'Would you like to go out and jump in puddles too, Oskar? Of course you would – what little boy wouldn't! But that wouldn't be good for you; you might catch a cold. Best just stay indoors.'

'Yeah, sure,' Oskar said. 'I don't want to go out, anyway.

I don't like rain.' He glanced at the window just in time to see a branch snap off one of the apple trees. What was going on at the top of the birch tree just now? He felt an irresistible urge to dash to his bedroom window. But he couldn't just sprint away from the table – he had to finish his meal first. He hastily filled his mouth full of porridge.

'You're quite the sensible young lad,' Grandma praised him. 'Very well raised. Why go stomping about in puddles! I'm just afraid you might get rather bored. What's a child to do, cooped up inside all day like in a prison cell? And your father already took all his children's books back to the city. Otherwise, it would've been nice for you to lounge in bed and read on a rainy day like today. Well, perhaps there'll be something you like on the telly.'

'I'll manage,' Oskar said. 'Thanks, I'm full.' He stood up, went to his room, and tore the curtain open.

The balloon was still there, swooping through the grey sky like a red bird in flight.

Oskar sniffed. All he could do was stare helplessly out the window and hope the balloon's string was wound tightly enough around the branch. And that the branch itself was sturdy enough. That the storm would be over soon. That the balloon wouldn't fly away from him.

At that moment, the balloon was yanked sideways with a mighty jerk, causing Oskar's heart to leap just as sharply in his chest and make him panic: *This is it!* But the balloon wasn't blown away; her string was very strong indeed. Oskar almost felt grateful to the cotton-haired boys' father who had tied it so tightly to her tail. If he'd just used regular thread, the balloon would already be zooming towards the horizon.

Oskar wondered if he should stay next to the window for

the entire day to keep an eye on the balloon. In a way, it felt natural – being at your friend's side till the final moment. But did the balloon even care? For her, the storm just meant a joyful dance. She hadn't a second to spare to notice that Oskar's eyes were trained on her the whole time from behind the curtains of rain.

So he went into the sitting room, deciding that he wasn't just going to stare out of the window all day long. He was still worried, of course – there was no avoiding that. And he thought he'd still pop into his bedroom from time to time to cast a frightened glance up at the treetop. Even so, he'd try to keep himself from doing it too often. He needed to find some other activity.

Grandma was sewing at the kitchen table.
'Turn on the telly, Oskar. Maybe there's a cartoon on,' she recommended.

So Oskar did, and flipped through all the channels. There was nothing good on – just some boring series for adults and the news.

But what if he were to *call* the television?

Oskar lifted the phone to his ear.

'Hello, telly.' He spoke softly so Grandma wouldn't overhear him from the kitchen. 'My name's Oskar. Do you have a minute to talk?'

'Hi, Oskar,' a tired and hoarse voice answered. It sounded like the telly was sick and in bed, a scarf wound around his neck and his forehead red-hot with fever. 'It's nice of you to call, but I'm feeling a little under the weather just now. I'm very ill!'

'What's wrong?' Oskar asked. At a glance, the telly appeared to be in perfect working condition. The screen wasn't flickering or fuzzy – a Middle-Eastern woman was reclining on a couch while a man wearing a turban and waving a sabre told her something.

'My tummy's a bit out of sorts,' the telly moaned. 'It's making strange noises. It usually happens every evening, but now it's in the middle of the day. And someone's talking inside my stomach even as I speak! Every now and then, someone sings there; sometimes they shoot guns; and occasionally I feel like somebody's driving a car straight through my guts! It rumbles like an engine! Some evenings, I hear strange animal noises coming from my belly, and sometimes they blow horns and bang on drums down there. I can't tell you how embarrassing it is – I'm actually quite modest and don't like to cause any trouble. I'm happy sitting quietly in the corner, not bothering anybody, but then, suddenly, my belly will start crooning and hollering! I'm afraid I'll be a disturbance and people will shoo me out of the room!'

'You don't have to worry at all,' Oskar consoled the miserable telly. 'People actually *like* to hear the sounds that come from your belly. And did you know that your stomach doesn't just make noises, it shows pictures too?'

'What?!' the telly cried in horror. 'What pictures?'

'At the moment, it's showing a dancing woman with a veil over her face,' Oskar said. 'And now there's a man in a red turban eating a slice of watermelon. It's a TV programme. People are actually very thankful for the things that come out of your belly, you know – you don't have to feel the least bit guilty for it. People *want* to see and hear them!'

'Really?' the telly gasped. 'And here I was, all distraught! I thought – how can it be that *I'm* the one plagued by such

a terrible illness! The table and chairs never howl and groan like me; not even the cabinet does. I'm the only one with a commotion going on in his tummy.'

'Yes, and that's why people love you. No one ever stares at the table or the cabinet for hours on end. But you're different! The whole family gathers round you to watch you together.'

'Then I suppose I've got a pretty useful belly,' the telly sighed contentedly. He didn't sound sick and miserable at all anymore, but full of vigour – a little like the man with a black beard who was now singing and galloping away on a horse in his belly.

'How brilliant it was of you to call me, Oskar! You've cured me. I won't be ashamed of the sounds my belly makes anymore. If people need to hear them, then by all means – come right over and listen as you please.'

'That's great,' Oskar said. Then he simply couldn't resist the urge anymore. It was as if some invisible force was pulling him towards the bedroom – towards the window looking out over the birch tree that shuddered in the stormy weather. The one and only thought in his mind was the question: *Is she still there?* 'I'm going to switch you off now, okay? I don't feel like watching these guys anymore.'

Oskar pressed the red button on the remote and the telly's belly went quiet. He ran to his room and peered out the window.

The balloon and the storm were still dancing.

31.

It was a grey and cheerless day for Oskar – one in which absolutely nothing happened, and he simply drifted in a cloud of stuffy boredom. At the same time, a prickly feeling of unease in his chest kept him from napping to pass the time. Time and again, he went to the window to frown at the gale raging outside and the branches bending in the wind – branches to which the red balloon was bound by a frail string. A string that could snap at any second.

Grandma darned socks, tidied up and cooked. Occasionally, she poked her head into Oskar's bedroom and tried to strike up a conversation, apparently trying to be entertaining, but he was too agitated to listen to her ramble on about strangers, dogs that lived a long time ago, and cats no one else could remember. Grandma's stories went in one ear and out the other without a trace. He'd comment absentmindedly with an 'Uh-huh!' or an 'Okay!' every few minutes, then dart back to the window like a soldier to his post.

Suddenly, a thought crossed his mind. What if the wind did rip the balloon from the tree, but instead of carrying her out of reach, beyond the forests and the fields, it swept her down into the garden instead, where it tossed her around until Oskar had a chance to catch her and bring her inside? He imagined hiding the red balloon under his bed and keeping her away from anything sharp or dangerous. That'd be incredible! He could place her on the windowsill so she'd sparkle in the rays of sunlight. He could play with her, and be the wind that made her dance.

This idea cheered Oskar up for a while, but then he started to have some doubts. The likelihood of catching the balloon if she got loose from the tree was extremely slim. He was in his room, far from the front door, and he'd need to dash outside as soon as he saw her take flight. That meant running past Grandma, who would try to stop him or at least demand he put on boots and a jacket, and there wouldn't be enough time for that. He'd make it outside in spite of her, but where would the balloon be by then? Far beyond the horizon! There wasn't a shred of hope that a storm like the one raging outside right now would leave the light little red balloon lying on the grass in peace to wait for Oskar's rescue.

He had to accept that he wouldn't be able to catch her. All he could do was hope the winds died down and the balloon stayed put.

The weather indeed improved that afternoon. First, the storm began to calm. The tree branches still swayed lightly from side to side as if stretching after a hard day's work. Nature seemed to be rather exhausted as a whole – blossoms and branches lost in the battle were scattered across the ground. The trees and bushes looked sweaty in the continuing drizzle, and almost out of breath.

Up in the treetop, the balloon had also stopped her furious bouncing and was now rocking on her string, seemingly exhausted. Oskar couldn't help but call.

'Hello, balloon,' he said gingerly. 'Are you able to talk now?'

'Why shouldn't I be?' the balloon replied. She sounded as carefree as always and without a hint of tiredness. 'Did you see the way I was dancing? My head's still spinning a little. I've never been to a party like that before! It was incredible!'

'That wasn't a party, it was a storm,' Oskar replied, feeling a touch irritated by the balloon's cheerful mood. 'You could've been yanked off the tree and blown away. I watched you from the window the whole time and couldn't stop worrying.'

'Well, that's *your* problem,' the balloon snorted. Her voice grew stubborn. 'I never asked you to watch over me, you know. If I'm asked to dance, then that's just what I'm going to do, because I *like* dancing!'

'But you could've popped!' Oskar insisted. 'If any one of those branches had poked you...'

'Enough!' the balloon yelled. 'I don't want to talk about things like that! Never, do you hear me? Goodbye!'

'Hold on...'

But the balloon had ended the call. Looking out of the window, it even seemed as if she'd turned her back on him from the treetop.

'You twit!' Oskar fumed. Since the balloon was no longer in any direct danger, he flung himself onto his bed and lay there flat on his belly until Grandma came to tell him the rain had eased.

'You can go outside if you put your boots on,' she said. 'Poor child, having to spend all day caged up like a prisoner. You must be bored stiff. Go outside and have a little breath of fresh air!'

So Oskar did. The air really did taste fresh from the rain. Drips sounded from every direction and the leaves glistened dully. The lawn squelched beneath Oskar's feet, leaving dark footprints in the wet grass.

His mobile started to make sounds in his pocket, so he lifted it to his ear.

'Hello, I'm calling from the shed!' announced a booming

voice. 'I'm the kicksled. The chair told me about you – she said that, back in the house, there's a boy with arms and legs who can talk to things. Do you have a moment?'

'Sure,' Oskar replied. It was obvious that the chair had told the various odds and ends in the shed all about him on her trip around the world, and his fame had spread. Oskar had no problem helping the kicksled out – it was pretty exciting to get to know the things in the shed and hear what life was like there. He had a few shed-friends already – the rusty nail and the hammer – but the shed was crammed with all sorts of other things too.

Oskar set off towards the shed as they continued their conversation.

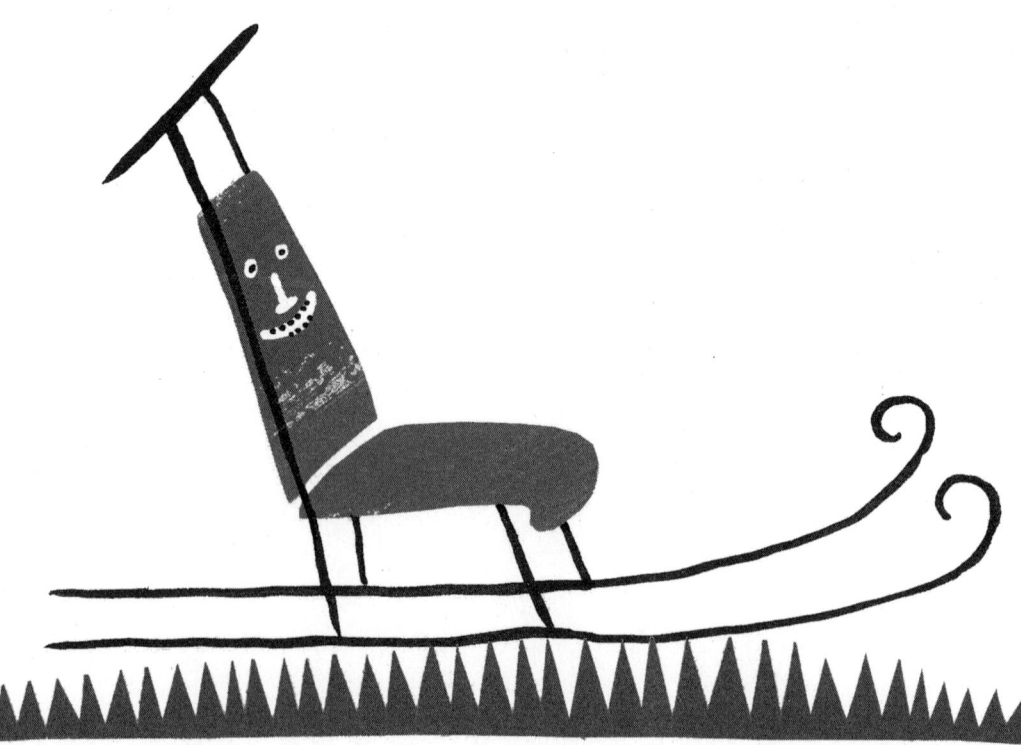

'I've got a bit of an usual request,' the kicksled began. 'I heard loud drumming on the roof earlier, and some of the wiser objects in here told me it was rain that was made this noise. I've never seen rain before, you see. Only snow! I'm only ever taken out of the shed when the ground is white. But things in here are telling me that the ground is *green* in summer! Is that even possible? If I could just get out the door and into the light for a minute, I could gaze upon that wonder with my own eyes. Would you be so kind as to haul me out into the garden for a little while?'

'Of course! It's already stopped raining, so you won't see that, but everything is still damp and dripping.'

'And there's not a snowflake to be seen?' the kicksled asked doubtfully.

'Not one,' Oskar replied. 'You're about to see for yourself.'

He stepped into the shed. The smells were different after the rain there too; it was muggier in a way.

'Where are you?' Oskar asked. The shed was so full of old junk that the kicksled didn't stand out anywhere at first.

'Here in the back corner, next to the bike.'

'Oh, now I see you!' Oskar said. 'I'll try to get you out.'

The kicksled was quite heavy and its long runners kept getting caught, but after a few strong shoves Oskar managed to get it moving. The sawdust and woodchips covering the floor allowed it to slide quite smoothly to the door.

'Daa da-da-da da da da daaaa!' Oskar cried into the phone as he ceremoniously pushed the kicksled into the garden.

A long whistle came from the other end of the line.

'You slick old sledder...' the sled murmured in amazement. 'Well, you were right as... rain! A snowball in the face; what can I say.'

'Is it totally different from winter?' Oskar asked.

'It's a totally different *world*!' the kicksled exclaimed. 'But a bit less nice, I'd say. I can't slide across this green stuff – it's not slippery enough.'

'It's called grass,' Oskar explained. 'You don't have to slide across it. You walk.'

'You can walk in winter, too, you know – but you can ride a kicksled just as well. Now, where's this rain I heard so much about, anyway? It was raining for hours on end, but I can't spot a single little rain drift, not to mention a rain mound.'

'Rain doesn't pile up. Rain is just water – it doesn't make drifts, just puddles.'

'What are *puddles*?' the kicksled asked.

'There aren't any here in the garden because rainwater soaks into the soil.'

Oskar suddenly felt very smart. He wasn't even in primary school yet, but here he was teaching things at Grandma's house like an actual headmaster!

'There are puddles on the road. I'll take you there so you can see!'

The kicksled was absolutely right – grass wasn't anywhere near as slippery as snow, which meant it took an awful lot of effort for Oskar to drag it along. Still, he'd promised the kicksled puddles, and puddles was what he would get. Luckily, there was a whole chain of them outside the gate, big and small, all brimming with brownish water mixed with dust from the gravel road.

Once Oskar had put him down, the kicksled stared at the puddles for a long time.

'The world sure is an incredible place,' he finally said, his voice full of awe. 'If only I could take one back as a souvenir...'

'That wouldn't really work,' Oskar said. 'Puddles aren't like rugs that can be rolled up and taken home. They're water; they'd spill.'

'Can't you pack one into a ball, like with snow?' the kicksled asked.

'Nope,' Oskar replied. He thought for a moment.

'Wait here,' he announced, then ran into the house. Grandma kept old glass jars of all shapes and sizes in one of the kitchen cupboards. There were hordes of them! Oskar thought he could take the kicksled a little jar without Grandma noticing it was missing. He trotted back to the gate with one and used it to scoop up some rainwater from a big puddle.

'Here you are!' he said to the kicksled. 'A genuine puddle you can take back to the shed as a keepsake.'

'Thank you, my friend!' gasped the kicksled. 'It'll always remind me of summer.'

32.

Oskar dragged the kicksled back to the shed, while looking up at the crown of the birch tree out of the corner of his eye. Did the balloon notice what he was doing? She had to – she generally kept an eye on everything, even a rusty nail lying in tall grass. Why shouldn't she be watching Oskar and the kicksled at the foot of her own tree? Was she getting curious? It had to be quite the spectacle – a kicksled on the green grass. Maybe she would call and ask: *What silly thing are you up to now, Oskar?* And Oskar would fill her in on everything.

But the phone in his pocket stayed silent. Oskar heaved the kicksled back into the shed and put him back in his original place. He put the little jar of rainwater between the sled's runners, making sure it wasn't too obvious. There was no need for Grandma to notice the kicksled's souvenir the moment she walked into the shed, as she probably wouldn't understand why a jar of water was there. At the same time, it was pretty unlikely the kicksled's prize would be easy to see, as the shed was so crammed with junk from floor to ceiling.

Suddenly Oskar's phone started making its familiar noise in his pocket. *Could it really be?!* he wondered in delight. Alas, it wasn't the balloon. An unfamiliar voice thundered from the magic mobile:

'Hello! Is this Oskar with the arms and legs?'

'That's me,' Oskar confirmed. 'Who am I speaking to?'

'The screwdriver,' answered the voice. 'I'm in a bit of a fix, you see – I've rolled off the shelf.'

'Which shelf?' Oskar asked.

'The one where the tools are stored, of course. You see, I was minding my own business next to the nail puller and the plane when, all of a sudden, something bumped into the shelves and there I go – shup! – right off the back. How's that for an accident! I suppose I was lying a bit too close to the edge, but how can I be to blame for that? I was right where I was last put.'

'Was that my fault?' Oskar asked guiltily. 'I'm sorry! I didn't realise. I was just pulling out the kicksled and I guess...'

'No, no, it didn't happen today,' the screwdriver reassured him. 'It's been... yes, I suppose about five years!'

'Five *years*?!' Oskar gasped. 'That really is a long time.'

'You can say that again! That's why I'm a bit het up, you see. How will they manage without me? The screws, I mean. Who'll tighten them when they get loose? I'm a hard worker and not one for lazing around. Tools should be lined up nice and neatly on their shelf and always at the ready, just like firefighters! As soon as anything goes wrong, they rush to the rescue on the double. But you see, I'm lying on the ground behind the shelf where no one can find me. I can't help anyone; can't turn a single screw! Be a good egg and get me out of here, would you?'

Oskar was sure rivers would start running backwards before Grandma started tightening any screws. That being the case, the screwdriver could just settle down right where he was without worrying about anyone noticing he was gone. Even so, Oskar knew you should always help where help is needed. It must be agonising just to lie in some dusty corner for five years. Oskar walked over to the tool shelves and studied them. There wasn't a screwdriver in sight on the ground in front of them, but then again, the caller *had* said he fell behind the shelves.

Luckily, the shelf unit wasn't fitted with its back against the wall, but rather with its side attached, which made things somewhat easier as Oskar didn't have to try and move it. Nevertheless, there was nothing easy about the task he faced, because there were all manner of crates, boxes, spools and old paint cans piled behind the shelves. They formed a kind of tower that stretched up taller than the shelf unit itself. Finding a screwdriver beneath that mountain of junk would be a very hard job, indeed.

'Can you see me yet?' the screwdriver asked. 'Try to hurry up, please! I feel so foolish chilling out down here while, somewhere, there must be thousands of screws jiggling loose or just waiting to be screwed in. I'm no lazybones – I enjoy working but I just can't right now! It's impossible! There's nothing to screw in back here. Please help me!'

'Easy for you to say,' Oskar grumbled as he slipped the phone into his pocket. He needed both hands for this job. He carefully started lifting the uppermost crates and cans down from the pile. Luckily, most of them were empty and didn't weigh too much. The only problem was that the whole tower was rather unstable. As soon as you removed one thing from one place, an avalanche started to form in another. A couple of paint cans rolled off the peak and clattered loudly as they hit the ground. An old washtub followed. Still, nothing ended up breaking and Grandma was far enough away to be out of earshot.

The screwdriver rescue operation became even harder once Oskar reached the lower boxes, because they were packed full of all kinds of odds and ends, and were as heavy as boulders. He tried to tug them to one side so he could squeeze between them and the shelves. Once the crack was wide enough, he had no problem wedging himself into it. Getting down on his hands and knees, Oskar started groping around the floor for the tool. It was dark in the gap, but then he thought he could see something. The screwdriver had rolled into a tiny space between one box and the wall. Oskar had to go flat on his belly to reach him, but finally he did.

'Phew!' Oskar breathed out as he pulled the screwdriver up into the light. The rescued tool was rather dusty from having been lost for five years, so Oskar wiped him clean on his shirt before pulling out his mobile.

'It took a while, but I found you!' he said. 'Is everything alright?'

'Everything is tip-top!' the screwdriver cried in delight. 'Much obliged, Oskar. I feel fit enough to go tighten some screws right away. I'm not the least bit tired – on the contrary, I'd be delighted to do a spot of work after mooching about for five whole years.'

'I don't have any loose screws for you to work on right now,' Oskar apologised. 'But as soon as I see one, I'll come and get you right away. I'm going to put you back on the shelf now, in the very middle so you'll never fall off again. Wait here.'

'Yes, sir! To my post!' the screwdriver declared ceremoniously. Oskar put him next to the other tools and started cleaning up the mess on the floor, trying to arrange the cans and boxes the same way they'd been. He didn't manage to stack an entirely identical tower, but it would do. Feeling rather worn out, Oskar went inside the house.

'Oh, good heavens! How dusty you are!' Grandma exclaimed. 'Where have you been crawling around? You've even got dirt all over your tummy.'

'I was in the shed,' Oskar replied.

'What were you doing in there? The shed is no place for playing. There are sharp, dangerous tools in there, like saws and axes. You could get hurt.' Grandma eyed Oskar nervously, as if she were afraid he'd already sawed off a limb.

'I wasn't playing with a saw or axe,' he tried to explain. 'I was... just looking at stuff.'

'The things in there are all old and broken; what's there to look at? I should load them into a truck someday and haul them off to the dump. Take that dirty shirt off right now; I'm putting it in the wash.'

Oskar tugged off his shirt, feeling cross. Grandma still didn't understand anything. There was no point in even trying to talk to her – you weren't going to make anything clearer, anyway. It was easier just to keep his mouth shut, let her go about her business, and think his own thoughts.

'Your trousers are covered in cobwebs, too,' Grandma sighed, clapping Oskar on the bottom. 'Don't go poking around that shed anymore; it's very dirty. You'll ruin all your nice clothes, and just think of what'll happen if you end up getting a splinter!'

Oskar let her to dress him in clean clothes and then ate dinner. Grandma pulled a box of marmalade sweets out of one of the cupboards.

'Let's enjoy a little snack now, too, shall we?' She put one in her mouth and washed it down with a sip of tea.

Oskar tried a couple of the sweets and once again had to admit that, out of all the sweet things in the world, marmalade was something he just couldn't stand. What's more, he'd once heard on the telly that marmalade was made with seaweed, which sounded downright disgusting. Oskar hated seaweed and refused to swim at any beach where you had to wade through it to get to the water. He was even less likely to eat it voluntarily. It made sense that all Grandma's cupboards only held worthless sweets. Typical.

Grandma was like a completely different species of human being. You couldn't have a normal conversation with her, she ate weird foods, and she did everything differently from how they did things in the city. Once, at the zoo, Oskar saw a turtle and a rabbit that lived in the same cage. They posed no danger to each other, but they weren't able to communicate either. The rabbit just hopped around and the turtle crawled along its own path. Oskar felt a bit like that rabbit right now.

He said goodnight and went to his room. As he sat down on the bed, he glanced outside at the balloon. She was still tied to the treetop, but somehow seemed sad. There wasn't a breath of wind in the wake of the storm and the balloon wasn't dancing like usual – she was completely motionless. Oskar suddenly realised how important she was to him and was overcome by the urge to say something nice.

He took out his phone.

'Hello, balloon!' he said.

But the balloon didn't answer. Oskar pulled the

blanket up to his chin. A fly buzzed up to the ceiling light to hear its fortune and, for a moment, Oskar considered calling him as well to ask questions about his own future.

But what could the light really tell him? Oskar was no gullible fly that actually believed the lamp's predictions. It would, of course, be nicer to fall asleep after hearing a happy fortune. But what if the ceiling light predicted something bad?

He decided it was better not to take the chance.

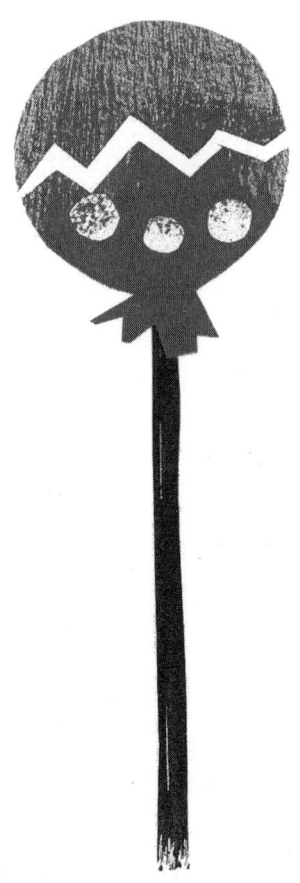

33.

The weather was fine again the next morning. Grandma hurried out to the garden, leaving Oskar to eat his porridge. Seizing the opportunity, he spooned most of it back into the pot. He wasn't hungry and there was nothing he could do to make this clumpy dollop more tasty.

Oskar's mobile started making noises in his pocket, so he picked up. It was the sugar bowl, which was right in front of him on the kitchen table. Grandma had put her there to spoon sugar into her coffee that morning.

'I have a rather large favour to ask,' the sugar bowl began with a quivering voice. 'Would it be possible to see my dear cream jug again? I miss him terribly and can't even sleep at night!'

'Of course,' Oskar said. 'It's no problem at all.'

'How wonderful! Would you tilt my lid down a smidgen too, please? And, if you'd be so kind, then move the salt cellar somewhere else as well. I don't want the cream jug to see her.'

'Why not?' Oskar asked curiously.

'Well, what if he ends up liking her more than he likes me?' the sugar bowl whispered timidly.

Oskar was just about to move the salt cellar to the shelf when he realized *she* wasn't just a lifeless thing that could be shifted around the kitchen willy-nilly either. The salt cellar certainly had her own plans, and was perhaps in the middle of doing something on the kitchen table right now. He decided it would be wise to call and check, just in case.

'Hello, salt cellar! I'm Oskar. Would you mind if I moved you up to the shelf for a little while? The sugar bowl would like to be alone on the table so the cream jug can look at her from the other room without any interruptions.'

'I've got nothing against a little trip,' the salt cellar replied. 'It won't be my first time on the shelf, and I've got a fair number of friends up there already. I'd be glad to pay them a visit. I just don't understand why the cream jug has to stare at the sugar jar from way over in the other room. Bring him to the kitchen! He's a dish of sorts too, which means he should certainly be allowed on the table. It'd be another thing if her suitor were a boot or a rucksack. Those things don't belong on a table – it'd be a scandal if dirty things like those were to climb their way up. But certainly no one in the kitchen would have any issue with the cream jug joining us!'

The salt cellar was absolutely right. Why should the cream jug and the sugar bowl have to be kept so far apart – one in the sitting room and the other in the kitchen – when they belonged to the very same coffee set? Oskar stood up, set the salt cellar on the shelf, and positioned the sugar bowl in the middle of the table. Then he went into the sitting room and opened the cabinet door.

'Hello, cream jug!' he said. 'You are cordially invited to the kitchen.'

'Come again?' the cream jug gasped. 'The kitchen? But that's where my darling sugar bowl is! Are we truly to be reunited? Oh, I am over the moon with delight! Are you taking me there now? You have my endless thanks!'

Oskar felt just like the pumpkin that turned into a carriage and drove Cinderella to the Prince's ball. True, this trip was in the opposite direction, with the prince riding to visit Cinderella in the kitchen. It made no difference, though, and Oskar was to give him a lift. He even made galloping sounds and trumpeted when he reached the kitchen table: 'Ta-daa! We're here!' After ceremoniously setting the cream jug down next to the sugar bowl, he declared just like the Fairy Godmother: 'You have until exactly twelve o'clock, because that's when Grandma will arrive!'

Oskar glanced back over his shoulder as he left the kitchen. The two seemed perfect together with their matching patterns, and looked as happy as clams.

Oskar sighed. Bringing the cream jug and the sugar bowl together had been so easy, but it was quite a different story with him and the balloon. He walked behind the house and craned his neck to look up. She hadn't drifted away overnight – he'd made sure of that earlier, of course, because the very first place his eyes travelled when he woke up was to the treetop. She was swinging back and forth, delicate and defenceless, and Oskar couldn't help but worry.

Funny – I can, and do, help every other thing I talk to, he thought. *The balloon is the only one I haven't been able to do a single good deed for yet. And I suppose I can't. Even so, she's still my very best friend. It's all so weird and unfair.*

There was one thing he could do, however – he could ring her, which was just what he decided to do now.

'Hello, balloon!' he spoke into the phone.

It rang for a long time, but no one picked up.

'Come on, answer me!' Oskar growled. 'You're right there at the top of this tree. You haven't flown away, you haven't... You're here and we have a chance to chat!'

But his red-coloured chunk of wood remained silent.

Oskar huffed and shoved it back in his pocket.

As soon as he had, the mobile started making a noise. He quickly pulled it back out. She *did* want to talk!

'Hi, there!' Oskar cheerfully answered. 'How's it going?'

But it wasn't the balloon on the other end of the line, but a soft, very shy and completely unfamiliar voice.

'Hello... Thank you for asking, I'm fine... I'm calling from the shed.'

'Oh, the shed,' Oskar echoed, trying to hide his disappointment. 'I'll be right there. What are you?

'I'm a vase,' the faint voice replied. 'That is, I *was*... and, in a sense, I suppose I still am. But I'm a little broken.'

'And how can I help?' Oskar asked, opening the shed door and stepping inside. 'Where are you?'

'In a big basket to the left of the door. I'm made of blue glass.'

'I see you,' Oskar said, lifting the blue vase out of a big potato basket to take a closer look. She was very pretty and shaped like a tall crocus flower with petals that curled back from the mouth. But unfortunately there was a chip at her base and a long, ugly crack running up her side.

Oskar set the vase down on a log.

'You look very nice,' he said. 'It's too bad that you had an accident like that. I'm afraid I really don't know how to fix you.'

'Oh, that's not what I was thinking,' she replied. 'No one can fix a broken vase. Actually, I wanted to ask... You see, I haven't held a single flower in oh so very long. Would it be possible for you to maybe pick a flower from the garden and bring it to me? It would just tickle me pink. I'll feel like my old vase-self again if I'm holding a flower, even though I'm cracked.'

She started sobbing.

'Don't be sad!' Oskar comforted her. He felt truly sorry for the vase – more than he had for any of the other things he'd helped so far. For some reason, she reminded him of the balloon and all the dangers she faced. 'I'm glad to help. Should I fill you with water first?'

'No, don't do that. I can't hold water anymore. I've got this awful crack in me and there's a chip missing... It would all trickle out. Just bring flowers. Wait... Oh, no!' she suddenly wailed. 'Without water, they'll wither right away! No, that won't do at all! I'm so foolish! Don't bring me anything. I can't hold flowers anymore. I'm no good for anything. I'm sorry I called and bothered you.'

'Nonsense!' Oskar protested. More than anything else at that moment, he wanted to do something nice for the miserable vase; to cheer her up *somehow*. 'If I can't stick a flower in you, then I'll find something else. Wait here, I'll be right back!'

Oskar ran out of the shed. The ground beneath the trees was covered in twigs that had broken off in yesterday's storm. Oskar picked up one that was just the right length and had enough smaller shoots poking out. He plucked off its leaves so they wouldn't upset the blue vase when they inevitably dried up. Then, he took it inside the house and went to get his felt-tip pens – the same ones he'd used to colour in his magic phone. Of course, he could have simply stuck the branch into the vase the way it was, but that seemed too dull and boring. She was used to holding brightly-coloured flowers! So Oskar started decorating the twig with stripes and polka dots.

He worked on his craft project for quite a while, the tip of his tongue poking out of the corner of his mouth. It turned out spectacularly! What had once been an ordinary branch was now as colourful as an Easter egg and looked like it had grown in a fairy-tale forest. Oskar thought the result was fantastic. With the branch in tow, he hurried back to the shed where the melancholy vase was waiting for him on a stump.

'What do you think?' Oskar asked as he poked the rainbow-coloured branch into the mouth of the vase. 'It's a flower that will never wither.'

'Oh!' the vase gasped. 'Marvellous! So colourful! How can I ever thank you, dear Oskar?'

'It's nothing.' Oskar grinned. 'I'm just glad to be of service to you and the other things.'

Though I suppose not all the other things, he thought and sighed as he moved the vase to a dark corner of the shed so Grandma wouldn't stumble across her.

34.

Grandma served chicken for lunch. Back in the city, 'chicken' meant a big slab of soft white meat or little morsels that were grilled to a golden brown and absolutely scrumptious. Grandma's chicken, on the other hand, meant a pile of bones of various sizes, from which you could maybe pry off a sliver of meat if you were lucky.

'Would you like some chicken?' Grandma asked. Without waiting for a reply, she served him a hefty drumstick with the skin still on it. Oskar poked it with his fork in disgust.

'Pick it up between your fingers and nibble at it,' Grandma said cheerfully. 'That's the best way to eat drumsticks. You can wipe the grease off your fingers when you're finished.'

Oskar tried to follow her instructions. He scraped the skin off to start with, as it looked totally unfit to eat. Then he cautiously tried gnawing. He managed to pry off a couple bits of meat, but the variety of bones poking through the drumstick made eating a real chore.

'Would you like a wing instead?' Grandma asked. 'Chicken wings are very tasty, too.'

That was somehow even *bonier*. The wing was impossible to eat without weird hard bits poking into the sides of your mouth. Grandma's chicken was like a completely different species of bird from the kind they ate in the city. The big chunks of white meat that Mum fried on a pan certainly had very little in common with what a real chicken looked like, and you might think they had belonged to a snail or some other boneless creature. Grandma's chicken, on the other hand, was like a monster out of a horror film with bones sticking out, and skin hanging from it in shreds.

Oskar pushed what was left of the chicken wing and the drumstick to the corner of his plate.

'Thanks,' he said.

'You've still got so much meat left on those!' Grandma exclaimed, her eyes widening. 'Be a good boy and peck those bones clean. Peck, peck!' she added encouragingly, then showed him how, by putting a bone in her own mouth and quickly moving her lips. When the bone re-emerged a few seconds later, it was bare indeed, without a speck of meat to be seen. Oskar glared at her. Pictures of cannibals he'd seen in books came to mind.

He sighed and was trying to find another tiny scrap of meat or two from the bones when suddenly he realised that he hadn't carried the cream jug back to the cabinet table. How could he have been so forgetful? The cream jug and the sugar jar were still nestled close to each other on the kitchen table like two school children who'd been up to some kind of mischief and were now afraid of being punished. It was a wonder that Grandma hadn't noticed them yet.

Oskar barely managed to think this before Grandma gasped.

'Dearie me, how did the cream jug get out here? It should be back in the cabinet. Did you put it there, Oskar? Don't you play with the coffee set – it's very fragile. The pieces are made of porcelain.'

Grandma stood up from the table.

'I'm putting it back, and I don't want you taking it out again. Dishes aren't toys.'

'Grandma, just let it stay!' Oskar protested, to his surprise.

He had never argued with Grandma before, always just accepting the fact that she wouldn't understand anyway and it was better to try and just do things behind her back. There was no way he could explain something like the chair being in the loo or the toothbrush lying under his bed. But why couldn't the cream jug just be left sitting next to his darling sugar bowl in the kitchen when it was something that made both of them so *happy*? The salt cellar had put it perfectly: the cream jug wasn't like a boot or a rucksack, which didn't belong on the kitchen table under any circumstances. Why did Grandma have to keep him locked up in the sitting room cabinet?

'You drink coffee every day and top it off with milk,' Oskar defended. 'You *need* a cream jug.'

'Oh, adding milk straight from the carton is just fine for me. This is a very precious coffee set and it isn't fit for using every day. We need to take good care of it.'

Grandma was just about to pick up the cream jug when Oskar swooped in and snatched the sugar bowl's boyfriend away.

'It doesn't *look* nice to pour milk straight from the carton,' he said with unexpected insistence. *Come what may, I'm not letting these two get separated again!* he thought. 'We certainly don't at home – Mum *always* uses a cream jug!'

'Well, that's no surprise to me,' Grandma said. She sat down. It appeared that Oskar's words had struck a chord. 'Your mother always has to have such fancy things. And I suppose she has every right to – people in the city do have different ways. You can get by with less fuss out here in the country; you don't necessarily need to use a porcelain jug.'

'But you *have* one! Why keep it tucked away in a cupboard?' Oskar wasn't giving up.

'For special days.'

'And how often do those special days come around?' Oskar asked. 'Look how perfect it is here with the sugar bowl. The table looks much nicer when they're together.'

Grandma seemed to hesitate.

'You're right that special days don't come all too often,' she sighed after a brief pause. There was a weariness in her voice. 'That's true. I suppose I'm just used to saving fancy things for special occasions... I wouldn't even have dared take out the sugar bowl, but my old one broke. Perhaps you're right, Oskar... Perhaps it really is just an old lady's funny habit.'

'I'll start drinking coffee in the morning, too, if I can use the cream jug to pour the milk,' Oskar promised, seeing that Grandma was starting to waver. He didn't especially like the taste of coffee, of course, but it wasn't the worst thing in the world if you added a lot of milk and sugar. What's more, he was prepared to suffer a little if it meant helping the happy couple.

'Oh, fine. It can stay.' Grandma smiled as Oskar triumphantly set the jug back on the table. He felt as if, for a brief moment, both of the dishes sparkled brightly, though it might just have been a ray of sunlight shining through the window. The chicken bones on his plate were glistening with grease, too, but neither of *those* had any reason to be ecstatic.

Grandma was suddenly out of sorts, somehow. She rested her cheeks on her palms and appeared to be deep in thought. Then she stood up, left the room, and returned carrying a photo album.

'I just had a funny urge to look at some old photos,' she said, almost apologetically, putting on her glasses and burying her nose in the album. Oskar peered from behind her. The photos were all of strangers, most of them young, laughing and looking happily into the camera.

'That's me,' Grandma said, pointing to a light-haired girl who was wearing a polka dot dress and eating ice cream. Oskar gaped at the picture in disbelief. Could that really have been his grandma? They didn't look anything alike.

'This was taken a few months before our wedding,' she carried on. 'Down at the coast. I was twenty-two years old. Quite a pretty lass, wasn't I?'

Oskar nodded. The grandma in the picture really was pretty. It was too bad he hadn't known her back then. They could have eaten ice cream together and gone swimming at the beach. He might even have been able to tell that girl about his magic phone. Maybe even about the red balloon...

'So it is. So it is,' Grandma murmured. Oskar couldn't quite understand what she meant, but he wasn't about to ask, either. She was somehow acting strange today. Grandma sighed as she stood up from the table, placed the photo album back in the trunk in her bedroom, and went outside.

Oskar stayed in the kitchen. The sugar bowl and the cream jug were snuggled side-by-side on the table. He considered calling them, but what did he really have to say? It was clear they no longer needed his help.

Instead, something called *him*. Oskar fished the phone out of his pocket. Naturally, a thought immediately flashed through his mind: *Is it her?*

Unfortunately it was a table knife, not the balloon.

'Knife's the name, treasure hunting's the game,' he growled in a raspy voice. 'I hunt for treasure high and low: in sausages, in cheese – everywhere. I slice 'em up and have a look inside. I peel potatoes 'cos who knows what they might be hiding under that skin! Carrots and turnips – I chop 'em up into tiny bits to see what's inside. I look for treasure in cakes, pies, even in strudels... I look in bread and rolls. Last autumn, I came upon a whole basketful of mushrooms, and I hunted for treasure in each and every one!'

'What would you do if you actually found treasure?' Oskar asked.

'I'd cut it up to see what's inside, of course! Maybe there'd be an even better treasure within! And then I'd slice that open, too.'

'So what do you want from me?' Oskar asked, in a not very friendly tone. The knife sounded a little daft, to be honest.

'I'd like you to help me search,' the knife replied. 'I get the sense I'm being bamboozled and the treasure's hidden somewhere else entirely. We'll start with the chairs, then move on to the table, the cups, and the plates.'

'Wait, *what* do you want to do with them?'

'Cut them up, of course,' the knife rasped. 'We'll slice them in half for starters and then those halves into quarters to see what's inside.'

'That is absolutely mad,' Oskar snapped. 'I'm certainly not going to help you smash up the dishes and furniture.'

'But they could hold treasure!' the knife insisted. 'We'll shred the curtains, too, then take on the sink. Let's get started!'

'No way,' Oskar grunted, and hung up. He tossed the foolish knife into a drawer – let it sit in the dark!

35.

Oskar walked outside and, before he knew it, found himself at the foot of the tall birch by the shed. It was bizarre how his legs seemed to take him down that path all on their own!

He craned his neck back and eyed the balloon. She was still up there, as round and red as ever before, so why couldn't they talk? Was she upset, or angry? Maybe she'd still been asleep that morning and that's why she hadn't answered?

Oskar lifted the phone to his ear.

'Hello, balloon!' he said. 'Talk to me, please!'

But the balloon was silent. Birds sang in the trees and someone was mowing a lawn far, far away, but those were the only sounds to be heard.

Oskar snorted. This was ridiculous! It was like going to the sweetshop with money in your pocket, but the shopkeeper at the counter simply refused to sell you sweets, only staring indifferently at the ceiling as if you weren't even standing there. Or like you were already sitting on a white carousel horse and the music was playing, but the operator couldn't be bothered to push the button to make it go round, and was just scratching his moustache and reading the newspaper while you fidgeted impatiently in your saddle, shooting him pleading looks.

It was the same with the balloon. Oskar had been afraid something bad might happen to her – he was afraid of it to this minute – because that would mean losing his friend.

There wasn't even the slightest breeze that could blow her away just then, but he *still* couldn't talk to her and there was nothing that could be done about it. All Oskar could do was stare helplessly at the treetop from below.

Fine, he thought, offended. *I'll just go and talk to other things then. They always answer when I call. They even call me themselves and ask for my help. And that's just what I do – I help them. I don't need that stupid balloon, anyway! Suit yourself and just keep swaying up there, waiting for dancing winds.*

Oskar's phone started to ring, and he raised it to his ear faster than ever before.

'Hello!' he cried cheerfully. 'Is that you?'

But the balloon wasn't calling.

'Yes, it is I,' a hesitant voice replied. 'Which is to say, I am the bike. Calling from the shed. You might remember me – I'm next to the kicksled.'

'Oh,' Oskar said, hiding his disappointment. 'I'll be right there. I was planning a trip to the shed, anyway.'

The bike leaning against the wall next to the kicksled was very old. And very broken. He did still have wheels, but his tyres were completely flat. The pedals were gone and he was also missing his seat – a hollow pipe poked out in its place.

'What seems to be the trouble?' Oskar asked.

'Oh, I don't really have any serious problems. I'm just resting here, living out my retirement. I got to spin my wheels quite a lot back in the day, but now I just doze here and reminisce about old times. But you see, sometimes I get this odd desire in summertime – what if I were to take another ride! It'd help me remember what it's like to have a dusty road crunching beneath my tyres. I don't intend to go all that far, of course; maybe just back and forth right outside the gate a few times. It'd let me stretch my spokes and air out my handlebars a bit.'

'I don't know how to ride you,' Oskar confessed. 'I've only ever been on a tricycle. Dad promised to teach me this summer, but now he's back in the city.'

'That's no problem,' reckoned the bike. 'You can't pedal me around like a proper bike anymore anyway. I don't even have pedals anymore, see? And my seat is missing, too – you can't just plop your behind down on a bare pipe! People aren't lollipops! No, I'm an old man now and all you can do is walk beside me. What do you reckon – do you have it in you?'

'I certainly do!' Oskar said. 'I dragged the kicksled all the way to the gate, and that was much harder. A sled can't slide on grass. You, on the other hand, have wheels.'

'Exactly! And they still go round, even if the tyres are flat. You're a good lad. The kicksled only had kind words to say about you – he was so glad to finally see summer. I always used to say to him: *Snow doesn't stay on the ground year-round, my dear sled; it melts away and then flowers bloom.* But he didn't want to believe me! Now he's seen it for himself.'

'Shall we go now?' Oskar asked.

'Why not!' said the bicycle. 'I've got nothing else going on, anyway. Let's give it a whirl, if you've got the time. It is a little embarrassing going out all broken in broad daylight, but what can you do? It's not like anyone'll be watching! And if someone does ask where you're going with a rickety old bike, just tell them you're taking me to the dump.'

'Okay,' Oskar said, chuckling. He hung up, as he'd need both hands to push the bike. Only Grandma worried him a little – there was no knowing what she might think if she spotted him walking a broken bicycle out the gate. Was he even allowed to go onto the road on his own? Cars sometimes drove by – rarely, but still.

But he couldn't go and ask for her permission, because then Grandma would want to know where he was going and why he needed to take the old bike with him. She'd say that he shouldn't play with a broken bike, and suggest he kick a ball around or play *Life* instead. No, there was no point in telling her. He just had to hope she'd stay busy in the garden and wouldn't notice him slipping through the gate.

Pushing the bike along was far easier than tugging the sled. The bike rolled along with a soft whirr and all Oskar had to do was keep him upright. Oskar felt like he'd grown eyes in the back of his head as they passed under the birch tree, because even though he didn't look up at the balloon, he could still feel her presence in a strange way. They got to the gate a moment later.

Now, I've got to really make sure that Grandma doesn't notice me, Oskar thought. He looked over at the vegetable patch, but Grandma was as busy as ever and didn't look up.

But I bet the balloon might've seen me. And might call and ask where I'm going and why I've got the bike with me. But the mobile remained silent in his pocket. Oskar nipped out the gate and onto the road.

The bike had said 'back and forth', so that's just what Oskar started to do. He turned to the right and walked until he reached the neighbours' property. He didn't want to go any further. There could be people outside in their garden, and Oskar didn't want anyone to spot him on his unusual walk. A little boy pushing a rickety bicycle wasn't something you saw every day. Someone might mention it to Grandma at the shop, and that was the last thing he needed. Oskar turned round and started heading back towards the gate.

But he didn't avoid witnesses, as the three white-haired boys came around the bend at that very moment.

The first idea to pop into Oskar's head was to dive head-first into the ditch. Maybe they hadn't seen him yet! That was hardly likely, though, because they were in clear sight. One of the smaller ones was already pointing at him. Oskar could feel his cheeks burning with dread. Why did he always have to run into these three balloon murderers!

He had no choice but to continue bravely on his way and pretend like walking with a broken bicycle was the most natural thing in the world – almost like taking a dog out for a walk. He quickened his pace. Could he get to the gate before they did?

Unfortunately, the white-haired boys were the first to reach it. They stopped and waited. What did they want? Had they hatched another awful plan for popping the balloon?

In any case, Oskar wasn't about to get all friendly with them. He planned to just say hi and try to get through the gate as quickly as possible. They could stare at him like dead fish from the other side of the fence as much as they wanted.

Oskar got to the boys, mumbled hi, pushed the gate wide open, and tried to get the bike through. Naturally, a wheel got stuck behind the gate post, and it was hard to keep the bike from falling over. He tugged at it desperately, feeling the boys' gazes on him. At last he managed to get the whole bike into the garden, where he leaned it against a rowan tree then turned around to close the gate. The bike fell over with a crash. Three pairs of eyes stared at him unblinkingly.

'Where'd you go with that old piece of junk?' the oldest one asked.

'For a walk,' Oskar replied curtly. He lifted the bike back up and started walking towards the shed.

'You're a little loony, aren't you?' Oskar heard one of them say behind him. He felt sweat bead on the back of his neck and didn't reply. At last, he'd reached the safe haven of the shed door. He took a deep breath. What a close call! No leaving the garden anymore – that much was certain.

Oskar leaned the bike against the wall next to the kicksled and spent a minute listening to his gushing words of thanks.

'It was all so familiar!' the bike said. 'Every pebble, every turn. Oh, how much I used to zoom up and down that stretch of road! Thank you, Oskar. It has been a lovely day, indeed.'

Oskar himself certainly didn't feel that way. As he left the shed, he noticed that the pale creatures had disappeared.

The balloon was still bobbing away, and this time Oskar couldn't resist pulling out his mobile and lifting it to his ear.

'Hello, balloon!' he said, not really expecting her to answer.

But a moment later, she did.

'Hello.'

'It's you!' Oskar exclaimed.

'Of course it's me. You called.' She sounded a little peevish. 'What do you want?'

'Why didn't you answer before?' Oskar asked.

'I didn't feel like it. And I can't just hang around chatting with you all day. I don't have the time.'

'So what were you doing?'

'All kinds of stuff.'

'I've been doing... all kinds of stuff, too. Did you see me take the bike out for a spin?' Oskar asked.

'I didn't notice.'

'How's that? We went right past the tree,' Oskar pointed out, not believing her.

'Oh, right. I guess I might have.' The balloon sniffed. 'Anything else?'

'You're in a bad mood,' Oskar said. He had wanted so dearly to talk to her, but this sort of conversation wasn't at all what he'd been hoping for.

'You think?!' the balloon snorted. 'Wow, you just might be right. And why shouldn't I be? Why should I be in a *good* mood when all you talk about is how I'm going to pop soon?'

'I was just worried...' Oskar stammered.

'Well, you don't have to!'

Both were silent for a few moments.

'Goodnight, then,' the balloon finally said.

'Goodnight,' Oskar whispered.

36.

Oskar was quiet and sulky all evening. He ate salami sandwiches with fresh cucumbers for dinner. They were actually delicious, but they didn't make him any happier. Grandma had even bought him a fizzy drink as a treat, but he still couldn't enjoy it that much.

Mum called from America just before Oskar went to bed. At first it felt a little strange to hear her voice on the phone and not think that the caller was the telephone itself. He'd spoken to so many things over the last few days, and undoubtedly Grandma's olive-green desk telephone had its very own voice and thought its own thoughts.

Nevertheless, Mum was the one on the phone now. She said it was just morning in America and that she'd already bought Oskar a few cool things and missed him very much.

'What did you buy?' Oskar asked.

'Well, a Mickey Mouse T-shirt, for one,' she said, and his first thought was that the shirt wouldn't be able to talk – it would just bark or growl. 'But I don't want to spill all my secrets yet. Let's make it a surprise!'

I wonder if things you buy from America speak in English? Oskar thought to himself. Mum asked how things were going at Grandma's house, what the weather was like back in Estonia, and if he was eating properly. Oskar replied that everything was fine, the weather was warm, and he was eating enough, at least in his opinion. Then Mum told him about life in America. As he listened, Oskar thought how strange it was that this phone call didn't give him any joy.

Just a few days ago, it would've made him the happiest boy on Earth, because he missed his mum and had never been away from her for so long. But right now he couldn't fully enjoy chatting with her. Something dark and depressing was gnawing away at him inside, distracting him. Mum was still very dear to him, but she wasn't enough. There were some problems that a call from Mum just couldn't fix.

'I'll see you soon, Oskar!'

Mum started to finish their phone call.

'Be a good boy and don't feel down. I'm still here and I think about you every day.'

'Okay!' Oskar replied. He hadn't actually ever been afraid of Mum disappearing. Mums don't disappear – they're just away for a while at work or somewhere else, and then they come back. Mums were something you could count on.

It was other things that could disappear...

Mum repeated how precious he was to her, wished him goodnight, and ended the call. Oskar brushed his teeth and went into his room. He felt oddly empty inside. Everything seemed so good on the surface – Mum had called, and she loved him; Dad loved him, too; Grandma also cared for him, as much as she could, and bought him fizzy drinks from the shop and everything, but he felt rotten all the same.

The balloon was swaying gently at the top of the birch tree. Oskar eyed her almost angrily, then rolled over onto his belly and called the pillow.

Almost immediately, the feathers' bright chattering came through the phone.

'Oskar! Oskar! It's so good of you to ring! Do you feel good, Oskar? Are we soft enough for you? It's too bad you can't see us, Oskar! We'd love to show ourselves to you, Oskar! We're so pretty, Oskar! Especially me! No, I am! Me! Me!'

'Hush, hush,' Oskar scolded them like a teacher. 'Stop arguing. You're all very nice.'

'But we want to know who's the prettiest! Oskar, let's hold a beauty contest! Oskar, you pick who's the prettiest!'

This led to a fresh surge of bickering.

'*I'm* the prettiest because I'm the softest! Hm!'

'*I'm* the prettiest because I'm the hairrrriest! Rrr!'

'*I'm* the prettiest because I'm the cutest! Tee-hee!'

'Hey, we can't hold a beauty contest, because you're all inside in my pillow,' Oskar interrupted. 'I can't just rip it open to pull you out.'

'But we want to show you what we look like, Oskar! We want you to see us, Oskar!' the feathers chirruped. 'We want to tickle you, Oskar! Oh, we certainly know how to tickle! Marvellously!'

'Especially me!' one of them squeaked. 'Because I'm the hairrrriest! Rrr!'

'I'm going to sleep now,' Oskar said. 'You all have a rest, too.' He hung up and slid the phone under his pillow. Chatting with the feathers was fine – they were funny and all – but it wasn't what he *really* wanted.

Oskar rolled onto his back and stared out the window until he fell asleep.

Next morning, Grandma made pancakes.

'Sunday morning breakfasts should always be better than just plain porridge,' she said. 'You be generous with the jam, Oskar – I've a whole cellar full of jars that need emptying before this year's berries ripen.'

Oskar had to admit that Grandma's pancakes were delicious, though different from the kind that Mum made. Mum's pancakes covered the whole pan. Grandma's were much smaller – four or five could fit at once. But on the other hand, they were much thicker. In any case, they were scrumptious, especially with strawberry jam.

The weather was nice too and everything seemed wonderful at first glance. But Oskar's mood hadn't improved even the tiniest bit overnight. He felt that even though there were heaps of brilliant things around, something absolutely essential was missing.

Grandma poured a splash of milk into her coffee from the cream jug, which was still nestled up next to the sugar bowl on the kitchen table.

'It really is much easier to pour,' she remarked. 'You're a good lad for taking it out of the cabinet, Oskar. It was just collecting dust otherwise. Young folk really are much wiser than old fogeys like me.'

Oskar bravely asked for a cup of coffee too, just as he'd promised. Grandma poured him a small cup, mixing it half and half with milk. Oskar dumped in three heaped spoonfuls of sugar to top it off, which made certainly made it more drinkable. He put the lid of the sugar bowl back at a tiny slant, just the way she liked it. How nice it was that the cream jug didn't have to gaze longingly at his girlfriend from the other room anymore, but could snuggle up to her right here. If only everything in life were that simple!

He was dying to pull the phone out of his pocket, but forced himself to focus on the pancakes instead. But the red balloon came to mind again and again as he stared at the droplets of strawberry jam that fell onto his plate.

I'm not going to call her! he resolved. *At least not today,* he thought three minutes later. *At least not right this morning,* he decided as he stood up and left the room.

Oskar had to find something to keep his mind off his friend. Last night's phone call from Mum and his idea that it might be interesting to ring Grandma's desk phone came to mind. Now was the perfect time to execute the plan.

'Hello, telephone!' said Oskar.

'Hello!' an astonished voice answered. 'Uh... Whom would you like to call? I'll connect you at once.'

'I'd like to call *you*,' Oskar replied. 'There's no need to connect me.'

'I'm sorry?' the telephone asked, sounding even more flustered. 'You're calling *me*? No one has ever called *me* before! You must be mistaken. Don't you want to ring your aunt or someone? Your uncle, perhaps?'

'No, you're the one I'm calling,' Oskar reassured her.

'Dear me, dear me! You called me! I've dreamed of this my whole life! I'd never have thought such fortune possible!'

She started crying with joy, so loudly that Oskar almost felt sorry for having bothered her.

'That was about all I wanted to say, really...' he said hesitantly. 'I'll talk to you later...'

'No, wait!' the telephone shouted. 'We haven't even started talking yet! You haven't asked me anything, but I've got so many responses, all prepared ages ago. Ask me about my health!'

So Oskar did.

'My receiver aches like mad every time it rains, and my cord feels stiff every morning,' she proudly replied. 'My ring has got raspier lately and my buttons are swollen too. It's all just aches and pains when you're an old lady.'

Oskar realised the telephone had had to listen to Grandma's calls every day and had started memorising them.

'Now ask me how Louise is doing,' the telephone demanded.

'I don't know a Louise,' Oskar protested.

'Ask me anyway, I'm begging you!'

'Fine. So how's Louise doing?' Oskar asked.

'Louise is doing just fine. She got herself a new set of false teeth and dyed her hair red!' the phone trumpeted. 'Now ask me about Beverley.'

Oskar was already getting annoyed by their conversation. What did he care about all those Louises and Beverlies and Grandma's other ancient friends!

'Okay. How's Beverley?' he asked anyway.

'Beverley bought a loaf of bread from the shop and found a mouse tail in it! The food they sell in shops these days isn't fit for eating – they should be ashamed of themselves! Now, ask me what Dorothy's grandson's name is.'

Oskar sighed and asked.

'Ambrosius Rigobert,' the phone announced. 'How dreadful!'

'Listen, I've got to go now,' Oskar said. 'I'll call you again some other time.'

He hung up. Calling strange numbers was truly risky. You could easily end up in an extremely odd conversation.

37.

Grandma said she wouldn't be working in the vegetable patch today, because it was Sunday.

'I'll tidy up in here instead,' she announced. 'The sun is shining, which shows up all the dust inside. This is no way to live!'

Oskar was baffled by Grandma's logic. Tidying up was work too, and one of the most boring kinds at that! Still, he kept his mouth shut and just went outside as Grandma filled a bucket with water and started scrubbing the floors.

He walked to the shed. It had become his favourite place over the last few days, as it was always cool and shady even when the sun was blazing outside, and it was packed with interesting things. Those things already knew him pretty well, and were no doubt waiting expectantly. He'd barely walked in and shut the door behind him before the phone started making its sawing sound in his pocket.

'Hello, Oskar here!' he said politely. 'How may I help you?'

Oskar felt like a doctor in a TV programme about life in A&E – one who strode down long hallways with a white doctor's coat fluttering around him, handing out pills and giving patients injections. The shed was, in fact, very much like a hospital, with old things in need of care heaped left and right. And here, Oskar was their one and only doctor.

'I'm a basket,' the voice moaned into the receiver. 'My tummy hurts.'

'Where are you?' Finding his patients in amongst all the odds and ends wasn't easy.

'Right next to the woodpile,' said the basket.

'Okay, I can see you now,' Oskar confirmed. He inspected the new patient with a stomach-ache: a medium-sized mushroom-picking basket with an old rolled-up coat inside.

'When did the belly pains begin?' Oskar asked, sounding just like doctors did on telly. 'Is the ache constant, or does it only happen sometimes?'

'It's aching nonstop and has been for a full six months! I've got food poisoning, I just know it.'

'What could have caused it, do you think?' Oskar asked.

'This coat, obviously!' the basket replied. 'I can't digest things like that! I'm a *mushroom-picking* basket – my tummy is used to mushrooms. Worst case, I might have some berries, too. But I'm certainly not meant to eat *coats*! I absolutely loathe the taste and they give me awful stomach pains.'

'Then I think the remedy is exceedingly simple,' Oskar said, pleased to have come up with the right solution so quickly and just like a proper doctor. 'We just need to remove the coat and then everything will be fine.'

'Easy for you to say...' the basket sighed. 'I've been flexing my belly muscles all winter and all spring, but it still refuses to come out. It's like the coat is stuck in there!'

'Certainly. We'll need to do a little operation to remove it, and that requires two hands. Luckily, Doctor Oskar has just the pair!'

'What a relief!' the basket cheered. 'Please help me, dear Doctor Oskar!'

Oskar cleared his throat and slowly reached out his hands. It would've been pretty slick to put on a pair of latex gloves, too – he'd have looked just like a surgeon! Alas, there

were none to be found in the shed, so Oskar decided to just imagine them. He seized the rolled-up coat and pulled it out of the basket in one clean pull.

'How do you feel now?' he asked.

'Oh, marvellous! My stomach feels so light. There's no pressure, nothing aches... Thank you, Doctor Oskar! How fortunate I was to meet you!'

'It was nothing,' Oskar said. He felt proud, just like a real surgeon after a successful operation. There was only one thing that bothered him – it was too bad the balloon hadn't witnessed his triumph. He could tell her about it later, of course... when he called her... But what if she was in a bad mood again?

Oskar banished these thoughts from his head. Right now he was a famous doctor who had many more important tasks ahead of him. For example, he couldn't just leave the coat lying on the ground – Grandma certainly wouldn't like that. She was the one who'd stuffed it into the basket and caused the poor thing so many awful stomach pains. Oskar had to find a new home for the coat, but one where it wouldn't cause anyone harm.

He decided to ask the basket for advice, as he'd been in the shed much longer than Oskar had and knew all its occupants well.

'I don't know anybody who eats coats!' the basket exclaimed. 'They're furry and bitter and, what's more, very heavy. Would *you* want a coat packed inside your belly?'

Naturally, Oskar would not. But it had to go somewhere all the same. He scanned the room and spotted an empty rucksack hanging from a nail. What about there?

'Hello, rucksack!' Oskar said. 'How's it going? Your tummy's not empty, is it?'

'*Sure* is!' the rucksack answered. 'It's so empty that it's rumbling. Just look at how thin and wrinkled I am! I'm so frail that the slightest breeze could topple me over or blow me away. How embarrassing! A proper rucksack should never be afraid of a little wind! A proper rucksack is as heavy as a boulder or a hill. I can still remember a time when I was full to the brim. Oh, how brilliant that was!'

'Is being full really brilliant?' Oskar frowned.

'Sure it is! Full rucksacks are beautiful. Believe it or not, but there were days when I weighed over three stone! A scrawnier chap couldn't even make me budge, much less swing me up onto his shoulders.'

'Would you like me to put a coat in you?' Oskar asked. 'It definitely doesn't weigh three stone, but it'll make you a little heavier.'

'Absolutely!' the rucksack cheered. 'Please, do me the honour of stuffing me full! Stick the coat inside, and why not join it, too? I'm as empty as can be at the moment and there's plenty of room.'

'There's no way I'm crawling inside you,' Oskar scoffed, even feeling a little offended by the offer. You don't say things like that to a famous doctor!

'And actually, I need to ask the coat if it wants to move into you in the first place,' he added. When dealing with the world of things, you couldn't forget for a second to be polite to every single one of them.

He called the rolled-up coat and immediately heard thick purring over the line. It was a sound that could have been made by a cat the size of a hippopotamus!

'Ah, that's right,' Oskar mumbled to himself. 'The iron told me earlier. Coats are clothes, too, and clothes don't talk. They just make noises.'

He considered how fortunate it was that people didn't have the ability to hear clothes without the help of a magic mobile. Otherwise, it would be impossible to walk around in public – all you'd hear is bleating and mooing, croaking and quacking coming from every direction. And just imagine going shopping in a big department store! The sounds would be deafening.

Oskar stroked the coat, which started purring so loudly that it sounded like a tractor was rumbling past.

I reckon it won't mind moving into a new den, Oskar thought as he took the rucksack down then stuffed the coat inside.

The rucksack immediately became fuller, his belly swelling out like a grape. Oskar hung him back on the wall.

'How do you feel now?' he asked.

'Oh, that really hit the spot!' the rucksack sighed contentedly. 'Though I've still got space galore for more! Perhaps you could find something else? If not, then even some stones from outside would do just fine.'

'I'm not going out to gather up rocks. It's not good for you to eat too much,' Oskar said irritatedly. The rucksack's greed reminded him of a fairy-tale wolf – like the one who gobbled up the seven billy goats.

'That's alright, I like it that way! Once I fit a whole tent and four sleeping bags inside me,' the rucksack boasted. 'I was absolutely groaning in glee then!'

'Your appointment is over!' Oskar announced curtly, and hung up.

38.

The phone started making the sawing sound again the second Oskar ended the call.

'Hello! There's someone here whose tooth is aching like mad,' something informed him. 'Be a friend and have a look, would you? Maybe you can help.'

'I'm sorry, who is this?' Oskar asked.

'This is the shovel talking, I've got no teeth of my own. But my mate here has a whole mouthful of them, unfortunately. And now one of them started to hurt! He didn't have the guts to call you himself, 'cos he's afraid of dentists.'

Oskar scanned the room, looking for the caller.

'I'm right here by the door, leaning against the wall,' the shovel said. 'And my companion's right beside me. He's a rake. Do something about him if you can, please. It's terrible to see the old boy suffering.'

The shovel hung up. Oskar found the rake and inspected his patient. The tool really did have a whole row of teeth sticking up, all sharp and made of metal. Oskar started to have some doubts. This wouldn't be as easy as pulling a coat out of a mushroom basket – treating a rake's toothache would be quite a challenge. Oskar himself had only been to the dentist once before. They'd found a little cavity, drilled a bit and then put in a filling. He'd had four teeth pulled out in his lifetime, too, but Mum had done that – not a dentist. They were baby teeth and were already so loose that Mum was able to give them a little tug and they came right out.

Oskar couldn't pull out the rake's teeth, as they were firmly attached to the rest of the object. Maybe a hacksaw would work to saw them off, but Oskar didn't have one, and Grandma would hardly allow him to start chopping up her rake, anyway. Nor did he have a drill, and he wondered – *could* you even drill into a rake's metal tooth? It sounded impossible.

Still, something had to be done. Oskar lifted the mobile to his ear and spoke.

'Hello, rake! I hear you've got a toothache.'

'That's right,' a miserable-sounding voice replied. 'It started last night. I was raking up some dead grass outside when all of a sudden there was this awful shooting pain!'

'Which tooth are we talking about?' Oskar asked.

'The fourth from the left. What're you going to do, doctor? You're not going to pull out one of my teeth, are you? I'm so afraid!'

'Don't worry, we can't pull it out anyway. Your teeth are made of metal and stuck to your head,' Oskar reassured him. 'I'm just going to take a little look first.' He crouched down and tapped the fourth tooth from the left. 'Does that hurt?'

'It hurts all the time,' the rake moaned.

Oskar inspected the tooth. He couldn't see any holes or scratches – just a few clumps of dried soil and one little blade of grass stuck to it. Oskar scraped them off with his fingernail.

'You should brush your teeth more often,' he said.

'I actually never brush them at all,' the rake replied sheepishly. 'Sometimes – not very often, I admit – I rinse them if Grandma forgets me outside and I get caught in the rain.'

Oskar prodded the sore tooth and chewed his bottom lip.

What might help the rake? What could he do for this toothache? There was no one he could go to for advice, because it was extremely unlikely that anyone nearby had ever treated a rake with toothache before. No one else had a magic mobile like Oskar's! It was dreadful to think that there could be thousands of rakes with toothache all over the world, but since people didn't know how to talk to them, there was no one they could tell and they just had to suffer in silence.

The rake's bleating wasn't much help. Oskar now knew the tooth hurt, but didn't know what he could do to help.

What would his mum do? Mum always knew how to make Oskar feel better. Sometimes she gave him a pill, sometimes cough syrup. And if there was nothing to give him, then she'd simply give him a soft kiss on the sore spot and say:

'Candle burn and magic mend, make our Oskar better again.'

That always helped.

Oskar decided to apply the same treatment to the rake. He gave the aching tooth a gentle, careful kiss and whispered:

'Candle burn and magic mend, make the rake's tooth better again!

'Well, how does it feel?' he then asked timidly. 'Does it feel a little better?'

'No,' replied the rake. 'It feels a *lot* better! It doesn't hurt at all anymore! Thank you, doctor! How on Earth did you do it? I didn't feel a thing.'

'Doctors' secrets,' Oskar said with a wink. He was thrilled that Mum's magic spell had worked so flawlessly. After placing the rake back by the shovel where he'd found it, Oskar scanned the shed. Were there any other patients in pain?

As if in reply to his question, the mobile started making its sawing sound.

'Hello! Doctor Oskar at your service!'

'I'm... I'm sick, too,' a very soft and somewhat shy voice said.

'Well, what seems to be the trouble?'

'I... I was stung by a bee.'

'You don't say!' Oskar gasped. He would never have guessed that bees could sting objects and hurt them too. 'Who are you and where can I find you?

'I'm on the floor next to the shelves,' said the victim. 'I'm a can of paint.'

Oskar walked over to the shelves and found the caller. She was quite an old can that had once held brown floor paint. Perhaps she still held a little now — why else would she be kept in the shed? In any case, she must have been stored there for ages, because Grandma's floors hadn't been given a new coat of paint in years.

He picked up the can and inspected her.

'So you've really been stung by a bee?' he asked doubtfully. 'You're made of metal. A sting can't get through that.'

The paint can was silent for a few moments, sniffling.

'You're right,' she finally admitted and started to cry. 'I wasn't stung. There's nothing wrong with me. Nothing except for being very lonely. I lied so that you'd pick me up. No one has held me in ten years, and I was afraid no one ever would again, because the paint inside of me dried up a long time ago. No one needs me!'

Oskar felt sorry for her.

'Don't cry,' he comforted the can. 'It's good that you called me. You can always give me a ring, even if you're as fit as a fiddle. I promise that as long as I'm staying here at Grandma's, I'll come to the shed and pick you up every day. Okay?'

'That would be very, very kind of you. Thank you, Oskar! I'd paint you brown from head to toe to show my thanks if I could, but unfortunately my paint is far too old and crusty.'

'Oh, there's no need,' Oskar said. No part of him actually wanted to be painted like Grandma's floor! He stroked the paint can a couple times more, then set it back on the ground.

The mobile started sawing again. *There are a lot of patients in here,* Oskar thought. He was getting tired of playing doctor. *This will be my last one for today, then I'm going back inside,* he decided.

'Hello!' Oskar said. 'Who are you and what seems to be the trouble?'

'I'm flying!' a voice cried from the phone. It was a voice Oskar would recognise anywhere. 'I'm flying! Oskar, I'm flying! Come and watch me! It's so amazing!'

Oskar felt time slow to a stop. His ears started ringing and his heart thumped as loud as a church bell. He pelted out of the shed.

All the time he was treating sick things in the shed, he hadn't noticed that a strong wind had risen outside. It was a wind that had torn the balloon from the treetop.

Oskar spotted a tiny red blob in the blue sky, drifting away towards the forest.

'Wait!' he shouted.

'I can't! I'm flying!' yelled the balloon. 'I don't know where I'm going and I don't know what's going to happen, but that doesn't matter! I'm riding the winds, Oskar! They're so fast! Bye! You were brilliant! I'm going to miss you! Kisses! I sent you an ant...'

And then the call broke off. The balloon was just a tiny dot among the clouds now. A moment later, she was gone.

Oskar stood in the middle of the garden and stared at the horizon in despair. Maybe the wind would turn back around? Maybe it could still carry the balloon back to him?

Grandma appeared in the doorway.

'Come and eat. I made borscht for lunch!' she said. 'It was your grandfather's favourite.'

Oskar walked inside without saying a word, not really seeing anything around him, his legs feeling like they were made of stone.

39.

The tears started to come when Oskar was eating, though they didn't drip into his soup bowl. His eyes brimmed with them and the world turned foggy.

'Dear me, your eyes are all watery!' Grandma said. 'Is the soup really that peppery? I didn't think I'd added much, but maybe it's turned out too spicy.'

She took a sip of the broth.

'Not bad, as far as I can tell,' she said with a frown. 'I suppose you're just not used to it. Your mum's cooking tends to be a bit bland. We'll just add some sour cream – that should make it better.'

She dropped a big dollop of sour cream into Oskar's bowl and mixed it with a spoon until the soup was no longer beetroot red, but pink.

'Now try.'

Oskar obediently ate his lunch. He didn't like borscht and never had, but that made no difference. Right now, he could be chewing on a sponge or black dirt – his thoughts were somewhere else anyway. Far away beyond the woods and the fields, where the red balloon was flying to meet her fate. He didn't care about the soup, didn't care about what Grandma was saying – the only thing that mattered was the fact that he could never call or see the balloon again. The magic mobile in his pocket suddenly felt totally useless.

He finished his soup without even realising it. Grandma gave him a look of approval.

'What a good lad!' she praised. 'I'd never have guessed that you liked borscht so much. I'll make it more often. It's wonderful to see a boy with a proper appetite.'

There was still a ringing in Oskar's ears which made Grandma's words sound like they were coming from far away, like they were being played from a crackly old record. He didn't reply; just slid off his chair then plodded outside.

'Yes, you go on and play!' Grandma called after him. 'I'm going to lie down for a bit and let lunch settle. It's okay to let yourself be a bit lazy on Sundays.'

She went into her bedroom, turned on the radio, and stretched out in bed. A few minutes later, she was already dozing. The sounds of people talking and singing floated through the airwaves. Grandma started to snore.

Oskar walked to the shed and stared up at the tall birch tree. Its crown now seemed disturbingly bleak, like an old Christmas tree without its decorations. One that sheds its needles whenever you touch it. One that was glittering and beautiful just a short time ago, but now stands stark naked in the middle of the sitting room, waiting to be thrown away. One that isn't even green anymore, but a shade of grey. The birch tree had turned grey in Oskar's mind now, too; even ugly. But no one would be throwing it away. The tree would stay standing next to the shed, its empty branches swaying in the wind as if nothing had ever happened.

He took a deep breath. Looking up at the empty treetop was terribly painful. Bitterly, Oskar decided he'd like someone to chop down the stupid thing. What was the point of the big birch without the red balloon bobbing in its branches, anyway?

Stretching out on the grass beneath its branches, he stared at the clouds swimming by. The balloon had been swept off in that same direction. She said she would miss Oskar. That he was brilliant. And she mentioned an ant right before she was cut off. That could only mean one thing – the balloon had sent him a kiss on an ant! Oskar's eyes filled with tears again.

Actually, it's good that she flew away, he thought. *I mean, it's better for her to have done that than to have popped right here at the top of the tree. That would've been horrible, much more horrible. Now I can just imagine she still exists somewhere else, riding on her breezes and dancing with them. I may not be able to see or talk to her anymore, but she still exists.*

Oskar remembered a book he'd once read about a little girl called Dorothy, who was carried by a cyclone to the faraway land of the Wizard of Oz. He wondered if the balloon could reach an enchanted place like that. A place where scarecrows talk and tin men chop down trees. She would never, ever have to worry about popping there. She'd stay as round and red as she was here with Oskar, forever.

He took out his mobile and pressed it to his ear.

'Hello, balloon!' he whispered softly. All he heard was static. He would probably never hear her voice again. But what if she could still hear him, no matter that she was miles away already and couldn't pick up?

'Balloon. I don't know if you can hear me, but if you can, then I just wanted to tell you that you're brilliant as well. And I miss you too. I hope you fly to the Land of Oz, where you can live forever. I'm going to call you every day and tell you what's going on. I promise! It doesn't matter that you can't answer. I just like talking to you.'

He paused.

'Bye!' he whispered, then rested the mobile on his belly. For a while, he simply laid there in the grass, staring at the clouds and the empty treetop and swatting mosquitoes away every so often.

Then the mobile made a noise. Of course: he and the balloon weren't alone in the world. Many other things existed, and he was a friend, helper, and doctor to them all. Oskar sighed and lifted it to his ear.

'Hello! Hi, Oskar!' a voice peeped. 'I'm a teaspoon. I had five sisters, six of us in total, but one disappeared two months ago. She and a teacup went to the kitchen table one evening, but she never returned. The last time the teacup saw her she was in the sink, but he lost sight of our dear little sister when the water splashed over him. Would you be so kind as to go and find her? We believe she's still somewhere in the kitchen, maybe under the table or behind the cupboard or somewhere!'

'Okay,' Oskar said, slowly getting to his feet. He was in no mood to play detective, but he had to help when asked, so he trudged back inside. The sound of snoring and a man speaking loudly on the radio about a world war were coming from Grandma's bedroom. Oskar closed the door between the kitchen and the sitting room.

He opened the cabinet drawer and inspected the five teaspoon sisters to find out what the missing one looked like. Then he checked under the table just in case, knowing very well that she wouldn't be down there – the broom would've found her ages ago. No doubt she'd slipped into a dark crack somewhere the broom couldn't reach her.

Oskar crouched in the middle of the kitchen, pressed the mobile to his ear, and called the missing spoon.

'Hello, lost teaspoon! I'm Oskar and I'm here to find you! Lost teaspoon, hello! Where are you? Give me a sign!'

'I'm here!' a frightened voice finally squeaked. 'Here, under the cupboard! Help! Help! It's so dark and dusty!'

Oskar crawled on all fours to the cupboard where the dishes were kept and tried to peer under it. He couldn't see anything, and the gap between the cupboard and the floor was too narrow for even his slender hand to fit between them. The cupboard would have to be moved a little bit if he wanted to rescue the spoon.

But that was no easy task. The cupboard was huge and heavy and had been probably been standing in the same place since the house was first built. Had it ever even been nudged this way or that before? It felt as if the piece of furniture had taken root in the kitchen floor. How was a boy of Oskar's size supposed to move it?

Still, he had to try – the teaspoon was sobbing so pitifully into the receiver. Oskar set his shoulder against the side of cupboard and shoved with all his might.

The dishes rattled in alarm, but the cupboard itself didn't budge an inch. Oskar pushed and pulled, making the dishes clatter louder and louder on their shelves, until finally a miracle occurred: the cupboard shifted with a horrendous screech, opening up a tiny crack between it and the wall. Oskar squatted and immediately spotted the tiny handle of the teaspoon amidst the giant dust balls that had collected there over the years. He was able to poke two fingers in to grasp her and pull her out.

Now I've got to push the cupboard back so Grandma doesn't notice, Oskar thought, looking with dismay at the dusty mess revealed in the crack. The cupboard had stood in one place so long that even the floorboards beneath it were slightly rotten, and he even noticed a gaping mouse hole in the wall. Oskar saw that the mouse had chewed itself a little tunnel that ran between the floorboards. And glinting at the bottom of that tunnel was something gold.

Oskar scraped away the dust. It was a ring! It must have rolled under the cupboard and fallen into the crack and out of sight at some point. No one would have been able to get at it for ages. But now the mouse had gnawed that crack much wider. Oskar fished it out and held it up in the sunlight.

The beautiful little ring hadn't tarnished at all while lying in the inky blackness under the cupboard. Unfortunately, Oskar didn't get a chance to properly inspect it in peace, because the door opened and Grandma's tired face poked into the kitchen.

'What's going on in here?' she asked drowsily. Then she noticed the cupboard had been shifted out of place, and her expression immediately grew stern.

'What are you doing moving the cupboard around?!' she yelled. 'That is certainly not a game to be playing! That's very naughty! It could have tipped over and then all my dishes would have been smashed! You could have been trapped under it! It's a very heavy cupboard, Oskar! What did you do that for?'

'There was a spoon that had fallen behind it,' Oskar explained. 'And then I found this...'

He held the ring out to her.

Grandma stared at it agape for a moment, then sat down heavily on a chair.

'Was that under the cupboard?' she asked. 'Oh my goodness, how hard I searched for it so long ago! I looked down there too, but I never could find it.'

'It was in a crack between the floorboards, that's why,' Oskar said.

'Oh my...' Grandma murmured, as if she didn't hear a word Oskar said. Her eyes were still locked on the ring. She tried to push it onto her finger.

'It doesn't fit anymore,' she sighed with a sad smile. 'That's

to be expected, I suppose – my fingers are much thicker now. But I used to wear it right here on this one. Your grandfather gave it to me. And I lost it two years later. That was fifty years ago. And it's been right here between the floorboards this whole time... Oh my.'

Fifty years?! Oskar was amazed. *That's ages ago!* He thought about all the pirate treasure in the books he'd read and films he'd seen; treasure that had to wait for endless centuries in shadowy caves for someone to find it. The ring's fate seemed identical.

'Fifty years,' Grandma murmured again, turning the ring over and over between her fingers. 'I can't believe I've finally found it again.'

Oskar tried to imagine what Grandma might have looked like fifty years ago. Probably similar to the girl on the beach in the photograph – young, pretty, and completely unrecognisable.

'Were you wearing it when you had the ice cream, too?' he asked.

'What ice cream?'

'The ice cream in that place on the coast. Where you were wearing that polka dot dress. In the picture, remember?'

'Oh, yes!' Grandma gasped. 'I *am* wearing it in that picture! Of course! That was the day he gave it to me!'

Grandma hurried out of the room and returned carrying the photo album.

'Here it is,' she said, pointing. Both of them stared at the old picture of a young, smiling Grandma with a gold ring on the hand that held her ice cream cone.

40.

Grandma took the ring to her bedroom and placed it in a drawer. Then she returned to the kitchen and, with Oskar's help, they nudged the cupboard back in place, causing the dishes to rattle uneasily again.

But before they did, Grandma used the broom to sweep up most of the dust from behind it.

'There's a lot of dust back here, but normally I can't wedge the broom between the cupboard and the wall. How lucky that you pushed the cupboard away – we found my ring and now I can clean a little, too. You know, Oskar, if you hadn't come to visit me this summer, then my ring would've stayed under the cupboard and I'd never have seen it again before I died.'

Grandma went outside once the cupboard was pushed back against the wall.

'I've rested and napped so much today that I should probably go out and do something useful for a while,' she said. Oskar noticed that Grandma almost looked younger – she wore a smile on her face and had a longer stride than usual as she walked towards the vegetable patch.

Oskar tiptoed into her bedroom. He'd had the idea the moment he saw the ring, but wasn't able to call it before Grandma went off to do some jobs. Now he carefully pulled open the drawer. The ring was there, nestled among an assortment of buttons, ribbons and balls of thread.

'Hello, ring!' Oskar said.

'Hello!' the ring replied. She had a nice, friendly little voice. 'Are you the one who found me under the cupboard?'

'That's right. My name is Oskar. Were you really there for fifty years?'

'I'm not sure,' said the ring. 'I can't keep track of time. But I was down there for very long, indeed. I remember falling, clattering against the floor, and rolling beneath the cupboard, and it was a smashingly good time! I didn't think for a second that I'd get stuck down there for good. I was certain someone would find me before long, then slip me back on their finger and sometimes take me off, and then I'd roll myself somewhere again just to have a good time. But no one did. Just some mice who visited every once in a while, and tickled me with their whiskers when they sniffed me.'

'Were you afraid?' Oskar asked, trying to imagine what it felt like to sit somewhere in the dark and be sniffed at by something much bigger than him – an animal about the size of a horse.

'No, why should I have been? I've never been afraid of mice. They're so funny. And what's more, I figured – to heck with it! I just had to keep a stiff upper lip. I was sure I'd make my way out someday. Rings are never in a hurry; we don't break or wear away. Well, turns out that I was right. I *was* found. *You* found me. Thanks!'

Oskar could feel himself liking the ring more and more. She seemed cool, wasn't afraid of mice, and didn't hold back from saying things like 'to heck with it'. She might have been under a cupboard for fifty years, but she didn't seem old at all. On the contrary – she reminded Oskar a little of his teacher at school, a young woman named Heidi, who took the time to have snowball fights with children and organised pyjama parties at the school. Unfortunately, Heidi had a baby before long and was replaced by a new teacher, Mrs Evelyn, who just sat on her chair the whole time, yawning and sometimes barking 'Hush, now! Stop your yelling!'.

'I saw you in a picture,' Oskar said. 'Grandma was wearing you. She was very young back then and was eating ice cream by the beach.'

'Oh, yes! I remember ice cream!' the ring exclaimed. 'Though I'm not sure if I can still recall the one we were having in that photo. There was so much ice cream! A tiny white trickle would run down her finger to me almost every single day. Sometimes brown. It was scrumptious!'

'Are you saying you ate it too? How can that be? You don't have a mouth!'

'So what? I can still taste things,' the ring explained. 'And I used to get lots and lots of ice cream.'

Oskar tried to imagine his grandma eating ice cream every day – it felt impossible. Grandma always ate burgers crammed with huge pieces of onion, and borscht, and macaroni-and-milk soup. An ice cream cone in her hand would look so out of place. Grandma standing in the middle of the vegetable patch licking a chocolate ice cream cone would be a strange sight.

Still, the grandma in the polka-dot dress in that old photo could easily have enjoyed an ice-cream cone or two. The two of them matched like bread and butter – she had that sort of sly, eager look in her eyes that someone with sweet tooth can never hide when they set eyes on a dessert. Only she wasn't like a *proper* grandma – she was...

That was it. Who *was* she, anyway?

And suddenly, Oskar realised: the ring was *in that picture*. The very same ring he was chatting to that very second, and which reminded him of his lovely teacher Heidi. She wasn't Heidi at all, though, but a young woman in a polka-dot dress in an old black-and-white photograph.

When Oskar talked to the ring, he was talking to his grandmother when she was young.

The two had been inseparable fifty years ago, enjoying ice cream together and tanning on the beach. Then the ring had rolled under the cupboard. Grandma grew old and barely resembled the girl in the photo anymore. But the ring stayed the same. The ring stayed young.

Oskar was amazed by his mobile. It really was magic. He could use it to talk to things that seemed lifeless on the surface. And now it turned out that it could even help him get to know his grandma better. The kind of grandma Oskar had never known. The kind of grandma he liked.

He did like the grandma he already had, of course. Grandma took good care of him – or at least she tried, even though it didn't always turn out as well as it could. Oskar could manage staying with her just fine. The only problem was that he didn't really know how to talk to her. There were so many things that were impossible to discuss with Grandma, or rather, so many things she wouldn't understand.

But the grandma who lived inside the ring – the young, sweet-toothed grandma – *she* definitely understood!

He could talk to her about anything!

Even about the balloon.

'I'm very glad I found you,' Oskar told her. 'I'm going to call you again tomorrow.'

'Please do!' said the ring. 'I didn't have anybody to chat with under the cupboard, but I'm actually quite the chatterbox. I enjoy chatting. And you know what else? Perhaps you could even roll me along the table a little tomorrow. It was an absolute blast the last time I did it, and all those years I was lost, I dreamed about rattling across the floor again. I just don't want to end up under a cupboard again. I've had my fair share of that already!'

She laughed.

'Sure, that sounds great!' Oskar promised. Grandma would never let him play with the ring, of course, but who cared about that when the proper grandma – the young, cool grandma – wanted to play!

Oskar slid the drawer shut. He heard footsteps outside – Grandma was coming in for dinner.

A little later, Oskar was back in his bedroom. Grandma had turned the telly on and already dozed off – he could even hear her snoring through the closed door. Oskar sat on his bed and stared at the birch tree with no one swaying in its branches anymore.

What was the balloon up to now? Where was she flying? Was she already in the Land of Oz, where the other balloons would make her their queen? He hoped so, at least.

Oskar missed his balloon. He had found a new, young grandma, of course, and that was brilliant too. But the balloon was different.

Oskar lifted the mobile to his ear.

'Hello, balloon!' he said. The phone hissed softly, like waves crashing on a distant shore.

'I just wanted to wish you goodnight. I hope you have polka-dot dreams.'

Oskar got up and went to the window. It was still quite bright outside. The sun hadn't set yet, but the moon was already high in the sky.

Noticing a little ant crawling along the windowsill, Oskar crouched down and studied the creature. It was plain to see the ant was carrying a tiny kiss on its back.

'Got it,' Oskar murmured happily. He gently touched the ant with his fingertip, scooping the kiss off its back. Having been relieved of its burden, the ant scurried away and disappeared into a crack.

Oskar tapped the kiss onto his cheek.

'Thanks!' he whispered, gazing up at the treetop. Above the tall birch tree, a full moon glowed through the hazy clouds like the pale shadow of a balloon.

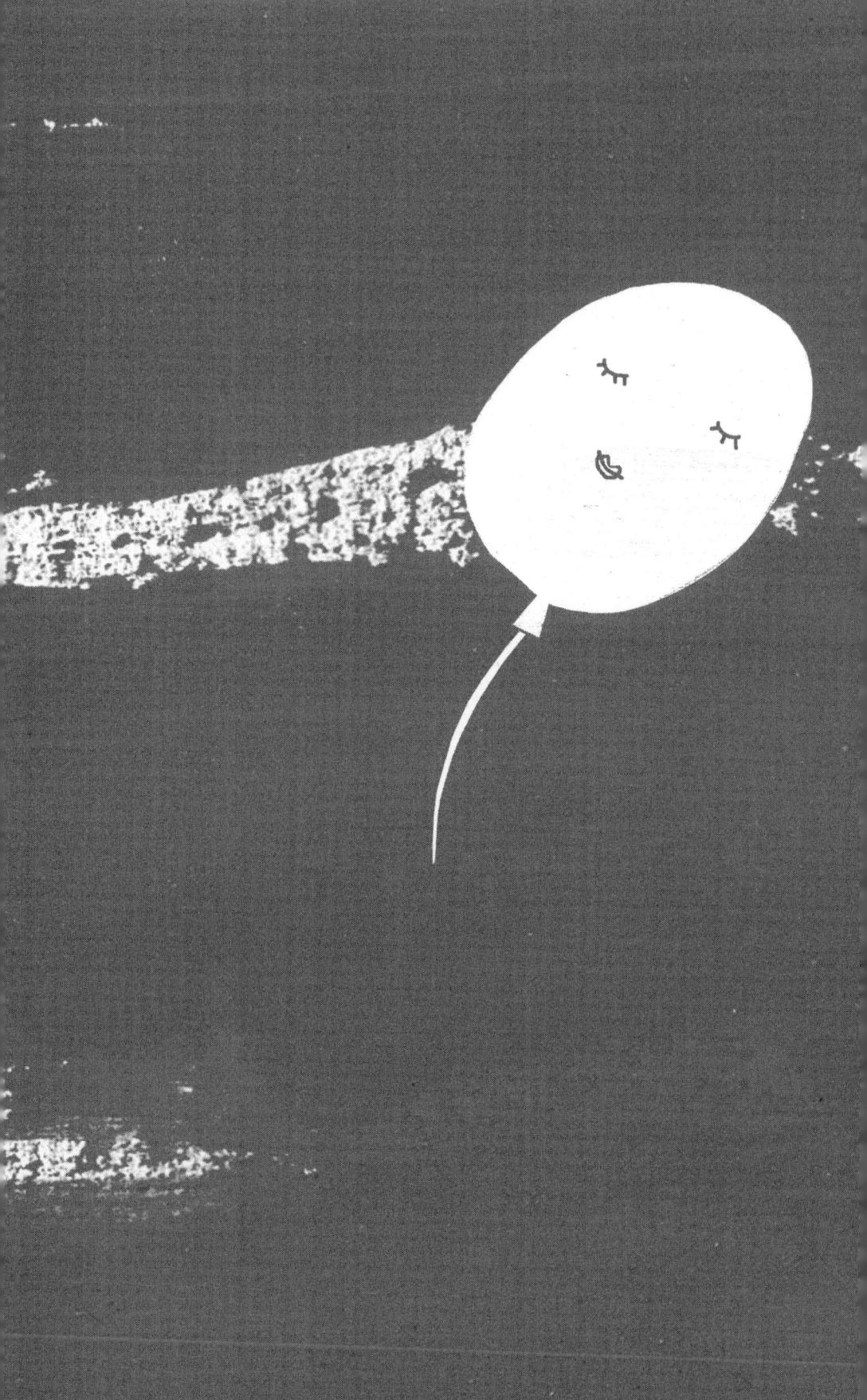

About the author

Andrus Kivirähk (1970) is an adult and children's prose and poetry author, a playwright, topical satirist, and screenplay writer. He is the most well-known and prolific figure on Estonia's literary scene today. He has written 12 books for children, all of which are kept in print and widely read. Kivirähk's children's stories are known for their rich fantasy and unique sense of humour. His writing is simple, the plots fast-paced, and the gallery of characters colourful and full of surprises.

About the translator

Adam Cullen (1986) is a poet and translator of Estonian prose, poetry, drama, and children's literature into English. His latest translations include Martin Algus's *The Lion* (Best European Drama, BBC Audio Drama Awards 2022), Jüri Arrak's *Panga-Rehe Stories* (50 Watts Books 2022), Peeter Sauter's *Don't Leave Me Be* (Tanooki Press 2022), Kertu Sillaste's *I Am an Artist* (Graffeg 2021), Tõnu Õnnepalu's *Exercises* (Dalkey Archive Press 2020, nominated for the Cultural Endowment of Estonia's Award for Literature), and Piret Raud's *Ellie's Voice: or Trööömmmpffff* (Restless Books 2020). A member of the Estonian Writers' Union, Cullen has resided in Estonia since 2007.

About the illustrator

Anne Pikkov (1974) is an illustrator, graphic designer, and book designer. She graduated in graphic design from the Estonian Academy of Arts. She has worked at an advertising agency, and as a visiting professor and the Vice Rector of Academic Affairs at the Estonian Academy of Arts. Pikkov has illustrated 14 children's books and contributed to the Estonian magazines *Täheke*, *Pere ja Kodu* and *Jamie*. She has received many awards at annual Estonian book design and illustration competitions. Her art is ornamental, laconic, spiced with humour, and evocatively expressive.